THE HARVEST

Christopher Hart was born in 1965 and educated in Cheltenham, Oxford and London. He works as a freelance journalist and lives all over the place. *The Harvest* is his first novel.

CHRISTOPHER HART

The Harvest

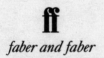

faber and faber

First published in 1999
by Faber and Faber Limited
3 Queen Square London WC1N 3AU
This paperback edition published in 2000

Photoset by Agnesi Text, Hadleigh
Printed in England by Mackays of Chatham plc, Chatham, Kent

A CIP record for this book
is available from the British Library

ISBN 0-571-20341-8

2 4 6 8 10 9 7 5 3 1

To Rosalind

No doubt but ye are the people,
and wisdom shall die with you

Job 12:2

(I have made
an elegy for myself it
is true)

Geoffrey Hill, 'September Song'

1   The Trap (1)

The sun shone down on a beautiful morning, edging the beech trunks copper and the beech leaves gold. The paddock lay like virgin land, the thin frost lay on it unbroken by human footfall, the grass only darkened here and there by delicate hoofprints where the deer had passed by when the mist still lay sorrelhigh, their sandy bellies brushing drops of dew from thistles, and had passed on and left the paddock still and silent as before in deep dreaming sleep.

Over the hill came Lewis Pike, a brace of moletraps in each pocket, dully clanking like some fantastic and redundant machine rusted the colour of the earth. A cloud of rooks arose from the wood's edge and circled, cawing laboriously, and went east and settled in a field beyond. He came down into the paddock where the mist lay thin now and the sun was slowly burning it away. He knelt and laid the moletraps down in his own shadow in the cold grass and squinted at the sun. The sun shone down.

He took a handful of earth from a fresh molehill and with it he rubbed the trim steel jaws. At the edge of the paddock he took a hazel stick and brought it back, hewing the end roughly with his pocketknife as he came and eyed the unseeable line between two fresh molehills. He stood astride the line and punched the stick down into the turf. There was no give. He pulled the stick out and wiped the clots of soil from it between forefinger and thumb. He eyed the puncture hole and hafted the stick down again half a foot from it. It gave. He pulled out the stick and tossed it aside and dibbed a forefinger in. There was the tunnel. He tore aside the turf with straining fingers and opened a rent in it wide enough to set the trap with his bare hand, well soiled so that it would smell barely human. He locked the eye of the trap between the two jaws and set it down transverse in the tunnel. He covered the tunnel again from the sun with the torn divots, scattered loose soil from a nearby molehill on it and wiped his hands in the wet grassblades. Then he stood and rubbed his palms together until they heated, opened his palms sunward and eyed with disgust the fat rolls of dirt that lay there. He shook them away.

He took the other three traps and the hazel stick, found three more tunnels and set the traps and then stood and walked west to the end of the paddock. There he found two sticks set upright. He pulled them out and knelt and eased the turf up from around where they'd stood and found the two traps, one gleaming like new silver in the earth. The other was forty years old and he had found it forgotten in the earth, sprung but empty, its catch quite gone but for some unidentifiable ghost of stuff, no more than the skeleton of an oak leaf, and now it always caught moles because it no longer smelled of anything but earth. In the new trap the eye was still locked empty between the jaws, but in the rusted trap he found a mole. He held the trap up out in the sunlight and the mole hung from the one jaw like a velvet comma. Its great paws like workman's hands, spades of flesh. He squeezed together the upper jaws of the trap between the heels of his hands and the mole dropped out on to the turf. The jaw had squeezed out purplish entrails from its belly. He dropped the trap and picked up the mole. He looked about him and up at the rooks' nests and saw no rooks in among the trees and he squinted up at the sun. Still it shone, whiter hourly. He turned on his knees until his back faced it and he brought the mole close to, in the shadow of his face, and nosed it as an animal would.

Then he paused and considered the mole, holding it in

2

the palm of his hand like some unexpected gift, but as if there was something in it that he did not understand and that he urgently needed to. Then he laid it down in the grass and picked up the trap and reset it and stood it upright on the grass. He lay down on his belly and held out his hand towards it. He extended his forefinger slowly towards the eye of the trap. He passed it through and pulled down until the eye popped out and the metal jaws banged shut upon his finger. He snatched his finger back in pain and the sprung trap dragged with it. Gasping with shock and pain he rested his hand on the grass and with the heel of the other prised open the jaws of the trap and released his finger.

He examined it with curiosity. An incomplete ring of blood seeped around the base of his finger beneath the skin. Soon it would be swollen and purple with all the capillaries dilated or broken and blood rushing to the scene of the outrage. He looked back and forth between finger and mole, mole and finger, until finally satisfied, as if some question had been answered or some peace vouchsafed. He took his knife and slit the moleskin from anus to snout and tore the naked body from it, rolled the skin loosely and wiped his knife clean and took the traps and put everything in his pockets and left the paddock and went home.

2   John Pike (1)

He entered the kitchen through the back door. His father stood over the table reading the paper with a mug of tea in one hand and the other thrust in his jeans pocket. He didn't look up.

Where you bin?

Trappin'.

Lewis dumped his camouflage jacket in the corner, crossed to the cupboard and took down a cereal packet.

Seen this? His father waved his hand over the giant headline.

Lewis poured out cereal.

Crooked self-serving bastards the lot of them. Can't believe they'll get away with it. Just votin' theirselves more money like that.

Lewis crunched mechanically on his cereal.

Anyway.

He drained his lukewarm tea, smacked his mug down on the table and crossed to the oven and took out a white linen bundle. He sniffed it sarcastically and said, Mm, lovely! Done to a turn. He looked at his son. Jesus, he said.

Lewis looked up.

Look at you. The honey monster.

Lewis grinned. The hungry monster. Starvin'.

I bet y'are. Leery, as Grandma would say. S'all that trappin'. He shook out the bundle. Catch anythin'?

Just the one.

His father held the antique garment out at arm's length and his face creased with sour incredulity. Bloody hell, he said. He shook his head with its mop of greying curls. Bloody *hell*.

John Pike worked at Farmer Gyles's Old Tyme Farmstead near Blandford. Five years ago he'd kept fulltime, working between Childoak and Dogdean farms until Dogdean laid him off and the hours at Childoak weren't hardly worth even the drive over there. Since then he'd signed on every fortnight and worked summers. At Farmer Gyles's Old Tyme Farmstead, pretending to be a farm labourer.

What an idiot, he said.

When he got to Farmer Gyles's he put on a stupid wig in a Portakabin there and a stupid straw hat and bloody *rouge*, would you believe, and hobnail boots and leather gaiters and baggy old corduroys and this stupid bloody linen smock and a red neckerchief and stood around grinning and looking stupid and saying, Oh ar, if any of the shell-suited grockles asked him anything. Only yesterday he slipped in the pigpen and got pigshit all over the arse of his smock and had to bring it home and handwash it. This morning the arse of it was yellow and still not dry, so he'd cooked it for half an hour on gas mark 2.

Smelt of chips but it seemed to do the trick.

Anyway, he said again. Another lovely day at Farmer Gyles's. What you doin'?

Lewis shrugged.

You could mend that bloody scooter of yours for a start. Hey?

He nodded.

Anyway. I'll be back six or soon after and you can do supper. Hey?

Stop saying that, he thought. Yeah.

Right. Oh and there's a letter from Katy there on the side.

He ducked out of the back door and was gone.

He used to nag Lewis about going to the job centre but not any more. He still worried about him. But Lewis thought little about his father. Children think far less about their parents than parents do about their children.

Unless maybe they're absent.

Lewis went out and walked down the lane to the stream overhung with willow and alder and brushed his arms through the leaves and catkins and came to where the stream slowed and the edge of a deep pond. Often he daydreamed, as he walked or sat by this dark water, of coming by here one day and seeing white limbs under the water like strange weed and of bending down and bringing her to the surface and stroking the velvet and mudbrown weed from her face and her limbs around him so cold and her body as cold as church alabaster monuments and of breathing life into her and her eyes opening and his mother smiling gently on him and looking at him and talking to him, talking to him . . .

He stood by that water for a long time and then he turned and went homeward.

Not yet ten and the summer days so long.

He watched morning television and a studio discussion about date rape and he lay and yawned and masturbated and looked often at the clock and sat through adverts for cars and holidays and tampons and insurance and cars.

He wished he could go and visit the Poet but he knew he wasn't welcome until after dinner. So he had dinner at half past eleven, baked beans from the tin, and then went to visit the Poet.

3   Gerald and Mary (1)

Gerald, the Poet, lived in an unkempt cottage at the end of a long chalk track. The cottage nestled on the hill against Hound Wood and looked out over the valley. Gerald had a beard and wore tweed and his wife Mary had a pale sweet face and long straight hair. Occasionally they came to the pub where he drank brandy and she drank beer. Most of the time they weren't seen in the village but were generally reckoned all right, if a bit eccentric.

Lewis came to the cottage at noon. He hesitated and knocked on the door. There was no sign of life. He knocked again.

After a while standing openmouthed and hesitating, he went round to the side gate and called.

Um . . .

There was a pause.

Hello? called back the Poet. Who is it?

It's me. Lewis.

Oh, Lewis. Hang on a mo.

There were scuffling sounds and then round the corner of the cottage came Gerald, shirtless and belting up his trousers. He saw Lewis with his mouth hanging open and roared with laughter.

Ha! I know what you're thinking, dear boy! But it's not that, is it Mary?

He looked back over his shoulder then gestured Lewis round into the garden.

Mary was still pulling her dress back over her head. Lewis looked down.

You're early, said the Poet. Not that I mind you catching us in the buff. It's more the interruption.

My watch must have stopped, said Lewis.

Never mind, said the Poet. Actually we were just reading Blake. You know, the old Adam and Eve thing, naked but not ashamed, like Mr and Mrs Blake sitting starkers in a tree reading Milton, down in darkest Surrey. Not what you think!

Lewis looked at the ground.

Do you know Blake?

He shook his head.

Oh, it's marvellous stuff and not difficult. Well, I say not difficult, I mean not difficult in the usual way. Which is not to say . . .

And the Poet was off.

Talking without pause, he led Lewis to the shade of the cherry tree and pulled on a jacket without a shirt and they sat in tattered garden chairs. Mary had gone inside to make cups of tea. Gerald never made the tea. She returned and handed Lewis and her husband their mugs and then sat crosslegged at her husband's feet, cradling her mug and looking up at him with her long hair shadowing her eyes.

Lewis sometimes wondered why he liked coming to see the Poet. Today, of course, he was lonely anyway with Allie at the vet's, but even when she was with him he still visited the Poet most days. He was happy just to listen and Gerald was certainly always happy to talk.

Lewis's attention returned.

Of course, the Poet was saying, Blake had some dotty notions about Stonehenge and the Druids, and even though we now know that the stones long pre-date the advent of the Celts and Druidism, one feels that Blake would have dismissed such merely *factual* evidence out of hand, and insisted on the truth of the heart's imagination, or some such Blakean nostrum. Or is that Keats?

Lewis didn't know. He saw Mary move her head slightly

and glanced at her. She was looking at him with an amused smile. He looked down again.

Remember *Tess of the D'Urbevilles*? Gerald was asking. Have you seen Polanski's film?

Lewis shook his head.

Pretty successful, I thought. Shot in Brittany, of course. Hardy's Wessex is no more. You must have been to the stones before they were fenced off?

Never bin, said Lewis.

What? laughed Gerald. Never even been to the stones? He laughed very loudly. Well, isn't that just typical! Still I can't talk, I'm a terrible hypocrite myself. All those years we lived in London, 'hated London' as Yeats called it, and never once did I visit the Tower! Never have done! Now isn't that just typical!

And he laughed very loudly again.

Mary laughed with him, more quietly, and Lewis saw her looking at her husband. Then she looked at Lewis. He looked back at her. They smiled.

Gerald was still laughing.

We don't even visit the monuments on our own doorstep!

It's not on my doorstep, thought Lewis. It's twenty miles away, the other side of Salisbury.

Ah well, said the Poet. There's plenty of time for you to go there, even though, alas! it is a site now ruined by concrete and barbed wire. You will go there one day, I am sure, to that place of legend and sacrifice.

He paused.

Wait a minute.

He fumbled in his jacket pocket and dug out a pencil and scribbled something on a piece of paper.

Many of my poems grow from single lines, he said. Like crystals.

He began to talk again.

In the cherry tree overhead a thrush was singing,

repeating phrases it liked, discarding others, pausing. The Poet talked on.

The sun was at its height and beyond the shade of the cherry tree it was very hot. The sun came round and fell on Mary's cheek and she turned aside slightly and caught it full on her face. She stretched her legs out before her and rested back on her elbow. Lewis drank in her every movement. Her legs were brown and smooth. She ran her fingers through the long grass and half closed her eyes.

For a week already it had been too hot and now the summer seemed to promise to stay that way. Lewis's grandmother had many a maxim and rhyme to prove that such a hot May meant a long hot summer.

The sun burned from a blank blue sky. By noon it reached 80° and still climbed. Only towards dawn did it seem cooler, a little. Everyone talked of another heatwave, of the hosepipe ban (already!) and shrivelled vegetables, of the ozone layer (a little uncertainly); many recalled '76. Lewis's grandmother recalled '21 and he wasn't even sure if she was just joking.

At night he lay naked on his narrow bed and watched the stars through the open window and saw the Plough wheeling about and Regulus disappearing and Arcturus slowly falling towards dawn. And no sleep came.

Gerald was now talking about Rogation Sunday of all things.

It was a marvellous service last Sunday, he said. You weren't there.

Lewis shook his head.

Pity. It was wonderful. Not that I'm much of a churchgoer myself of course, not a regular pagan like me. Small time for the pale Galilean and all that bollocks. No, but this was different, quite evidently the survival of the old pre-Christian celebration of spring. May Day and all that. I'm surprised we didn't have a damn maypole there. It was all about cocks and sex really.

Lewis bowed his head.

But good on the vicar for holding it out of doors, at least. That was a bold stroke. God knows who we prayed to. They prayed to their pale Galilean I suppose, while I murmured a few words to Gaia and Cybele and Isis and whatever gods might be. The old dears next to me would have had a fit if they'd have known. *An 'orrible pagan in their midst.*

And Gerald roared with laughter.

Now then, he said at last. How about a glass of cider? Mary, be a love would you and go and . . .

Mary was already on her feet and gliding towards the kitchen.

Excellent stuff, real Somerset scrumpy. The real thing. Now then. What are you doing with yourself today?

Lewis shrugged. Dunno. Collectin' . . .

You should be out in the fields, said Gerald, gesturing vaguely about. How sweet I roamed from field to field And tasted all the summer's pride. You haven't read Blake, you say? You really should, you know, he's jolly good. I could lend you a copy.

No, but Rogation Sunday was very fine, though. We all stood in the churchyard in the hot sunshine with our heads bowed in prayer. I fancy we looked a little like the peasants in Millet's 'Angelus'. And the old vic led us in thanksgiving to the forces of nature and fecundity. Quite splendidly ironic, really, for the worshippers of the dying god to be . . . Ah, Mary.

She brought a tray with three glasses and a brown bottle and set it on the grass. She poured out the cider and handed a glass first to Lewis and then second to her husband. She took the other glass and sat sideways and sipped the cider gently.

One does get a terrific sense of old pagan England from some of those services, though. Old earthy, peasant England, in those prayers for rain and those thanksgivings for ripe fruit and plump corn. Cranmer must have known his stuff! He laughed. I just can't wait to see the Harvest Festival!

They drank their cider and it was strong and sour and flat. Gerald smacked his lips. Lewis felt it tart in his belly.

We could do with praying for some rain now, couldn't we? said Gerald, looking around in the blank sky.

Lewis nodded. Had none this month, he said.

Awful. Quite frightening really. Seems that all these predictions of global warming are coming true after all.

Lewis bowed his head and plucked up grass and smiled to himself, doubting it very much, remembering nights in March when the east wind had seared his eyeballs and grated his cheeks raw and when he'd walked the fields before dawn through hoarfrost so thick it had lain on his boots like snow. He said nothing, drank his cider.

But Mary saw him smiling and thought how sweet he looked when he smiled.

A wasp had got into Mary's glass. It lay on its side, caught in the sticky meniscus, dabbling its helpless legs. Mary held the glass near the rim in her left hand between thumb and third finger and extended her forefinger toward the wasp. She tried to flick it free with her fingernail but instead caught it and trapped it against the side of the glass. The wasp curled round like a prawn and stung her on the pad of her forefinger.

Oh shit, she said, snatching her hand away and letting the glass fall into her lap where the cider spilled out on to her dress and the glass rolled away. The wasp fell sozzled into the grass. She snatched her stung finger towards her.

Oh God, said Gerald. Oh darling, oh look I can't, Lewis . . .

He sat and writhed in his chair and screwed up his face in vicarious pain and looked frenetically about, anywhere but at his wife's finger.

Oh Lewis, can't you . . .?

Lewis knelt opposite her and took her forefinger in his left hand and looked closely.

12

What? What? cried the Poet.

It's OK, Lewis said to her. Wasps don't leave a sting in.

Still hurts like hell though, she said.

Does it darling? cried the Poet. Does it really?

Yeah, Lewis said to her. It'll pass.

She managed a smile. You're all sympathy.

He shrugged.

I'll have to go and sponge this dress. Come on, you can help me find some cream. He's useless.

Oh darling, protested Gerald.

Secretly rather enjoying the drama, Mary padded over the grass in her bare feet with Lewis following awkwardly after.

Behind them, Gerald seized the cider bottle and ground the heel into the grass until the wasp was broken beneath into three constituent pieces.

Little bugger, he said.

He poured himself another glass and wondered why the world could not be as simple and beautiful as his dreams.

The cottage kitchen was cool and dark. The couple had changed little. The floor was of flagstone and there was an open range and a long kitchen table of pale ashwood patterned and hatched with knifecuts and worn smooth by generations of hands and elbows.

Bathroom's at the top of the stairs, she said. See if you can find some cream or something, there's a love.

Lewis trod gingerly up the narrow cottage stairs that creaked beneath his every footfall. The bathroom was bright and yellow and bunches of lavender hung from the wainscot. He found a tube of cream in the medicine cabinet over the washbasin. He looked at himself in the mirror. Bloody *hell*, he thought.

When he came back down to the kitchen Mary was standing at the sink, sponging her dress. As he entered the room, she lifted it up from the hem and held it out like an apron over the sink. The thin cotton wrapped tightly around her bum and her legs were bare to the thigh and long and smooth and brown. She threw him a glance over her shoulder and her hair fell across her face as she did so.

Avert your gaze like a gentleman.

He bowed his head but his eyes didn't move.

She stood up on tiptoe and her legs were taut with slender muscles. Then she dropped back on her feet – he heard a little slap on the bare flagstones – and lowered her dress and shook it out as best she could.

That'll do, she said. It'll soon dry out in the sun. We're not expecting a visit from the Queen, are we? She came over to him.

So you found something.

He showed her the tube.

Go on then, she said, holding out her forefinger to him like a little girl. Show me your bedside skills.

Shaking a little, he squeezed some cream on to his fingertips and replaced the cap. He put the tube in his pocket and held her forefinger and rubbed the cream over the swelling. She winced.

Sorry, he said.

It's OK.

He kept rubbing gently until the fat white cream vanished into the skin.

Very good, she smiled. Doctor Lewis. Come on, let's have some more cider.

Lewis followed her back out into the sunshine.

Is that a mistle or a song thrush? Gerald asked Lewis, pointing up at the cherry tree.

Song, said Lewis.

How blithe the throstle sings! . . . te tum te tum, come out into the life of things . . . Oh, what is it? Let nature be your teacher!

Gerald chuckled.

I once wrote a very short poem on that theme, he said. 'Nature's like Nietzsche – A dubious teacher.'

He laughed uproariously.

Do you like that little epigram?

Mary poured more cider for Lewis and herself.

No, said Gerald. Unadorned nature leaves us only bare forked animals, alas, much as we may dream of a return to some pristine Eden.

He sighed.

They sat in companionable silence for a while, listening to the song thrush and then Lewis drained his glass and stood up.

You off? asked Mary.

Better be, he said.

Ah well, come again, said Gerald. You know you're always welcome. Bring some juicy village gossip next time, eh? Murder or adultery or at least a heartrending tale of the unspoken love between a man and his sheep, eh? Eh?

And he laughed.

Lewis set his glass on the tray and nodded and turned away.

4 Mary (1)

And Lewis Pike went walking the high downs.

In the village Mrs Percy would be opening the shop again after her dinner. And Lewis could picture Mrs Whitaker going in and taking about twenty minutes to buy one book of second-class stamps and a tin of catfood because there was after all so much to talk about, especially the weather, and that funny new couple at Pound Cottage, never still from one minute to the next. Mrs Percy folding her brawny arms across her gingham housecoat and pursing her lips awhile and saying she didn't think they'd be here long, they'd find the village too quiet for their liking.

And Maurice in the churchyard, strimming around the gravestones, grass seeds and halms and insects whirling around his head and clinging to his sweaty forehead and him wiping them clear away and working on. But stopping to watch without word or expression as the bloke from Pound Cottage comes haring back through the village in his flash new car to halt at the door and rush inside for something he's forgotten. Rushing back out again and flinging a sheaf of papers on the passenger seat and doing a tight turn and driving back to town. Maurice watching all without word or expression and then lowering his head and working on.

In her converted chapel the lady novelist would be settling down in her lovely morning room to work on her latest novel. Gazing out of the window and nibbling her fountainpen, deep in thought.

In her cottage with its thatch badged and bare like the coat of an old dog, loony Mrs Martin standing at her kitchen window that she keeps closed mostly nowadays for fear of burglars and strange men and talking softly and without pause to the birds that fill her garden. Her smile vacant and serene.

But Lewis Pike went walking the high downs.

He met no one in all those acres and miles. Those high downs empty of shepherds, those fields empty of ploughmen and nodding horses.

Those lost landscapes.

He was back in the kitchen going through his pockets when he found the tube of cream he'd used on Mary's finger. He slipped it back in his pocket and walked back up the lane, pondering and biting his lip. He came to the foot of the track and stood a long time. Then he set off up the track fast and came to the Poet's cottage.

He went through the side gate without calling out and entered the garden and found with excitement and fear Mary standing with her back to him playing a hosepipe on the runner beans.

He came up near to her.

Um . . . he said.

Ow! she yelped and wheeled round. When she saw him she laughed and clutched her hand almost to her throat and let the hosepipe hang loose from her other hand, water seeping silver through the grass.

God, Lewis, she said. You gave me a shock.

Sorry, he said.

He couldn't help glancing at the hosepipe.

She looked down at it too and bent it back for a moment to cut it to a trickle.

No ban for us, she said proudly. Our own spring water and it's supposed never to run dry.

Oh yeah, said Lewis, remembering. He wondered if that was true, even in '76. He'd ask Grandma. She'd remember.

He's out for a walk, she said. Usually is, this time of day.

Lewis glanced down at his watch. It was just on 4.30.

Too damn hot if you ask me, she said, stroking back her hair. Her forehead was streaked with sweat. What brought you tramping all the way back up here? she asked him, then immediately wished she hadn't, in case he had no real excuse and should feel embarrassed.

But it was OK.

Lewis produced the tube of cream from his pocket and awkwardly held it out. You left this, he said. I mean, I took it. By accident . . .

Mary laughed. Oh Lewis, you didn't need to come all the way back just for that. I think I'd have made it through the night without it.

His hand began to drop and she saw his sweet hurt face. She reached out and he gave her the tube.

Thanks anyway though, she said gently.

How's your finger?

She looked surprised. Oh – still hurts and a bit swollen, but not too bad. She looked around. Hasn't stopped me watering the beans though.

Lewis looked at them. They were growing well. But it was too soon in the day to be watering them, the sun too high in the sky.

Shouldn't be watering them yet, he said. Sun'll scorch the leaves.

Lewis Pike! she cried, half cross, half amused. You're becoming a typical interfering little old countryman. At your age! How old are you?

He grinned sheepishly. Seventeen.

One of the reasons we *didn't* want a cottage in the middle of a village is *precisely* because we knew we'd get interfering old boys coming round and leaning over the hedge and telling us exactly what we were doing wrong in *our* garden!

Lewis grinned more broadly and thought immediately of old Tom. That was him to a t. Mary was sharp, in a funny way.

Anyway I'm hosing them round the roots, not on the leaves, so they won't get scorched. And if you tell me one more thing I'm doing wrong I'll hose *you*!

Without thinking, he said, I don't mind if you do, I'm that hot.

Right, she said wickedly and turned the hose full on his chest and loosed it.

He leapt backward under the blast of chilly water and gasped and laughed out, and Mary pursued him and soaked him. Then she relented and played the water up in the air where it scattered into silver drops and fell on them both alike.

They were quickly soaked and laughing. Lewis's hair was plastered to his head and his shirt clung tightly to his skinny chest. Mary shook her long hair and water flew off from it in an arc of sunbright droplets and some fell on him and across his face and he thought he could smell Mary and whatever shampoo she used, apple or peach or strawberry. He let the droplets rest where they fell, not brushing them away, letting them stay like something precious and never to be recaptured.

Jesus, laughed Mary. I think that's enough for now. I'm feeling cold already.

She dropped the hose into the grass and walked over to the side of the cottage out of sight and the water ceased flowing. She came back with her face raised up to the sun and her teeth shining white and scooping her hair up with her thumbs back over her ears. She stood with Lewis and her blue cotton dress clung tightly to her, showing clearly her breasts and her nipples that the cold water had made hard.

God, she said. We'd better dry out.

I, said Lewis, looking down at his watch. I better be getting back. Ought to cook dad's supper.

So soon?

You don't know what he's like before he's had his supper.

Mary smiled. Men! she said. Tuh!

Anyway, said Lewis, turning away.

Oh well, said Mary. Thanks for bringing back the cream, that was sweet of you.

'S OK, said Lewis.

And – well, you know. Come again.

She was stroking her bottom lip absentmindedly with her swollen waspstung finger but her eyes were fixed on his. He looked downwards.

Yeah, right, he said, and swung towards the garden gate.

5 The Wren

He laid two big pork chops on the grill and then he boiled up some water and put a heap of potatoes in. After a few minutes he added some carrots. He looked at the chops and turned them over and turned the grill down. He stood staring out of the window, humming. A wren was in the hedge, singing louder than all the other birds in the garden.

The phone went and it was his father.

Oh Lewis, hello, I dunno if you've cooked supper yet, only there's this event on here tonight and I can do some overtime. Is supper done yet?

Just about to start, said Lewis.

Well, whenever you want it, said his father. I'll grab something here. They're laying on a real spread so there'll be plenty left over, I bet. Anyway, least I don't have to wear the bloody costume tonight. I'm just showing people around, it seems. So.

So that means we'll not be collectin' Allie tonight then?

Oh buggery, I'd clean forgot about her. Oh Lewis, I'm sorry, it'll have to wait till tomorrow night now. You'll have to phone them up and tell them at the vet's.

OK, said Lewis. All right, I'll see you later.

Yep. Not too late, I shouldn't think. You eat summing now.

Yeah yeah, said Lewis.

He picked up the phone and dialled the vet's number. After a long time a woman's voice answered. He said nothing. She spoke again. He still said nothing. He put the phone down.

He ate the two pork chops and some of the potato and

scraped the rest into the bin and covered it with bunched-up newspaper so that his father wouldn't see it.

He watched television and it was all bright colours and laughing people and a competition of some sort but he took nothing in. He turned it off and went upstairs. After a while he came back down again, snapping open an air rifle with a tin clenched between his teeth. He fitted a pellet and snapped the rifle shut and went slowly over to the kitchen window.

He thought the wren would have gone by now, restless as his own beating heart, but he could still hear it there in the hedge. Thick with summer's growth, he'd never see it. He leaned on the sill and sighted the rifle on the hedge and waited. At last the wren reappeared on top of the hedge and clear against the blue sky, so small and plump she looked almost spherical. He closed the sight on her and though she still twitched and moved so restlessly about on the hedge he fired at her just as she opened her wings. She tumbled into the long grass.

He dropped the rifle and raced outside and found her fluttering in pain in the grass like a fledgeling fallen from its nest and the strong song of life and territory was gone and the voice too was now only a helpless fledgeling cheep. She was as if shrinking towards death. He picked her up and one wing trailed on tiny broken bones. The pellet had punched a neat hole near the shoulder and taken feathers with it and passed into the body. She sat in the palm of his hand, not struggling, her heart vibrating, head cocked at him. She was beautiful. He would never kill another wren. He closed his other hand gently over her to rest her in darkness and looked about and when he lifted the roof of his hand off her again she was dead of a burst heart. He laid her back in the long grass and left her for the flies.

Then he returned to her as an afterthought, his heart beating as the bird's had done, swollen with inarticulate feeling as if about to burst through the breastbone and his breathing irregular and troubled. He vowed he would never kill another animal again except to eat. That was different. That was hunting.

After a moment's hesitation he knelt and made a sign of the cross over her, then he stood and looked around and made another sign over his own breast. He did all this troubled and vague, not understanding. The Poet had once said 'life is sacrifice'. He went back into the house, eyes searching, not understanding.

He went out walking again, as restless as a bird. Already that day he had walked twenty miles or more and still wasn't tired or felt no tiredness. He walked over Swallowcliffe Down and struggled to phrase his yearning for what was still and for ever unattained. He was here, always here, but – such strangeness in this – on Swallowcliffe Down, yearning for Swallowcliffe Down. At last he came back and ascended the hills beyond Hound Wood and on the top of the hill overlooking the valley and the village he sat on a limestone outcrop where the soil was thin and sheltered by furze. He lay back and watched the sunset change over time. Pale, barely distinguishable pink bunched into livid salmon weals over the darkening horizon towards Dorset. Cloud turned smokegrey and heavy but that was only the failing light and promised no rain. All the sky that had been bare blue all day was bruised and wounded now that cloud was coming over.

Around him in the cropped tough grass fluttered yellow rockroses. He plucked absently at a rockrose and then pinched through its stalk with a caked thumbnail and rolled it into a humid ball between forefinger and thumb and flicked it from his palm. Then he crawled about and pinched through all the rockroses he could find and tore their petals and rent them and flung them about him.

Afterwards he examined the sunset again with animal curiosity, cockheaded. He imagined a bow and he fitted an

23

arrow and fired it into the sky but however he strained his mind's eye it fell far short of that distant gold buckler, the sun, and scudded with a mocking whisper over the grass in the valley below. Then he rose and shambled downhill and broke the invisible arrow beneath his boot heel and went home.

He was in bed when his father returned and he knew that he had been drinking. He laboured up the stairs and pissed noisily into the toilet bowl then he lurched into his bedroom and Lewis knew he'd fallen asleep immediately, fully clothed, across the bed and would wake tomorrow with a parched mouth and maybe a dead arm.

No sleep came to him. He thought of Mary a lot. He imagined he fought for her in some battle on a hill and led a glorious charge, the sun bright on his sword and bright on the sheen of blood that lay thinly over his bronze armour. His death was prolonged and glorious.

He dreamed with his eyes open, watching the clouds scudding over the sky with no fall of rain and the heavy-leaved branches of the trees tired and swaying. And no sleep came.

Sometimes when he knew that his father was asleep next door and wouldn't stir for hours he would get up and go out into the garden and crane up at the stars or he would go down to the river and wade kneedeep and naked, remembering its brown floods only three months ago when it was so swollen with spring rain. Or he would lie and soak himself, shivering, the heat given off his skin driving the fish away downriver, his head alone raised, and then stand and masturbate as his skin hummed and warmed and the night air wrapped around him.

6   The Town (1)

He knew his father must be feeling rough the next morning because he was sitting down and drinking tea and he hadn't bothered to make a pot which he did usually. He ate nothing but steadily drank his way through mug after mug of sweet strong tea.

Morning! said Lewis brightly, close to his ear.

His father turned his head slowly. You bugger, he said. You'll feel it one day, my boy. One day you'll know what it's like an' all.

Lewis grinned and helped himself to a bowl of cereal.

How was it anyhow?

Oh it was all right. Investors or summing wanting to have a look around. London types, suits an' all, but very polite really. Polite chaps. Remembered my name, or one of 'em did. Ah, hello John, he says, how's things?

Lewis grimaced.

Anyhow after they'd all packed up an' gone an' we were all munching our way through all the nosh they'd left cos they didn't eat hardly anythin' –

And the cider, said Lewis.

And the cider, he acknowledged. Farmer Gyles's Genuine Old Tyme Farmhouse Cyder or summing daft. Wicked stuff an' all.

Depends on how much you drink, said Lewis loftily.

His father gave him an evil look and went on. Anyhow, where was I?

The nosh, said Lewis.

Oh right. Yeah well, after we were all tuckin' into the

sandwiches an' vollavonts an' smoked salmon an' roast beef an' all kinds of things, Will says to me, he says, Of course John, you know what all this is about, don't you? An' I look blank so he leans close up and says, Well it's all pretty much hushhush at the moment but I've heard they want to do the same sort of thing up near you. Oh yes? I say. He gives me the old nod and wink and says, Up at Hound Wood apparently.

Lewis stopped chewing and laid his spoon back in the bowl and raised his right hand to his mouth and bowed his head.

Anyway, he says, that'll suit you, eh John? Not far to walk in the morning if you got a job there, eh? Save a bit on petrol there, eh?

He drank his tea. A long slurp.

Which is very true, of course. Though whether it'll ever come to anythin' I dunno.

He looked at his watch and drained his tea and set his mug down on the table and stood up.

Ah well, he said. No rest for the wicked.

He looked down at his son and felt an upwelling of unsought sadness. He hesitated. Then he said cheerily, You going over to see Katy today then?

Lewis looked up. What d'you mean?

She says in the letter, haven't you even looked at it yet? You can go over an' see them any time. You could go over and see 'em today. Nice day for it.

I was going to collect Allie this morning.

What, all the way to Shaftesbury?

Wunt take long. Couple of hours.

Yeah, an' back again. An' she won't exactly be up to walkin' yet, now will she? Now don't you be daft. We'll go over and get her tonight, she'll be fine till then. You 'op on the train and go and see your big sister, eh?

Lewis nodded.

And don't worry about supper tonight, I'll pick us up

some fish and chips or summing. You go an' see Katy.

He still wondered whether to go and get Allie.

He would walk up over Gallows Hill and join the oxdrove along the chalk ridge leading almost all the way to the hill of Shaftesbury. He would walk the oxdrove between its high hawthorn hedges and meet no one and pause only in gateways to look out over the sunlit sweep of the valley and across to Whitesheet Hill or south to Pentridge. And he would walk back with Allie at his heels and her tongue hanging out and bubbled with saliva in the heat.

But instead he went upstairs and took his money and left the house and walked north and caught a train at Tisbury to Yeovil Junction.

He walked from there into the town, to Katy's flat in a block near the ringroad where she lived with her husband and two children.

Oh Lewis, you might have phoned to say you were coming. Come in then.

Katy looked tired and stressed. He followed her into the hall and sitting room. The baby was crying. The television was on. Kenny the toddler stared at him for a moment and then waddled over and thumped him in the groin. Then he sat down and stared at him again.

Shush shush, said Katy, picking the baby up and holding it on her left shoulder and patting it on the rump. She swivelled gently. Shush shush. At each turn the baby's face came into view, wrinkled and inflamed and demonic, eyes sightlessly fixed on him with implacable hatred. His palms were sweating and he felt dizzy. He felt very close to turning and running out.

Here, you stay and talk to Kenny. I'll be back in a mo. He knows quite a few words now, don't you, Kenny?

Kenny looked up at his mother and said nothing.

Katy disappeared into the bedroom.

Lewis knew what she was doing. He pictured the baby at the breast, that demonic squashed face, the breast swollen and blueveined. He felt physically sick. He sat down gently on the edge of the sofa and held his head in his hands, hoping he wasn't going to be sick.

The spider plant on the telly was faded almost milky white. The flat smelled of baby and milk and static and thick carpet and dust and central heating. He was sweating heavily and tried to calm his breathing. The carpet under his boots was horribly soft and thick and the sofa was too soft and squashy under him and the television blared at him and he wished he could just set it all on fire. He couldn't believe how nauseous he felt. All these babies staring and jostling him, all these electrical beams and voices crowding in on him, and none of them making any sense, none.

He knew Kenny was staring at him. He didn't look up but he knew his nephew was staring at him wide eyed. Da, said Kenny. He squatted and banged his palms flat on the carpet. Da. Da. Lewis saw clouds of dust arise from where he banged the carpet. They formed into a plume and slunk mysteriously under the door and he watched them go. His mouth was caked with dust and milk, his brain was banging with blood. All these bodies and babies and smells and milk and no point to it anywhere, no point at all. He could make sense of nothing.

Kenny was getting to his feet and coming towards him. He didn't know if he could stand it. Kenny had something in his hand which he held out towards him. It was the remote control.

Da, said Kenny. Dat. Da.

Lewis kept his head down and did not move. Kenny repeated his words until he got bored and dropped the control and waddled back and sat suddenly by the television, not looking at it, his whiteblond hair dyed with the bright colours of the cartoon.

Lewis could sense his sister about to come back. The

panic in his stomach was unbearable. He would either have to shit or puke. She would offer him tea or coffee and which should he have? He didn't know, he couldn't see any point in choosing one rather than the other. It didn't matter. Tea, though. He would say tea. Kenny would have orange squash out of a smelly plastic beaker and it would leave an orange stain around his mouth. Katy would wipe it away with a tissue.

He struggled to his feet and ran into the toilet and locked the door behind him. He sank to his knees and threw up in shallow desperate retches, gripping the edge of the bowl and shuddering. Strings of saliva hung from his mouth. He wiped them away with the back of his hand. He laid his forehead on the cool white rim of the bowl and it felt good. Jesus, he breathed.

Lewis? called his sister. You in the loo?

Just a minute! he called back.

He stood and flushed the loo and ran the cold water and it smelled metallic and chemical. He ran it over his hands and splashed his face again and again and drank a little water from a cupped hand and looked in the mirror. He was ashen grey and his mouth hung open like an idiot's. Most of all he hated his own hunted eyes.

He smoothed the water from his face and shook his hands and breathed deeply and went back into the sitting room.

Kyra's asleep now, said Katy. Bit of peace and quiet. Do you want tea or coffee?

Tea, he said and sat down again.

Are you all right? she asked.

Yeah, fine, he said.

She made them both tea and handed him a mug.

So – how's dad?

He's OK.

And you? No work yet?

He shook his head.

Oh well. You will, I'm sure. It's just a matter of time. These things are getting better, I'm sure they are. Have you thought of doing some computer course? Andy says you can always get jobs in computers nowadays. It's having no skills to offer that's the problem. Andy says they've had loads of orders these past two weeks, things are really picking up.

She sipped her tea.

I still think you'll have to move though, if you really want a job, Lewis. I've said you can come and stay here for a bit while you're looking for something.

He nearly laughed hysterically. He bowed his head and clenched his teeth. His own sister and she really had no idea. So far away.

I bet you'd find something in Yeovil pretty quickly. I mean, honestly, you're not going to find anything in the village, are you?

He said nothing. Bowed his head.

I mean, I know you love it and all that, but it is a bit full of old fossils, isn't it? It hasn't exactly kept up with the twentieth century, has it?

She paused and then thought maybe she had said enough. How's Tom? she asked.

He's gone to Bournemouth, said Lewis. College.

Won't he be back for the summer?

Lewis shrugged. He didn't add that Tom's brother was squatting in Blandford with a three-hundred-pound-a-week heroin habit. Why tell her? Why not?

It's not good for you, all this being on your own. I bet you don't eat properly when Dad's not there, you look as thin as a rake as it is.

Lewis couldn't even remember what he had eaten yesterday. Not for the past week.

Anyhow, sighed Katy. I mustn't nag you, I suppose. She hugged Kenny. We're all very Happy Families here, aren't we, Kenny?

30

Kenny snuggled up close to his mother and chewed his finger and looked at Lewis sleepily.

Daddy's got lots of orders, and we're off to Florida next month. She smiled at Lewis. Not enough hours in the day, Andy says. I'm sure if you wanted to he could take you on – at least for the summer. But like I say, it's up to you.

His gut ached or his stomach or his bowels. He had to go. He stood up and said, I'll just go to the toilet.

Katy saw he hadn't touched his tea.

His bowels opened in a steady stream and he cradled his face in his hands and shivered.

When he came back, Katy said, Are you sure you're all right Lewis?

Yeah, I'm fine, he mumbled. Look, I've got to go.

But you've only been here a few minutes.

Well, yeah. I said I'd get some things for Dad in town. Tools and things.

Well, look, I'm sorry if I nagged you, she said, holding her arm out to him. You know it's only because I care about you. I just think you'd be a lot happier . . .

'S OK, said Lewis. Don't worry. I'll . . . you know . . .

There was a pause. She felt helpless.

Oh Lewis, she said. She tried to smile maternally at him and found she couldn't. He seemed so distant and so sad. Again she reached out an arm towards him.

You take care now, d'you hear?

Yeah yeah, he said. Grinned.

OK. Well, come and say goodbye to Uncle Lewis, Kenny!

Uncle Lewis! Again he felt a rush of laughter that he swallowed down.

Kenny half hid his face against his mother's leg and looked shyly at him.

Lewis waved at him and managed a smile.

Katy talked some more. Lewis thought how plump she had grown, yet she looked tired. Then he said goodbye and that he would see them again soon. Katy said they'd all come over for dinner one Sunday, and then he left.

He paused only briefly on the street corner to look back at the flats where Katy lived and his eyes were brimming and wet but they burned brightly too, like fire seen burning underwater.

He went into the town centre to the busy shopping streets amid the crush of people, not knowing why. He felt guilty. He stumbled there among the strange faces and the crowds like some unpalaced king stumbling lost and drunken among paupers. Pausing to tremble on the margins of a main street he tried in vain to remember where he was and then thought that after all it did not matter where or who. Hair or woo, he thought and giggled. Passersby regarded him strangely. Take me back, he thought. Take me back . . .

He was hungry. He went into a supermarket. The aisles were crowded with plump shoppers, mothers and children and babies, and he kept at a distance from them.

He went up and down the aisles in their antiseptic light. He passed the bays of fruit and smelled the summer smell of their ripe skins. He hovered at the delicatessen counter and eyed the cold ham and the cheese and he passed by the racks of fresh baked bread and his stomach groaned with the sweet pain of hunger. Yet though he had money in his pocket he bought nothing. Though he was almost giggling with hunger the food on the shelves disgusted him as if it were just so much flesh and blood and he passed by, seeing and smelling it out of his strange asceticism, and shunned it and left the supermarket emptyhanded and lightheaded with hunger, walking away from the people with their loaded trolleys.

Though he wanted desperately to catch a train and get back he carried on walking with an aimless determination, feeling obscurely that he must be heroic and go on as if on a quest. Then on the outskirts of the town he came to a shop that had plastic crates out on the pavement filled with

32

canvas haversacks and boots and faded army fatigues and in the window there were knives. He went in and at the back of the dark shop he saw racks of crossbows for sale. He fingered the price labels and found one he liked for £80. He had just over £5 in his pocket. He looked over at the man behind the till and away again.

Need any help, mate?

Lewis shook his head.

Nice, aren't they? Beautifully made.

He nodded. Then with great courage he asked, What sort of bolts does this one take?

The man swivelled in his chair and reached up on the shelf and showed him a box of bolts, slender aluminium rods with bluntish tips. Lewis nodded.

He left the shop and walked for another half an hour and came to a newsagent's on a corner among residential streets. As if in a dream and as if protected by an unseen power, he went in and asked the woman for some chewing gum and paid with his five-pound note. When the till drawer opened he was ready and his hand darted forward like a snake's head or a blackbird's beak stabbing at worms and snatched the ten-pound notes from the till. The woman slapped his arm hard and screamed as if with real terror and slammed the till drawer shut but it was too late. He ran from the shop and ran very fast into the main street, his legs pumping and his hands flat out and taut like knives. In a park he stood against a willow and counted out the notes to £140 and panicked and tore five of them in half as if knowing he was not entitled to them and threw them in a litter bin. He returned to the army-surplus shop and bought the crossbow for £80 and a box of bolts.

No targets? asked the man.

No, said Lewis, then panicked and said yes and so bought some cardboard targets with his loose change. He returned to the station and caught the train home.

7 Blackberries

Seeing Katy always brought back memories of childhood. He stared sightlessly out of the train window and remembered that time they all went blackberrying, Dad too; it must have been a Sunday, he guessed. He was six or seven maybe, Katy a little older, and wasn't there one of Katy's friends with them too? Becky? They carried those little tupperware boxes they used for packed lunches that smelled of plastic but by the time you had only a handful of ripe blackberries in the bottom you couldn't smell the plastic any more but only fruit and autumn.

He was wearing shorts, he remembered that now.

They found brambles all along a woodland ride that was overgrown with deep green grass around long dark puddles. After the summer, here it was still green and wet. They picked heavy boxes of blackberries and his wrist ached just from holding his boxful one-handed. Then it began to rain suddenly and heavily. And she – Mum – said they could get back to the car going through the shelter of the woods but Dad said they couldn't, they'd have to go back up the track. They must have had an argument. They often did. Dad said there was no way he was going back through the wood, you couldn't get through the other side. Mum said she wasn't going back up the track, they'd get soaked to the skin. They stood at the edge of the wood arguing, Dad with his shoulders hunched and hands in his pockets, scowling. Then he walked off up the track on his own, the heavy rain making his shirt transparent, clinging to his broad back.

Come on then, said Mum brightly. Let's beat Daddy back to the car.

They followed her, Indian file, into the wood. At first it was easy going. The rain had stopped and they followed a dry woodland path between tall pines. The sun came out and flashed through the needles overhead. He remembered nursing his tub of blackberries carefully to his chest, determined not to drop a single one. He looked down and began to count them as he walked. He stopped when he got to twenty-five. There were far too many.

When he looked up he saw a fabulous bird sitting on a branch with its tail hanging down almost to the ground. Also in the trees were cymbals and gongs and chimes hanging down. Ahead of him his mother and Katy and Becky stopped and looked around. Katy looked back at him and he knew that she saw what he saw. Then without another word they walked on.

A horse, white or sundappled, passed among the trees ahead of them. It stopped at a woodland pool and stretched a foreleg out and lowered its head and drank. Then it raised its head and looked at them briefly and then walked on and vanished into the trees.

From behind a dark bush arose a cloud of little birds, each one a bright different colour. They chattered and screamed as they whirled about their heads like coloured ribbons stretched between the trees and then they flew away.

Other birds sang and could be understood. They sang songs or hymns. Other birds just chattered. Looking up, Lewis caught glimpses of brownskinned children high in the trees, dangling from branches and caught by the sunlight above the canopy and they saw him looking up and giggled and disappeared.

They walked for hours and stopped at a pool and drank like animals and walked on again. They saw more coloured and chattering birds and deer and horses and fantastic garlands of flowers hanging from the trees.

A fly buzzed in his face. Lewis waved it away and glanced across at the passenger opposite him, a middle-aged woman, and shifted his chin on to his other hand. No, he was remembering bollocks now. He was just day-dreaming. He was always daydreaming nowadays.

After that they emerged from the wood and had to scramble through swathes of bracken and then bramble and nettle to reach the path. The brambles were laden with blackberries but they didn't stop to pick them. They were too busy holding back the curving brambles from their bare arms and legs but still the thorns caught them and left needle cuts across their skin. They all got stung as well and it started to rain again. Still nobody spoke to each other but each battled on through the thorns. It was exhilarating in a way. It was like trekking through a hostile jungle and though they didn't speak they held back the brambles for each other or thrashed them down with sticks.

They didn't beat Dad back to the car. He was already sitting behind the wheel when they came in sight. They could see him through the steamed-up windows. He saw them coming and got out of the car. He still looked cross.

Look at you, he said. All wet and muddy. And you've got cuts all over you.

We had to get through some brambles, said Mum.

You'll all need baths tonight, he said. He flicked the front of Lewis's T-shirt lightly. And *that*'ll never come out. Lewis looked down. Where he had clutched the tub of juicy black-berries tightly to his chest there was now a wide stain of purple.

OK OK, said Mum, don't go on. At least we picked some blackberries.

I *told* you you'd never get through that way. I do know this area, you know, I've lived round here a few years myself.

Oh ar, she said. Never bin out of the village, me.

Now don't start, he said.

You were the one who started it.

36

Oh for Christ's sake, woman, just shut up!

She shut up. Then she started to cry softly.

They drove home in silence.

Lewis raised his chin from his hand. There was a red mark where his chin had been pressing. He got up and walked down the carriage to a seat where no one could see him, wiping his eyes dry on the backs of his hands.

8 Mrs Martin

In the garden he took one bolt and honed the blunt tip tirelessly with a sandstone for an hour or more until the sweat streamed from his forehead and dripped from his nose upon the now scratched and gleaming bolt. He fixed a target on to a piece of quarter-inch plywood with drawing pins and nailed that to two staves which he set deep in the ground with a mallet. He loaded the honed bolt into the crossbow and cranked back the ratchet and knelt in the grass and steadied his aim and loosed the bolt at the target.

His aim was good. The bolt punched straight through the plywood and buried itself up to the flight.

Lewis Pike looked up and grinned like a fox.

He took the bow and the bolts and the staves and the target and hid them all carefully behind the logs in the shed where they wouldn't be found at least until September.

He walked out and along the lane and rolled himself over the gate and climbed up the field and skirted the edge of Hound Wood. The smells of summer were rank and drowsy, the nettle leaves already dark green and stringy, the bare earth baked grey. Dust kicked up where he trod.

He leaned against a tree trunk and watched a treecreeper spiralling up another trunk and resting back on its strong tailfeathers. But he heard little and few birds sang. The wind was to his left and he scrutinized the dark wood but could see no antlers still or slowly moving. There were oval droppings shiny and black at the wood's edge and he knew the roe deer were in there but he could see or hear nothing, no bark of alarm or kids' birdlike *peep*. Soon it would be the rut and the stags would bellow with taut necks in Ashcombe Bottom beyond and would run as he had seen them each summer, nose to tail with the does in figures of eight in a marriage of lust and fear with each year a greater stiffness in their winter limbs and so driven into lust by summer's heat to escape that winter's coming.

But Lewis's head thrummed and he imagined what it would be like to see the men and the diggers in the heart of Hound Wood, gnawing at it, bringing destruction to the wood and bringing his father work. But when they come I'll be gone, he thought. Somewhere, fuck knows where. But I'll not work here.

The incomers would start a campaign against the development. He almost grinned satirically at the thought. Mrs Armitage and her cronies. They'd get up a petition, you'd get in protesters, didikoys and gyppos, travellers, all sorts. And Lewis Pike who knew every tree and leaf in that wood would do nothing except visit the wood daily as he had done for years until he could come there no more for the diggers and excavators and site tape dividing the land. Yet now he loitered a moment with his hand gripping the stock of his invisible crossbow and behind certain trees he paused and raised the crossbow and fired off invisible bolts, bolt after bolt finding its mark in the chests and backs of men.

And then he turned from Hound Wood and started to descend the meadow, past late-afternoon rabbits, ghostgrey, pausing from nibbling to listen and watch and then fleeing into the earth. And Lewis Pike felt in that moment that he knew it all and understood it all as everything goes into the earth: that the human is a strange brief flower from a few millennia since to a few millennia hence, a mere stone's throw in time and then gone. That fantastic potentate quite gone and his restless, homeless heart stilled at last and his imperturbable subjects, the animals, will go on just the same. Nature stirs and things are restored. The human

39

passes by and nothing changes. The silent old stone Eden slumbers on.

He crouched in the long grass. Across the meadow near the river was an old woman stooping to pick rushes. He screwed up his eyes and stared at her. She was oblivious to the rest of the world. He thought he could hear her humming to herself. There was no one else about. They were quite alone.

Then he recognized her as Mrs Martin. Loopy Mrs Martin. He was nervous. About what she might do next. He was the only one around. She was as mad as a badger, everyone knew that. She might do anything.

She looked as if she was wearing her nightie anyway. It billowed around her when she stooped and in the sunlight betrayed her tiny frame, her very bones. When she had collected enough rushes she held them aloft in her right hand as if they were a torch. Then with her left hand raising the hem of her nightie, demurely and ladylike, she turned and stepped through the reeds and into the river.

Lewis darted forward. She *was* going to do something loopy, he knew it. He'd have to . . .

She didn't get very far. With her right hand wobbling over her head, her tiny feet caught between large stones on the riverbed and she fell, kneeling, looking around her bewildered, her other hand still holding up the hem of her nightie though now floating on the surface of the water and the torch of rushes held high over her head as if they might still cast some light on her confusion and loss.

Lewis ran down through the meadow to the river's edge.

Er . . . Mrs Martin? he called out.

She looked around and up at the trees, gapemouthed. She looked everywhere but in his direction.

Jack? she said.

He didn't know what to say. He stood there helplessly, wondering if he should just wade in. Wade in to her and

40

pick her up. He thought she would weigh no more than a bird, than a dying wren.

Jack? she said again. Is that you?

It's me, he said. Lewis Pike.

Lewis Pike, she repeated slowly. What a coincidence.

She tried to get up but only lurched to one side and Lewis could see she was about to topple over into the river, as inflexible as a statue. There was hardly enough water flowing to drown a kitten but maybe still enough, he thought, to drown an old loony like Mrs Martin. He splashed over to her and grabbed her arm and swung her upright again. He was shocked at the looseness of her skin, as if it wasn't attached to the bone at all. As if she was just a jumble of unconnected bones held together by a sack of rice-paper skin. He pulled her to her feet speechlessly.

She stared at him. Jack, she said. I knew you'd come.

He helped her back towards the bank. He saw that both her knees were bleeding, thin watery blood trickling down her shins where it mingled with the river water, or maybe it was just that she was so old and that her blood was as thin as water anyway.

He sighed when they got to the bank. Out of the water and back on dry land it was as if sanity and lucidity returned, at least for a moment. She heard him sigh and took it as a reproach.

Oh dear, I'm so sorry, she said meekly.

Her helplessness made him feel grown-up and responsible. What were you *doing*? he asked.

Wide-eyed she replied, Why, looking for my poor Jack that's dead.

That last word was a full stop to the conversation. They walked back up the path by the river and he opened the gate and they walked out into the lane. She leant on his shoulder. She was barefoot and the lane was cruelly gravelly. There was also fresh cowshit everywhere from where they had passed by for milking.

Do you want my socks? he said.

She looked at him as if *he* was the mad one. Don't be ridiculous! she said. I have socks of my own. Whatever would I want with your socks? Jack, you do say the queerest things sometimes!

She laid her head against his shoulder. They walked on in companionable silence.

Back up the lane to the village Maurice saw them coming a long way off and came towards them and took her other arm and together they led her into the village shop and sat her down. Mrs Percy popped out the back to make a cup of tea.

Lewis sloped off. Mrs Percy and Mrs Whitaker talked over her head as if she wasn't there. Maurice stood looking uncomfortable on.

Poor old thing, said Mrs Percy. Hasn't been the same since her husband died.

So I've heard, said Mrs Whitaker. Must be very lonely. That generation had it very hard, it seems to me.

They really did, said Mrs Percy. Someone told me that in the first war a third of the men from here went and never came back. Of course it was in the second war that Jack Pike died. Somewhere out in the Far East.

Mrs Whitaker looked queryingly at her. Mrs Percy mouthed more quietly, He broke her heart, so they say.

Mrs Whitaker nodded. Poor old thing.

9 Jack and Rose (1)

It was haymaking time.

Over in a distant field a small grey tractor was lumbering and behind it walked a pair of men. That was Alfred and his son, young Tom, and that little terrier he took everywhere with him. The tractor had a little chimney that spewed dark smoke. In a nearer field, mown two days before, its upside nicely dried now, a horse was dragging a swathe turner. A man walked behind. And in the corner of the field, bearing hay from the neighbouring meadow, stood a highsided hay-cart, almost obliterated by its load. Its ironbound wooden wheels stood taller than a man.

A young man in his early twenties was hitching a couple of heavy horses to the front. He wore a collarless white shirt and old suit trousers and a bowler hat. His forearms were cut and scarred and brawny. When he had hitched up the horses he laid his hand on the leather collar across the back of the right-hand horse and spoke softly. She was the strongest and gentlest horse he'd ever worked with. He'd had some kicks in his time but never from Bess. She shifted her dinnerplate hooves and began to lean forward. The man raised his voice and made noises of encouragement.

Geeaah! Gerraah!

Both horses now leaned mightily into their collars. The leather creaked and groaned across their backs and the traces tautened and then with dreamlike slowness the spokes in the wheels began to turn and the cart moved forward. The man shouted more words of encouragement, and then, once the speed and rhythm of the cart had been established –

a very slow walking pace – he fell in beside it, still resting his arm against the lead horse and humming a tune.

Anyway, he said into the lead horse's twitching ear, speaking softly like a lover, you'll eat most of this load yourselves, won't you, you greedy great buggers!

The haybarn was two miles away. It would take him well over an hour.

He waved across at the older man behind the horse-drawn swathe turner. Last load from that one! he called. The man raised his hand. He looked weary. He had been mowing and turning since four this morning when the dew still lay heavy on the watermeadows and the grass cut more easily.

The younger man knew how he felt. When he had got the cartload back to the farm and unloaded the hay into the stackyard with his brothers, who had walked on ahead for now, he would return here to keep the older man company. They would finish about seven. They would drink a flask of cold tea together and hope for clear sunshine all day tomorrow. The day after, they'd come up here and take the last of the hay in. It was a fine summer this year and the hay was early.

He hadn't been going more than a few minutes when he heard footsteps behind him. He looked round.

Well, good afternoon, Rose Parsons!

Good afternoon, Jack Pike.

The girl was perhaps eighteen and very pretty. She looked both shyly and confidently at Jack. She wore her hair old-fashioned and long.

Where are you headin' then?

Homewards.

He summoned up his courage and nodded towards the cart. You can hop on if you want to.

She laughed at him. Well, you may not have noticed it, Jack Pike, but I am walking *faster* than you and shall be home long before.

44

He looked a little hurt. What's there such a hurry for? he said.

She relented a little. Very well, she said. I'll walk with you a little way, in case you get scared on the long lonely way 'ome.

He looked so solemn she laughed at him again.

They fell in to walking side by side.

He jerked his head back. Bringin' in the hay, he said.

She looked back at the load. I surmised as much, she said.

So, he said after a while. How are you keepin'?

She took it as a family enquiry. We're very well, thank you. And you?

Aye, well enough, he said. After a while he said, We heard from brother Ernest t'other day. Seems he's doin' very well for 'imself down in the town.

Is that so? she said. What's he doin' there again?

He's a commercial traveller, said Jack. He was very proud of brother Ernest. Goes all over Hampshire, Dorset, all over. An' 'e still sends ma a something every week.

Rose Parsons smiled to herself and nodded.

They were approaching the steep part where the track dropped down to join the lane.

Here, said Jack, you best stand behind the cart till we're past this bit. Better safe than sorry.

She did as he said and watched with admiration with her hands shading her eyes from the setting sun as Jack led the horses gently down the slope. He prayed the load would hold. Despite the cart's high sides the hay was mounded still higher above them. Only last year they'd left it drying too long and when they piled it into the cart it wouldn't hold, it was so light. They'd lost tons of it.

The great horses leaned back into the cart and braced their front legs out straight. The polechains tightened. The cart rumbled slowly down, its bulk filling the space completely between the high hedges. Then a wheel hit a large flint. The cart shuddered and stopped.

Bugger, said Jack Pike.

He rested the horses. There was no point trying to drag the cart over an obstacle by main force, not on a slope like this. He might lose half the load and he didn't fancy any more pitchforking today.

He ducked down and looked back.

Well, ain't that just the case, he muttered. The flint had somehow eluded the front wheels and stuck fast in the path of the back left, wedged hard into the drybaked chalk and, at a vertical angle, a perfect block even to a wheel that size. Beyond that he could just see Rose's legs. He heard her voice calling from the other side of the mountain of hay.

Beg pardon? he shouted back.

I said, What's the matter?

Got a flint caught under the wheel, he said. I'll 'ave to shift 'er.

Ahead of him he saw Rose crouch down on her hands and knees and look back at him. They stared at each other under the cart and both started laughing.

Well, said Jack, it's the first time I ever held a conversation under a haycart.

Rose agreed. Where's? . . . Oh, I see it, she said.

Now you leave it alone, he said. I'm not 'avin' you gettin' stuck under 'er wheels. He added with callous joviality, T'd slow me up no end!

Oh you're such a gentleman, Jack Pike.

'Tis what all the girls say.

He began to crawl under the cart. He reached the back wheel and grasped the flint with both hands. It was the size of a haunch of venison. It was firmly wedged between chalk track and wheel. He couldn't budge it.

Rose watched him struggling.

You'll have to back up the cart, she suggested.

He looked up at her sourly. I *know*, he said.

So I'll have to move the stone.

Their eyes met for several seconds and then without

another word he crawled back out from under the cart and spoke to the horses. He slapped Bess on the chest. The horses leaned back and the polechains tightened and the cart creaked back a few inches.

That's it! he called. Now, mind you don't get yourself in front of that wheel!

She scrambled under the cart and shoved with both hands but moved nothing so then she sat between the two back wheels and braced her feet against the recalcitrant flint and strained her thighs and, after a little give, the flint fell outward. She pushed it clear with her hands and got out and stood up. Before she could call out, the cart had started to move forward again on its stately way, unimpeded. She followed behind to the bottom of the hill. Once Jack had steered the cart round into the lane there was room for her to skip down the side of it and join him at the front.

We did it, didn't we? she said.

He stared at her for a while and then couldn't help smiling despite himself. We did, he said.

They walked on. Aye, he said. You're more use than some girls I could mention.

She reflected on this. Then she breathed in and said, Is it true that you're walking out with . . .

But her words were drowned by an approaching din overhead. They stopped and looked up. Two planes buzzed low heading north. Up over Whitesheet Down and were gone. They stared after them a while.

More 'n a hundred mile an hour they can go, said Jack. Two hundred even. Fly to the moon an' back soon.

Yes, but they're not carryin' half the hay in Wiltshire, are they? Rose pointed out.

Jack ignored her. Just think, he said. They could fly to Dorchester and back before we even get home. Further than that even.

That's just daft, said Rose.

He smiled at her and they walked on. Looking down at

47

her boots she said, Do you think there'll be a war, Jack Pike?

He shrugged. Everyone says so. I dunno. He thought about the planes. About the things he had heard in the Horseshoe. I suppose, he said.

Will you fight? she said.

I suppose, he said.

10 The White Horse (1)

Lewis was quite a hero in the pub that night.

They drove over to the White Horse at Compton Wake. It was their nearest local now. At Sunday lunchtimes it was invaded by people driving from the towns, but most nights it was too quiet and remote to be anything but local. The pub in their village, the Horseshoe, had finally shut down four years ago. So now the White Horse was pretty much the nearest and meant a drive over. But the lanes there were quiet.

And news of Mrs Martin had already got around.

What an old dingbat! said Dave Mabey. She'd be floating out to sea at Christchurch by now if it wasn't for you.

What'll happen to her now, I wonder? said Dennis from behind the bar.

She'll 'ave to go in an old folks' 'ome, won't she, now? said Dave Mabey. You can't 'ave 'er wanderin' around like that, can you?

John Pike looked over at Lewis. And why not? he said quietly. She does a lot less harm around the place than you, Dave Mabey, you big yobbo.

Lewis and his father grinned at each other conspiratorially.

Another pint?

A Coke, said Lewis.

When John Pike came back from the bar, Lewis said, She kept talking about Jack. Who's Jack? I thought her husband was something else.

So he was. John Pike took a long draught from his fresh pint and set it down. Buggered if I can remember. Mr

49

Martin . . . He turned to Dennis. What was Martin's Christian name, Dennis? Buggered if I can remember.

Dennis stared down at the pump handles for a while. Me neither, he said.

John Pike turned back. Oh well. It wasn't Jack anyhow. Might have been . . . Peter? Or Paul? Began with a P, I think. He was from Kent and an unfriendly customer too, never mixed much.

So who's Jack? Lewis knew he was on to a trail here like a hound after a wounded fox. His father grinned slyly. Well, he said. Who do you think?

Light dawned. Granddad?

Exactly, said John Pike. My old man. Jack Pike.

What, and he and Mrs Martin . . .?

Now don't you go jumping to conclusions and blackening my old man's name, said John Pike affably. She wasn't Mrs Martin till latish in life. She was Miss . . . Weathered it was. Anyhow. No, my old man was a goodlooking devil apparently and he must 'ave walked out with Mrs Martin, Miss Weathered, for a while. Not that that meant much in them days, mind you, just a kiss and a cuddle on a Sunday afternoon, my mum said. Not like girls nowadays, drop their knickers for any bloke that takes their fancy.

Lewis grinned. That sounds a good idea, he thought. Where can you meet these girls?

No, said John Pike. Walking out meant just walking out in them days, mostly. There was terrible trouble for any girl who got herself in the family way. Anyhow. Some time after that my old dad must have fallen for ma and he fell for her in a big way. He was a decent man and I'm sure he didn't do anything unkind or nothin' but Jeanie Weathered never got over him. It was quite a few years later that she married this chap Martin and they lived mostly away from here. And I don't think there was ever much love in it. No children or nothin'.

Lewis nodded. It seemed so odd that these old women,

Mrs Martin, his grandma too, could still be in love at that age, and with a man dead nearly half a century. But maybe not so odd when you think about it. He nodded again, this time to himself.

The door of the pub opened and an incongruous trio entered: Gavin (the vicar), Mary and the Poet, all talking and laughing together like old friends.

Aha! cried Gerald on seeing them there. Pike One and Pike Two! Thought I might bump into you here. What's your poison?

He bought a round of drinks. He had a double brandy himself and he and Gavin brought the rest over. Mary sat between Gavin and Lewis. She was wearing a short blue dress that became shorter when she crossed her legs. Her legs were very brown.

Gerald rolled a cigarette. He asked Gavin if he smoked. Gavin shook his head.

The body is a temple of the holy spirit, said Mary. Gavin smiled at her.

I suppose that is a reason for not smoking, he said. But I'd sound a bit pious coming out with a line like that in here, wouldn't I?

Quite true, said Gerald. The tavern is the last home of paganism and earthly delight, whichever way you look at it, and no place for preaching. Fortunately, padre, you're not wearing your dogcollar at the mo and could well pass for an offduty . . . teacher? A geography teacher, perhaps, with that beard?

Both John and Lewis Pike were taken aback at how familiar the Poet was being and relieved to see that Gavin was perfectly capable of taking a joke.

Offduty teacher maybe, he allowed. But not a *geography* teacher, *please*.

I quite agree, said Mary, setting her drink down and wiping her forefinger over her lips and patting Gavin on the knee. Geography teachers have notoriously unkempt beards that sprawl all over their faces, and are often a horrible gingery colour.

What, geography teachers? said Gavin.

Mary giggled. No, their beards, she said. I'm happy to say that I have never undergone the trauma of seeing a geography teacher naked, and thereby discovering whether they are gingery all over. Although I could well believe it. I could believe pretty well *anything* of geography teachers.

It was turning into one of those inebriated nonsensical conversations that Lewis loved. He wished he could join in but he could never talk fast enough. His father wore a baffled smile.

Whereas you, Reverend Harris, went on Mary, have a neatly trimmed, ecclesiastical, and mostly fairish beard. She reached out and stroked it briefly with the back of her fingers. Very *kempt*, she said.

Lewis felt insanely jealous. What a flirt, he thought. And Gavin a married man.

But just what is it that you have against geography teachers? asked Gavin. Something serious by the sound of it.

Ever since we went on a geography field trip to Telford, said Mary. There was an incident at the back of the school coach involving myself, a boy called Robert, and a king-size Milky Way, which led to my being told off by our geography teacher in front of the whole class. Mr Peckitt, his name was.

Beard?

Gingery, affirmed Mary. Unkempt. She stroked her dress down demurely. And he called me some very unkind names indeed.

Gerald roared with laughter. I bet he did too! You never told me that story before, darling. What are the full details?

Later darling, later, said Mary.

Gavin was by now looking distinctly embarrassed. Another drink anybody? he asked.

Everybody wanted another drink. It was that kind of evening. The Poet asked for another double brandy.

The drink of poets! he informed everybody. Algernon Swinburne's favourite, algolagniac Algy. Burst into tears if he saw a vase of cut flowers.

They talk too fast, John Pike was thinking. They talk too fast and they use words that don't mean anything. Like Lewis, he was wondering how to join in.

Gavin returned with the drinks, hoping the conversation had moved on from naked geography teachers, only to hear Mary turn to Lewis with, Well you must have had the most recent experience of the species, Lewis. What do you think?

Tossers, said Lewis emphatically. All teachers are tossers anyway but geography ones are somethin' special.

There you are, said Mary triumphantly.

They tell you, said Lewis, getting animated, I mean you think they're goin' to tell you about these places with these really good names, like, like . . .

Samarkand, suggested the Poet. Alexandria.

Right, said Lewis.

Gethsemane, said Mary, mindful of Gavin's presence. Anastasia.

The banks of the Guadalquivir, said Mary liltingly.

And all you get, said Lewis, is stuff about population growth. And coal.

They all nodded.

It does indeed take a very special kind of talent, said Gerald, to make such a subject as geography dull. A toast: to the extinction of geography teachers!

They all drank.

You're very quiet tonight, said Gerald to John Pike. All well?

John Pike smiled self-deprecatingly. I'm wonderin' how to keep up with you all! he said. You all talk so fast!

Gerald laughed. Indeed we do, he said. And it is all complete drivel. He paused for thought. Yes, he said, although we've lived in the country for three years now we probably still move at an urban pace. Not at all good for you.

We're slowing down though, said Mary languorously. Some of us more than others.

Where were you before, anyhow? asked John Pike.

London, said Gerald.

Ah, said John Pike.

Exactly, said the Poet. Not much to add to those two dud syllables. Lun–dun. The toll of a funereal bell.

Oh darling, you do exaggerate, said Mary. You loved it while you were there.

Loved it? cried the Poet. Loved it? How could any intelligent and sensitive person love that . . . that *skidmark* on the devil's underpants? No: love–hate he corrected, love–hate at best. Nobody can simply *love* London.

John Pike chuckled. The Poet glanced at him.

No, it just reminds me, said John Pike, you all talking nineteen to the dozen the way you do and London an' all. This group of people come in 'ere, oh must 'ave been a year ago now or so, young couples they were, down for the weekend, and there's only a few of us regulars in 'ere, an' old Maurice. And this group, they weren't rude or nothin', but just loud, and they talked so fast! And moved their hands about like mad, and tore around the place, exhaustin' just to look at them. And in the end old Maurice, 'e goes up to them and asks them where they're from and of course it's London. And Maurice, 'e waggles his 'ead at them like this – John Pike did a very good impression of Maurice waggling his head – and 'e says to them, Now I could tell you were from London because you're *go go go*!

Everyone laughed, Gerald especially loudly. Oh marvellous! he cried. Marvellous! 'Go go go!' Priceless!

John Pike looked quite embarrassed.

Ah yes, said Gerald, *go go go*. That's London all right. Never a moment's peace.

John Pike didn't say any more. He was remembering where his wife – his ex-wife? – was living now. Somewhere in London, he believed, though he would never know an address. Somewhere on her own, in a flat, earning a living somehow, 'finding herself'. He swallowed hard. He knew she was lost to him.

There were days, said Gerald – Sundays mostly, and believe me, Sundays in London are *particularly* awful, when the sky is grey and the streets are quiet and mournful and the week's traffic has died away and the fumes are settling softly and poisonously on every pavement and rooftop, on every hand and face, and everything is the same colourless colour . . .

Mary looked around. John Pike's head was bowed, every word hurting, but she caught Lewis's eye and then Gavin's. Gavin was just thinking what a good preacher the Poet would make, how articulate, how persuasive . . . apart from his paganism, of course. His fervent paganism might be a slight impediment to an ecclesiastical career, even in the modern, latitudinarian C of E. He grinned back at Mary.

I remember afternoons, said Gerald, such afternoons, lying on the grass in the park opposite, Victoria Park, Hackney's finest, hoping and praying that we wouldn't be set upon by any passing pitbulls, and I would say to Mary, Ah my fair one, my beloved, do you not yearn for the fields and the hills and the stars? Let us then take to the road with nothing but a sack upon our backs and a song in our hearts, carefree and poor and proud! Let us wander like a breeze without a goal, let wandering itself be the goal! Ah, come away, fly away with me, my beloved, my love, we will steal out one night into the deserted streets with no more than a handful of gold sovereigns in our pockets, I with my mandolin, and you shall dance, and I shall play, on the windswept corners of streets or in smoky taverns for a crust of bread until the spring comes, and then when the first crocuses begin to appear beneath the sad willows and the

London planes in the parks, we will head west out of the great city, smoky and populous and much like hell, hand in hand like two fugitive children and follow the stripling Thames out to Goring or Pangbourne and there hitch a lift on a gaily painted barge with pots of rosemary and oregano on the roof, and then we will set off on foot over the long white roads of Wessex, the endless chalk tracks under a blue sky, and then the moors, to Cornwall, or over to Ireland, to Cork, and across the mountains by pony and trap to Galway town and the green hills of Connemara . . .

Is he on drugs? John Pike whispered to Lewis quite seriously.

Mary overheard him. Not just now, she said. Just lots of brandy. He tends to get very verbose when he's drunk. And he's verbose enough sober. So you can imagine what it's like.

Gerald tailed off. I'm sorry, he said. Was I rattling on?

Just a little bit darling, Mary said sweetly.

Anyway, said Gerald, such dreams are all behind us now, because we *have* successfully made the Great Escape, and come to live in blissful tranquillity in the heart of rural England.

Hm, said Gavin. Not always that tranquil, you know.

Well no, farmers have got to work, and drive tractors and that sort of thing. But the noise of agricultural labour is surely just one of the perennial sounds of the countryside, like the blackbird's song.

Yes, said Gavin. And the sound of bickering villagers. That's another of your *perennial sounds of the countryside*.

Dear oh dear, said Mary, patting him on the back of the hand. You *do* sound misanthropic. Any juicy gossip?

Not really, said Gavin, stretching and sighing. Let's just say that I foresee an almighty kerfuffle over this year's Harvest Festival. Last year it was Easter, and the unchristian presence of eggs that suddenly upset one staunchly . . . puritanical parishioner.

Who was that? asked Gerald.

My lips are sealed, said Gavin. But she has lived here a lot longer than I have so I must be careful. Fortunately she was in a minority of one so we got round the eggs problem without any actual killing taking place.

Eggsellent, said the Poet. I mean, *un oeuf* is *un oeuf*.

Lewis thought this was brilliant.

Darling . . . said Mary.

Sorry, said Gerald. And couldn't help adding under his breath, for no obvious reason, Omelette, Prince of Denmark.

So, resumed Gavin. That little skirmish was defused. He paused. Or am I mixing my metaphors?

Gerald thought about it for a while. Yes you are, he pronounced. You can't defuse a skirmish, only a bomb.

Oh well, whatever, said Gavin. We escaped without bloodshed is what I mean. But this time I foresee a rather more divisive split between the old guard and the incomers.

Ah, said John Pike. That'd be nothin' new. Though I always think we get on well enough in this village.

Hm, said Gavin. It's all to do with one or two of the more . . . *forceful* ladies in the village getting a bee in their bonnets over a corn dolly.

John Pike looked mystified.

They want to revive the tradition in church, said Gavin. Build a lifesize corn dolly or something. Sounds dreadful to me, as well as completely bogus. I don't know.

Splendidly pagan though, said Gerald. Harvest and sacrifice and all that.

Yes, said Gavin. But if you recall, we're still C of E hereabouts, at least nominally. Not actually *pagan*.

Gerald laughed loudly. *Touché!* he cried. Oh *touché!*

John Pike drove home very carefully.

They're a funny lot, he said. A lot of fun though, hey?

Yeah, said Lewis.

That Mary, said John Pike. She's a right one though, she is. A real *femme fatale*.

She certainly is, said Lewis in what he hoped was a weary, man-of-the-world tone of voice. She certainly is.

11   The Daydream (1)

Mid afternoon.

He lay in the garden, sunk in lethargy. The sun was past its height but the air was hot and there was no wind. The sky was a bare blue. He tried to make clouds come over but none came. He stood and wandered near the hedge and with an absentminded smile he brushed his hand against a nettle leaf until his skin was stippled with white spots. The pain was there but he didn't feel it. It was there but it was no part of him. It was just a hand at the end of an arm. He regarded it curiously, academically. It was pain but it didn't hurt. Not that. Other things might hurt but not that. It meant nothing. He could associate it with nothing. The pain was meaningless and would pass and was for nothing. Perhaps all pain was meaningless, but he rebelled at that thought.

At last he sank down into the grass and his head fell back and he closed his eyes. He remembered the time – or did he imagine it? – when he was wearing shorts and playing in the garden with Katy and some other shadowy figure he couldn't remember. Then he went inside the house and his mother was there and she was very young and had friends round to tea. Lewis didn't look up at any of them but he knew Mrs Armitage from the village was there. Bossy Mrs Armitage from the village whom his father was always rude about.

The women all stopped drinking tea and looked at him staring with eyes like fearful horses' eyes. A dozen or so staring faces of women.

Hello Lewis, said his mother very slowly. You've been climbing trees.

All the women nodded.

Someone prodded him in the back and he was made to walk into the centre. They surrounded him in a horseshoe shape and scrutinized him closely. They were muttering to each other. Some of it made no sense but one said, A nice-looking boy.

Taller than Timmy, said another.

They stood and crowded towards him. Then one of them opened her mouth and tried to sink her long yellow horse's teeth into his hand. He snatched it away, bleeding and tingling, and ran from the place in terror and ran down to the stream and tried to plunge beneath the water to hide himself but the water was too shallow. And behind him he could hear the women coming for him.

He awoke in a muck sweat. Runnels of sweat ran into his eyes and stung. He gasped and wiped his face with his hands and shook his head violently. He rubbed his face again hard until it prickled with salt and sunburn and then he went into the kitchen and drenched his head with water.

Later, he could no longer resist the temptation to use his crossbow again. He found a rucksack in the cupboard under the stairs and went out to the shed and stowed the crossbow in it and a couple of bolts. He held the rucksack up for inspection and hoped the outline of the crossbow through the canvas wouldn't show. Then he set off through the village towards the estate woods, reckoning Jim would have given the pheasants their evening feed by now.

12 The Woods

And in the woods that day he forgot his vow never to kill an animal again except for meat and he killed a magpie and a blackbird and a song thrush and narrowly missed a second magpie and also missed a nuthatch and a woodpecker. Then he felt disgusted with himself. If he could kill a rabbit, something for the pot, he knew he would feel better. Better with the rabbit's blood . . . He climbed an oak at the edge of the wood and crawled out along a bough and loaded up the crossbow. He waited with an infinite animal patience until the first rabbits appeared. In slow motion he aimed the crossbow but scraped the heavy stock against the bough and the rabbits heard. They stopped nibbling and listened and took a wary hop or two towards their burrows and stopped and listened again and sniffed but could smell nothing. Lewis froze, his arm in cramped agony. He prayed that the rooks would not start their cawing and warn the whole wood. After some minutes the rabbits were hunched and eating again and he took aim and fired his bolt. It struck the rabbit directly behind the skull and went through and stapled it to the ground. The other rabbits vanished. The rabbit was not dead. It squirmed under the bolt in slow motion and its screams were terrible. Lewis almost fell out of the tree in his haste and dropped the crossbow and ran to the rabbit and, pressing down on its arched skinny backbone, he pulled out the bolt and broke the rabbit's neck. He wiped the bolt clean of blood in the grass and then retrieved his crossbow. He held the rabbit up by the hind legs and shook it so the little drop of blood fell from its nose. He

61

wondered about its last agony and tried to understand, and then he dropped it into a plastic bag and into his rucksack.

He killed a fat woodpigeon that looked surprised as it died and when it was dead he found its crop full of beans and he smiled. It reminded him somehow of a year or two back when he'd stamped on a snake and when it was dead and its mouth fell open, out hopped a live frog.

Lastly that day he killed a single pheasant. It was too easy and pheasants were too stupid and he despised them for it. It was a fine cock bird too, but he knew his father would be angry if he took it home so he laid it hidden among the rotting bluebell leaves and left it for the foxes. Not meat for him but for the animals. The other birds he treated with dignity. He bowed to them or made a sign of the cross over their torn bodies outstretched, even over the magpie, that braggart, that troubadour, that sneakthief who looked like a survivor even in death. But not over the pheasant.

13 The Church

Returning through the village with the rabbit and the woodpigeon crumpled in his bag, feeling like some returning hero, he paused and went into the church. No one was in there.

It was a proud and well-cared-for church, for in these remoter parts the god Christ was still widely worshipped. The villagers loved their church, its companionable emptiness. Lewis and his father came on Christmas Day morning but not otherwise. I'm a regular churchgoer, regular as clockwork, his father liked to joke. Every Christmas, without fail. Chuckled.

Lewis stepped into the church like a manmade cave with its oak canopy supported on limestone beechtrunks. A stone copse, a cool asylum from the sun. He stared at the old memorial tablets, read them slowly, his lips moving. One he stared at especially, two Grecian maidens in marble in cascading robes weeping over a funerary urn. He ran his fingers over the marble. Their hands held aloft, their breasts bared, weeping, weeping since 1806, he thought. It was one of the Sedleys. Jane Sedley, beloved wife . . . The Sedleys who were up at the big house until 1946 when the last Mr Sedley died, aged eighty-two, by some strange reversal of nature outliving both his sons by decades. The big house where new owners since had come and gone like the seasons, the latest being Mr Van der Whatsit. Veen.

Lewis stood on the altar steps and craned his head and read the big brass plaque again. 1914–1918, *For those who gave their lives in the Great War* . . . Lt. G. Sedley, Capt. M. Sedley, aged nineteen and twenty-one. Ypres 1915, Somme 1916. And then the other ranks. (There were no Pikes on the brass plaque. What did the Pikes do during the Great War? What they had always done. They snared rabbits. They caught fish. They killed hawks and dug potatoes. They endured.)

Slowly Lewis read out the other names, his lips moving. His lips said, *For those who gave their lives* . . . His lips read of Pte. Hall and of Pte. Sellars and of Pte. Watson and of the three Wilkins brothers who all died together at Ypres in 1915. He wondered if they died with Lt. Sedley, whether at the last they joked together there in the trenches before they went out together to die. Lewis's grandmother told him that the fourth and last Wilkins brother came home in 1919 and never spoke again. She said that summer was long and George Wilkins walked the fields and murmured to the birds and some said they'd seen him with flowers in his hair, though others said that was just malicious talk. His grandmother said that certainly he never spoke again though before he'd gone to France he'd loved a girl, and he never looked man nor woman in the eye again in all his life.

There was another brass plaque for 1939–1945. It had fewer names on it but Lewis read them too.

His head was bowed when he heard the heavy latch go and the south door creaked open. He stepped in close to the wall and recognized one voice immediately. It was Gavin. The 'new vicar' as everybody still called him though he'd been here nearly two years now.

We're just about half way there, Gavin was saying. And that's safely tucked away earning 6 per cent meanwhile.

Although the cost of the work isn't getting any less either.

True, true, agreed Gavin. But, you know . . . another long hot summer of fêtes and coffee mornings and we might do rather well. Some of the PCC even suggested a church carboot sale.

Not a bad idea, said the other man. Might make a mint.

Well yes, it's just that I had visions of cars parked all over the churchyard. A little disrespectful to the dear departed, don't you think?

Gavin had that jokey tone to his voice. Even on Christmas Day when he preached his short sermon, he seemed desperate to keep that jokey tone to his voice. Lewis hated it. He was a traditionalist in church matters.

The other man shrugged. Needs must, Gavin, needs must. Either that or pray for a miracle. A magic money-box or something.

Gavin smiled. God helps those who help themselves, Don.

The age of miracles is past, heh?

Well . . . said Gavin. At least I'm not like some of my senior colleagues who go around saying God is dead.

Don chuckled. It does seem a bit like biting the hand that feeds you.

Well . . . said Gavin and said no more.

The two men stood with their backs to the altar and their hands clasped behind their backs and looked up at the tower. Lewis followed their gaze. The ancient wall was patterned with cracks like scars and damp clung to it like sores.

Don pointed out one particular crack that emerged from the corner of the tower and crossed the wall almost to the other side.

That's the one, he said.

It's not going to fall down just yet, I hope, said Gavin.

Not *just* yet. It's lasted eight centuries, I reckon it'll last a few more years. But which would you rather have, a car-boot sale or the tower dropping on your congregation?

Gavin sighed. Well, when you put it like that . . .

What about the application?

Still under consideration, said Gavin. You know what they're like. Of course we should get something, but unfortunately we're not the only church with a problem like this.

No, agreed Don. And your rich philanthropist parishioner?

65

Mr Van der Veen, smiled Gavin. Not a churchgoer but very amenable with his chequebook, yes. I think if we got near to the appeal target he'd top us up, but I don't really like to ask him again just yet. He was a great help with the hall. Besides, we don't want to make it too easy for ourselves. The rest of us should make an effort too.

Suffering is good for the soul, said Don.

Something like that, said Gavin.

The two men continued to discuss matters. Lewis inched out slowly from the wall and began to tread gently down the altar steps. He didn't expect to escape from the church unnoticed but neither did he want them to see him here, so near to the altar. He felt he might be trespassing on something.

But as he moved something caught his eye. On the white marble of the altar steps, an unearthly red spot of blood. For a moment his scalp prickled with cold sweat and he thought he must be bleeding. Then he reached his hand back and felt his rucksack and understood. Stupid of him. The rabbit must have bled more than he realized and the blood had leaked from the plastic bag and soaked through the canvas to drip on to the floor. Lewis panicked and wiped the wet blood from the rucksack and thrust his red hands into his pockets and strode down the aisle. Gavin heard the steps and turned, a little startled.

Ah, Lewis Pike, he said. Hello.

Lewis managed a weak smile and headed for the south door.

Didn't see you there.

Just . . . lookin' . . . Lewis managed to mumble and opened the door and escaped back into the sunshine.

Gavin and Don exchanged wry smiles.

One of the old school, murmured Gavin. No job, poor lad.

Just as long as he's not nicking the church silver, said Don.

Later the two men went up the chancel towards the vestry door and as they halted Gavin noticed a bright spot of red on the altar steps. He frowned and looked up at the roof. Then he knelt down and saw that it looked like blood. He tutted and took a handkerchief from his pocket and wiped the blood away.

Although Lewis wanted nothing more than to get away and hide, without troubling to understand why, he hesitated beside the church noticeboard. The cracked and faded board usually gave out nothing but a list of this month's services in the five parishes, and maybe an imminent fête. But today a big yellow poster hung there. Harvest Meeting, it announced. Lewis laboriously read every word. There was to be a meeting at her home to discuss plans for the Harvest Festival. Come Along and Share your Ideas, it said. The contact name was Mrs Armitage at Wardour House.

Lewis screwed up his face and walked back up the lane homewards.

14 Allie

He waited, restless and fidgeting, for his father to return home, standing at the kitchen window for half an hour with outstretched fingers. He had already gutted the rabbit and pigeon and left them to hang.

At last he heard the car and was outside the cottage with the doorkey in his pocket before the engine had stopped.

Bloody hell, you are in a hurry, said his father. Hop in then.

They drove into town.

What you bin up to today, then?

Not much.

How was Katy?

Katy. That seemed like ages ago. Oh, she was fine.

And the kids?

Yeah, said Lewis.

Tsss, said his father. Dunno why I bother asking. I'd do better ringin' her meself to find out anythin'.

Oh, she's all right, said Lewis.

When they got to the vet's Lewis was almost sick with excitement and dread. The girl said they should have informed them that they weren't coming over till today. John Pike looked over at his son and said nothing. Then the girl brought Allie round and she looked wobbly and thin and sheepish and had a big white collar on her neck to stop her scratching her stitches. It made her look a bit like a choirboy. Lewis giggled at her and she looked immediately hurt and ashamed and moved her tail feebly. So Lewis sank down on his knees beside her.

Hey girl, he whispered. I'm sorry. The collar's great. He ruffled her fur.

She looked at him with her old brown eyes and her eyes smiled and she looked away. She was ready to leave.

John Pike paid the bill and made jokes about having to do overtime to pay it off. Or sell the dog, he joked. Not that we'd get much for her now.

Lewis looked up at his father then back at Allie. Come on girl, he said and led her outside.

Loves that dog, said John Pike. Loves her more than anything. How long d'ye reckon she'll last?

The girl shrugged and looked sympathetic. I don't think Mr Wood can say. It was a big operation, her whole body's still like in trauma. But if it hasn't spread – a few more years, maybe.

Let's hope so, said John Pike. There you go then love. He handed her the cheque.

Outside a terrier puppy was yapping furiously at Allie. Lewis glared at it. Allie looked away with disdain but he could tell she was bitterly ashamed to be wearing the stupid collar.

When they got in the car Lewis asked how long it had to stay on.

At least a week, said his father. They'll have to have another look at the stitches then to see how they're doing. Maybe a week.

There you are girl, said Lewis nuzzling her between the ears. Back to normal in a week.

When they got home Lewis said he wanted to take her for a walk.

Not too far now, said his father. The girl at the vet's said she was still, like, in shock.

OK, said Lewis. Won't be long.

He walked away down the lane at a gentle pace and Allie walked at his side, wearing her collar with as much dignity as she could muster, which wasn't much. She couldn't forget about it. She tried to poke her muzzle under an interesting gate at one point but the collar got in the way and she turned away in disgust.

Come on girl, said Lewis, walking on ahead, pretending not to have noticed this embarrassment, and Allie broke into a trot after him, believing he hadn't seen. They were as close as two minds could be.

He talked to her quietly about all that had happened, told her everything of the past week. When he said the word 'rabbit' she cocked her ears and looked around. When he mimed the action of the crossbow she looked briefly puzzled and then bored. As her heart began to beat harder and her blood warmed from the exercise and as the myriad sounds and odours bombarded her and invaded her she became more distant from him though they were still linked by an invisible equality. But she would not tolerate a patting or a fondling from him now, not for now. She walked further from him, she lingered longer when he called her. She was out in the world now, less humanized, more purely animal, and she must be strong to survive. Later, nearer to sleep, he could stroke her. But not here, not now.

It was at a bend in the lane with a hint of dusk on the horizon over the farther fields with Allie lingering thirty yards behind him that he heard the car coming. He stopped and looked back. Allie seemed to be oblivious, her muzzle skimming deliriously over horsedung. Allie! he called and she heard nothing. The car appeared, going too fast round the corner, and didn't even brake when the driver saw Allie and his face showed white shock. Allie turned her head to look at the last moment but the collar prevented her from seeing anything in time and she moved only slowly. Then the car went over her.

The car braked violently between her and Lewis. He raced back past it and found her on her feet looking shame-faced. Her collar was crumpled on one side but otherwise she seemed unscathed. She looked ashamed at her own clumsiness yet she had managed to roll under the car and out at the back without injury. But she knew her clumsiness could have been fatal and her every instinct told her to be ashamed. A dog that trips and falls, or is deaf, or cannot smell, will not live long.

Lewis stood beside her and looked back at the car. It was a high 4×4. Any other car would have killed her. The woman in the passenger seat was looking anxiously in the rear-view mirror, the man was already out of the car and walking towards him, talking to him though Lewis could hear nothing. In his pocket his hand gripped tightly on the moulded plastic handle of his knife.

He recognized the people. They were the incomers who'd bought the farmhouse up the valley that had absolutely nothing wrong with it and had had builders in all year doing alterations and doing up the barn. Fuckin' yuppies.

The man was facing him now, moving his hands in apologetic gestures and looking down at Allie with an expression of relief and talking, but Lewis could not hear a word. There were floods of words. At last he stopped talking. There was a pause. Lewis said very slowly and quietly, though the man heard and looked as though he had been struck, *Drive slower*.

Then he clicked his tongue to Allie and turned away and boy and dog walked back down the darkening lane. The man gazed after them for a long while so that his wife wondered and then he returned to the car and told his wife it was OK, thank God, and they drove back to the farmhouse.

He put Allie to bed and tried to make her comfortable with that wretched collar. She fell asleep easily.

Lewis did not fall asleep easily. Heartful and restless, he lay naked on his narrow bed and watched the wheeling stars and felt his heart pumping with too much blood and

71

too fast, too full of warring passions. His forehead was ridged in thought and he could decide on nothing. He wondered when it was going to come together and start making sense and he wondered if it ever would. The last days passed before him in a meaningless chain: Mary – Allie – the yuppies – his crossbow – his dreams – the bleeding rabbit. And he felt convinced that there must be some pattern to it and that something was there, some message or warning or some command, if only he could understand it.

All this is not enough. What must I do? he asked.

15   The Daydream (2)

He was fantasizing about Mary.

Mary sat on a swing wearing only a loose white shirt. She smiled to him and ordered him to sit with her. They started kissing. In the distance he could hear a howling wounded dog. He felt very small, clinging to Mary like some ridiculous insect. He did everything he was told to do. Later he found her standing over Kenny at the side of the house. Kenny lay on recently dug earth. He was curled up and peaceful, like grandfather when he lay dying. Kenny's throat was cut and his cock had been cut off too. Blood had seeped out and stained the earth smooth and shiny. Mary pointed her knife at him. I thought it was time for him to be harvested, she said. Now you do as you're told.

Then they covered Kenny's body lightly with soil though his bones still showed through like white chalk in the dark earth. Then Lewis sat on the lower branches of a beech tree and chirruped like an insect. He knew it would soon be his turn and he too would lie curled up and peaceful in the earth and no one would ever know he had been there.

She was calling. It was time for him to go.

He awoke from the nightmare or dream that seemed to have a fit ending and he felt strangely calm and sated. He got up and went downstairs and out into the garden. The night was a cage of shadows. An owl's cry. He felt it might after all be beginning to make sense.

He went to the shed and retrieved his crossbow and went inside and stowed it under his bed. He felt tired now. He fell asleep to the terrible and quiet sound of the mind steadily feeding on itself.

16   The White Horse (2)

On Friday night his father returned home from work late and they had a quick supper and then his father said, Come on, I'll buy you a pint.

When they pulled up behind the pub John Pike smiled softly and said, Ah, I see the Mabey brothers are here. Surprise surprise.

He nodded towards an ancient Land Rover with a new aluminium roof bolted on to it. The Land Rover also had shiny black bullbars on the front.

They heard someone down here talking about how dangerous them bullbars can be to kids and the like, said John Pike. Next week Dave Mabey turns up. Same old jalopy. Bloody great new bullbars on the front. Says him and Gary nicked them off a Range Rover in Tisbury.

John Pike shook his head. Almost laughed, not quite.

Inside the pub the Mabey brothers had already had six pints of lager each and were just going on to the cider. And they'd been smoking dope all afternoon. Nobody asked where they got their money from. They were both on the dole. Lewis was still a little afraid of them, especially Dave when he'd been taking speed. Dave Mabey wore a camouflage jacket with no shirt and long stringy hair hung down either side of his weasel face. He wasn't one to pick fights but he'd been in quite a few all the same and taken his knocks and his thin nose was broken and canted to the right and his temples had their scars from broken glass. They nodded benevolently to John and Lewis Pike when they came in. Dennis behind the bar started pulling two pints.

Old Tom was in the corner too with his ancient terrier, Jimbo. People said that Tom had had that dog since he was a little boy and they had grown old and arthritic together. Tom bought one pint each evening, drank it very slowly, and he wore the same old winter coat in all weathers. Even now. Normally it hung open from his skinny shoulders but in a cold snap he'd bind it tightly around him with twine. There's not many left like old Tom now, Lewis's father told him admiringly.

How do, Tom.

How do.

They joined him at his corner table without further exchange. Jimbo pulled himself up on to his rickety legs and nuzzled Lewis's hand blindly. He could smell Allie. A few sniffs were enough and then he folded himself up in the corner again. Old Tom looked down and poured a puddle of beer from his glass on to the flagstones between the dog's forepaws. Jimbo lapped slowly.

So how's tricks, Tom? John Pike asked him.

Tom grimaced. Too bloody hot.

Certainly warm. Dunt do any harm at work though.

Tom nodded and grimaced.

There was a pause while they drank their beer and then Tom nodded again at Lewis.

Saw you out t'other night walking your dog. She all right then, back from vettery?

She's fine thanks, said Lewis, heartwarmed.

Nice dog she is. Bloody stupid collar an' all but a nice dog. Bet she 'ates that collar.

She does too, said Lewis.

'Im 'ad a collar on 'im once, said Tom, thumbing at Jimbo. Couldn't keep it on 'im for love nor money. Scratched it off straight away and then tore hisself open along 'is stitches like 'e was diggin' for one of 'is own bones. Daft mutt. He cuffed Jimbo gently on the muzzle. 'E lived though. 'E's bin through worse than that an' lived.

Have another, Tom?

Tom ruminated a while while he considered this offer, rolling a slender cigarette from a tin. Ah, well now. Don't mind if I do, John.

Started on their second pints, Lewis felt emboldened to say, Mind you, she nearly got run over that evening.

Tom eyed him.

Straight back from the vet's we went out for a walk and she was standin' in the middle of the lane when a car comes too fast round the corner and goes straight over her. She just rolls out the other side with not a bruise on 'er.

Lewis took a deep breath.

You never told me that, boy, said John Pike.

Lewis shrugged. She was all right.

Did this car stop?

Yeah, said Lewis. He was aware of the Mabey brothers listening in from the bar. Fuckin' yuppies.

Lewis, said his father.

All right then, *bloody* yuppies, said Lewis.

Old Tom chuckled.

That lot from up at the farmhouse.

Eversfield?

Yeah. They're driving this big 4x4 with not a mark on it. Which is 'ow Allie rolls right under it and gets away with it.

What did they say then?

Oh, the bloke gets out an' comes over an' 'e's gabbin' away saying like 'ow sorry 'e is an' all. An' I just look at 'im an' say – Lewis suddenly thought how good it sounded – I just say to 'im, *Drive slower*. Then me and Allie walk away.

There was a pause while Tom ruminated on this and then he smiled slowly.

That told 'em, he said. I like that.

Lewis grinned widely. Well . . . he said.

Drive slower. I like that. Tom sipped his beer and added,

77

They got to learn though, these new folks, they got to learn.

He looked down at Jimbo.

Reminds me of before the war, he began. John and Lewis eyed each other and his father winked and they settled back for a long anecdote.

What war's that then, Tom? called Dave Mabey across the bar. The Boer War? They cackled.

Old Tom's expression betrayed nothing. Aye, he said, clasping his hands in concentration. Must have bin, now, let me see – 1892 . .

The Mabey brothers whooped together and drained their ciders in delight and ordered again.

Anyhow, said old Tom. There's this city gent commutes down from London at weekends. One of the first week-enders 'e must ave bin. An' 'e was an awful toff an' just about everybody 'ated 'im though of course we was always very polite, always were in those days, very deferential like. I don't just mean 'e was an incomer but 'e was a real toff, sun shone out of 'is arse, talking to everyone like they was muck an' all, demandin' this, complainin' 'bout t'other. Your uncles, Tom nodded to Lewis, your great uncles, that is to say, they really 'ated 'im. 'E was always offerin' 'em work in 'is garden, Help you out a bit, eh, old boy? 'e used to say to 'em, Bit of easy work, eh? Or even to *their* father, your *great* grandfather, Because I know you're not up to proper farmwork now, 'e'd say. Well, you can imagine 'ow old man Pike took to *that*.

An' we all thought 'e was a pouffe an' all. An' 'e 'as these couple of Alsatian dogs with 'im all the time. Now you didn't see many Alsatians in those days, least not round 'ere you didn't. Fact they may've bin the first I ever saw. Anyway, we were all quite impressed by the dogs if not by the old queen hisself. An' 'e puts up this notice on 'is gateway saying Private – No Admittance. Now that's the field that leads over to Summerfield Church and there's bin a footpath there since Adam and no one gave a tinkers 'bout

78

footpaths and rights of way an' all that anyway in those days except those that run across the estate. So, anyway. Then he goes and sets 'is dogs on this old dear's spaniel and they tear it up real bad. I think the poor animal died, I don't recall. Anyhow – do you remember old John Willow?

John Pike nodded. I do, Tom.

Ah well, 'e died a while back. Anyhow 'e had this little terrier, only young, couple of years old, an 'e swore it'd take on anything it met if only 'e gave the word. So we all put bets down at the Horseshoe – in them days, you know – an' 'e goes out to that field with the little terrier tucked up inside 'is overcoat. An' these two Alsatians come racing across from the house like on cue. An old John Willow 'e takes this little dog from 'is coat an 'e sets it on the ground like a bloody clockwork toy an' 'e says to 'im quiet like, *kill*.

Tom sipped his beer slowly and relished the tension.

An' that little dog, 'e goes straight for one Alsatian, no hesitation. Jaws on the windpipe like a clamp. Hangs there. T'other dog is snapping around 'im but 'e can't do nothing. Minute later the first dog's dead. Terrier jumps up. Does the same to t'other. In a couple of minutes you've got a couple of dead Alsatians and one little terrier with 'is tail in the air like a young man's cock.

The bar dissolved in laughter. Dave Mabey nearly choked himself with a lungful of cider and his brother had to beat him urgently and violently on the back.

And you know what? added old Tom. That terrier of John Willow's there was this one's ancestor. He nodded down at blind Jimbo. Great grandfather or summing. No, more than that. An' I'll tell you summing else an' all. I never did rate Alsatians much after that.

The chuckles gradually subsided. They didn't know whether it was true or not, exactly, but you never knew with old Tom. You never could tell.

Tell you what, though, said Tom. Another funny thing only a couple of weeks ago. That Taylor family, the wife she

79

says to me t'other day, You know, Tom, our little Sammy's awfully off his food, don't you know.

Tom's attempt to do a posh accent was excruciatingly bad, but everybody laughed because they knew that Tom also knew it was awful.

She says to me, You're an old hand at dogs aren't you, Tom? I just nod, mysterious like, an' I says, Just you leave 'im to me, Mrs Taylor, for a week or so. I'll soon 'ave 'im eatin' again. Oh, will you, Tom, she says, oh, will you really? Certainly will, Mrs T, I says, never you worry about it. I'll start 'im on wild rabbit tonight, dogs love that. Wild rabbit with maybe a sprig of thyme. Hm. Tom set his pint down and pondered for a moment. Hm. Maybe I overegged it a bit with the wild thyme. Anyhow. That's what I tell 'er. An' she looks at me all impressed like with her big blue eyes an' all. Good-lookin' lady an' all.

Steady on now, Tom, called Dave Mabey.

Anyhow I takes the dog off of 'er. Real little pooch, this Sammy. Little bloody pooch with these sleepy eyes. I takes 'im 'ome. Pops 'im in the woodshed with a bucket of water and locks the door.

People are beginning to chuckle again.

Week later – laughter erupts – I takes 'im out again. Bit wobbly on 'is legs, little Sammy is, but none the worse for wear. Takes 'im back to Mrs T. There you go, Mrs T, I says. One happy hungry little dog. You'll find 'e'll eat most anything now. Oh Tom, she says, you *are* a marvel, you really are. How much do I owe you?

Tom sipped his beer.

Oh, fifty quid should cover it, Mrs T, I says. Are you quite sure? she says. Quite sure, I says. I nearly wants to add, Yeah, a bucket of water don't cost much more than that nowadays.

Old Tom and his stories. Wicked, cunning stories, a little cruel. But survivor's tales. Lewis could have listened to them all night.

But Tom's voice was in danger of being drowned out by the rising tide of noise and chaos. Dennis behind the bar had been hitting the rum hard and now laughed with his girlish high-pitched giggle whenever the Mabey brothers said anything funny, and often when they did not. Then Mad Ken turned up on his moped and came into the bar to commence his usual rant about his ancestor Black Ken the Pirate. The bar was lit by a few bare candle bulbs on a wooden chandelier and it was Ken's habit to seize this chandelier and give it a violent shove so that the light and shadows in the pub swung violently to and fro and Ken could pretend they were all trapped below deck in some dreadful storm. Ha ha! he roared like a pantomime pirate. Ha ha! This takes me back to the time we were aboard the *Hispaniola*, a-buccaneering on the Spanish Main, and a fearful storm blew up out of the Gulf of Mexicky . . .

Lewis felt he was surrounded by lunatics. His father urged another pint on him but he asked for a Coke. At the bar he watched his father down a whisky chaser before his next pint, then turn and lean on the bar and watch Ken and his antics. Old Tom clicked his tongue at Jimbo and muttered to Lewis with a wink, Time for us old 'uns to depart, lad, and crept out of the pub unnoticed by any other. There were a few minutes' embarrassment just after Tom left when Gavin the vicar arrived and sat at the bar to have a pint and be friendly. He sat wearing an open-necked shirt and said Don't mind me and tried to make conversation. The others smiled benevolently but not directly at him and minded him intensely. He might be a decent enough bloke but this wasn't the place for him, at least not on a Friday night. It wasn't right.

Lewis thought he should come striding in here with a long white beard and blazing eyes, brandishing a staff and denouncing them all as sinners, or else he should not come at all. He should be apart. He looked across at Gavin, bent like a cuphook over his pint, and he thought how weak he looked and he despised him a little. It was much better when he was here along with the Poet and Mary.

Then Gavin said, Well, cheerio, and left.

Ken resumed his antics. The Mabey brothers began to roll a monstrous spliff quite openly on the bar. Dennis was too far gone to realize what they were doing.

Oi, Ken! shouted Dave Mabey. Seen the Great White Vole lately?

The Great White Vole was another of Ken's strange obsessions. He abandoned his piratical persona in an instant. Ah, he said mysteriously. The Great White Vole of Wiltshire. No, I've not seen it abroad of late. Have any of 'ee?

All shook their heads solemnly.

No, Ken went on. Not these last few years. But tes a terrible creature, they do say. Some tell that it is the size of a sheep, while others have told that they have seen such a beast more the size of a horse, and terrible fleetfooted to boot. Ah. He bowed his head. What times we do live in. He raised his head again and adopted a grim mien. It stalks the hedgerows of the land, and falls upon its prey with a terrible . . . *eek*!

Lewis's stomach ached from laughing. Ken should have been on the stage. Everybody said that he should have been on the stage.

Ah, he resumed. Mayhap it has moved on. He rolled his eyes wildly. Mind you, the Great White Vole of Wiltshire, though a fearsome beast, is as nothing to the new strain of Killer Voles over in East Anglia.

That right?

Indeed it es. They're only a small vole but they stop at nothing. Why, only a few weeks ago my friend James was out walking along a towpath in Suffolk, on 'is holiday 'e was. By 'isself. An' 'e's just gettin' over a stile an' 'oppin t' the ground when 'e sees this vole up ahead of 'im. Well, James looks at it and dunt think nothin' of it. 'Tis only a vole after all, though he thinks it's strange that the little bugger doesn't plop straight back in the water as soon as it sees 'im. So 'e starts walkin' towards it and the creature just stands there, bold as mustard, occupying the middle of the path and not budgin', just fixing 'im with 'is beady little eyes. Now James pauses and thinks to 'imself, What the 'ell! I can't be frightened of a bloomin' *vole*! And just at that moment when 'e paused, the vole came at 'im. That's 'ow 'e describes it, the little animal just *came* at 'im. In a trice James is up and over that stile and runnin' for 'is life.

Some moments later, 'e looks back. No sign of the vole. But James is shakin' like a leaf. Took 'im all 'is courage just to tell me the tale an' all.

Ah yes. He nodded his head ponderously. The East Anglian Killer Vole. Not a big animal by the usual standards, but savage. *Savage*.

Somebody bought Ken a pint and told him he was a nutter. Lewis wondered if the evening would seem to him more normal if he was drunk or stoned too. He sipped his Coke and smiled slyly to himself. *This place*.

More people turned up. The Beatties. Roy and his wife. She's brave, thought Lewis. That Mr Pollock who drank whisky and never spoke a word to anyone.

Ted Beattie and Ken started some nonsensical exchange across the bar.

Oi you, why are you wearing that nasty jacket?

Nasty? said Ken. Nasty? I'll 'ave you.

No you won't, said Ted. I used to play the piano standin' on me 'ead.

Your 'air's all slipped off though.

Ah, now you're takin' the piss.

Are you the police?

Get along with you.

You want pissin' on, you do.

Get on with you, you're drunk.

Lewis wished he could follow the conversation. Evidently

83

he hadn't drunk enough. Ted and Ken seemed to understand each other. They were brothers-in-law.

I'm drunk? I'm not drunk. I'm 'appy. 'Appy as Larry.

Get on with you. Where's your car tonight?

Where I left it. Where's yours?

Your 'ead'll hurt tomorrow.

Least it'll still 'ave 'air on it.

Dah! Jacket . . . Mr . . . Nasty Jacket Head . . .

Dah! Get away with you!

The pub finally shut about midnight when Dennis was too drunk to man the bar any more. John Pike drove home in second gear all the way and with all the windows open. There was even a way home that took them off the road altogether and through the estate woods and brought them out in the field behind the house. But it didn't seem necessary tonight.

Lewis watched his father stumble into his bedroom hiccuping and then went and lay on his own bed and thought about his father: decent, baffled, ashamed, frank, drunken, kindly, sad . . .

17   The Downs

His father worked again on Saturday. Busiest day of the week, obviously, he said. We'll go over and see Gran tomorrow, all right?

Lewis nodded. Fine.

He watched some cartoons and ate no breakfast and then called Allie and went out walking. He wanted to take his crossbow but he didn't dare.

He walked up the shady track towards the downs, the track brindled with sunlight. The sun was strong and roared through the summer leaves. As he walked, Lewis talked to Allie or he named the flowers softly to himself. Past a clump of mallow on rocky ground, the bees going mad about it. Past yellow archangel and stitchwort. (The names were like poems to him. He knew all the flowers. Even his father said Lewis knew his flowers, teased him for it.) Past cow parsley thin and straining in the shade of the lane and finding no light. A dayflying moth skittering among dead leaves. The old track overarched by hawthorn and hazel and field maple. He found garlic mustard and rolled a young dark leaf between his forefinger and thumb and smelled his skin stained green. He knew it all. He pierced his thumbpad on a rosethorn and pinched a spot of blood out and drew it in a trickle down his thumb and then let a drop fall to the ground and gazed down on it and then walked on. Allie was up ahead, her muzzle deep in the ivy, her tail a semaphore. Past bindweed with its leaves too glossy and tropical, past bluebells' brief flowers now turned to pragmatic green pods. He split open a pod and found the row of seeds like tiny white balloons clinging to the seam. Fairy's balloons, his Grandmother had told him, showing him years ago. And he had believed her. Past soldier beetles lazing and copulating on the lacewhite heads of umbellifers. Past silverweed perpetually wintry with its sheen of hoarfrost. May blossom blowing down on him, speckling his hair, and the woodland paths ahead of him snowy with fallen blossom. Past purple vetch and tiny speedwell, arches of wiry cleavers, past herb bennet flickering under hawthorn, and fields of green barley beyond growing on the thin downland soil never to have been ploughed, bare grasslands by nature.

He walked on, thinking how primitive plantain looked, somehow upside-down, and seeing a peacock butterfly and a speckled wood and a yellow brimstone startling against the dark leaves, fluttering and restless as his own restless heart. He saw a ladybird cupped in a grass stalk like a spot of blood and through the long grass dayflying moths arose in clouds at every footfall. It was everywhere and without end and beyond expression and he could not name it but he loved it beyond telling and swore never to forsake it.

He walked on, smelling ramsons deep in the umber caverns of the wood. And then at last he was out and free upon the bare sweep of the downs, chalk shoulder and chine, with the short springy turf beneath him and the lark ascending with its strong glad song ringing in his ears. He could barely breathe for the joy of it, his country: the freedom and delirious solitude and the ease with which he could fly up and away into the blue beyond if he chose to.

He lay back in the grass and gazed skyward and felt himself falling into that infinite blue. (Allie sat with him a moment, cock-eared and puzzled, and then tired of waiting and moved away to sniff around, blissful and without thought.) He clasped his hands behind his head and concentrated on making the clouds move by the power of his thoughts. Beneath his knuckles the grass was so dry, needing only a spark to make that field a furnace.

Then he took to the track again between the coarse grass where insects everywhere hummed and gathered and copulated. The track was dazzling white in the sun's glare, broken only by lumps of flint holed or hollowed and calcified in chalk looking like scatterings of lambs' skulls. For though at this time the scales of the year are weighted towards life, death's mementoes are ubiquitous, as in winter's blackest depths small reminders may be seen, black ashbuds with their promises of new green leaves, neither life nor death triumphant. And it was in winter when the animals were so much less visible that Lewis had most pity and feeling for them and honoured them most, and their unfathomable patience in a world of wounds and frost.

He walked on higher still and closer to the sun along the white chalk track across the downs with his eyes burning. It was too hot. He met no one. He bent and whimpered beneath the sun's summer holocaust, sanity's balefire, the patient dog at his heels, boy and dog both pained with thirst and no water to be found in all that wide dry sheep country. Those bothies untenanted, those dewponds bygone, those bare hills shepherdless.

Thus Lewis Pike went walking the high hills and lonely downs, following the long white roads of Wessex and finding no place of peace in all that beloved country. Until at last after many hours boy and dog stepped from the track into the cool green lane of the tunnel, tongue-parched and footsore and went their way homeward.

18 Grandma (1)

On Sunday afternoon they drove over to see Grandma.

She lived in the cottage she'd moved to when she married Jack Pike, John Pike's father, and she had never moved since and never would. She had never been to London and for some years now not even to Salisbury, though Lewis recalled her telling of their twice weekly journeys into town when she was a girl on market days. The same days of the week, Tuesdays and Saturdays, that they've had there for seven hundred years, she used to tell him, waggling her finger at him as if imparting some profound moral lesson. And when he was very young and heard this he had been confused and pictured her going to Salisbury twice a week for seven hundred years and had thought, No wonder she needs to sleep after Sunday dinner.

Now he knew that some of her memories must be feigned. She couldn't possibly remember the weather of 1921, she wasn't even born then or only just. And yet at other times still, when she gazed at him with her clear blue eyes and wagged her finger solemnly, he didn't dare to doubt. It seemed to him as if time's strictness might on occasion relent, and the memories and stories of others might somehow seep through the years and become her own. She was a river of stories and memories and who could say which were hers and which were not? Something impersonal in that trove of stories and that mythical record of one small village's triumphs and cares and small unremarked agonies.

Over two hours that short journey from the village to

Salisbury could take in those days by cart, she said. Now in those days Salisbury was a long way off. People talk now about just popping in to Salisbury to do some shopping or what have you. Dint do much popping in in those days, I can tell you. Hard work it was for six or eight months a year. In summer, of course, with the long days, it was more of a jaunt, especially if we took the oxdrove over the downs. Driving the sheep into market on foot, though. That was the finest sight and one you'll not see ever again.

His grandma's words always lulled him and made him dreamy and he pictured everything she said. He saw the oxdrove in summer baked hard and flat and easy where the sheep had been driven for hundreds or thousands of years ever since men in coarse clothes and bronze buckled belts about their waists first walked it. And he pictured Salisbury market square a mass of fat sheep in their pens, no cars then, and sweaty auctioneers, and every building around the square a pub in those days, with farmers drinking their ale and fingering their coins and notes in their jacket pockets.

Sometimes John Pike would urge her to write down all her stuff, write a book. But she would just purse her lips and say, There's far too many books around nowadays already.

She took them into the cool front room which was never used but for visitors and never at all in winter. Lewis would rather have sat in the snug kitchen but Grandma wouldn't hear of it. You don't use a dinner fork to dig potatoes, now, do you? she would say, or some such odd saying of hers which he never heard anyone else use but which nevertheless made perfect sense in its own way.

The front room had a faded three-piece suite and an old upright piano on which Grandma could sometimes be persuaded to play 'Little Brown Jug' after a few glasses of sloe gin.

So then, Lewis, and what are you doin' with yourself these days?

He hated these questions though he knew his grandma meant them only kindly. She cocked her head at him like a little bird and her eyes were birdbright.

Oh, keeping busy, he said, hating his own words, thinking what a pathetic old man he sounded. Mustn't grumble, he wanted to add sarcastically. Could be worse, would be worse. He said, Gardening and suchlike.

He works on the estate garden from time to time still, said his father, stepping in. Very good gardener he is too when he's a mind to it. Never 'ave the patience myself but Lewis here enjoys it, heh?

Lewis nodded.

Oh well, that's nice. It's good to do something you enjoy. Here, have a piece of cake.

Though he loved his grandma deeply, Lewis felt the familiar surge of irritation whenever she used words like nice. He didn't mean to but he couldn't help it. He suddenly wanted to blurt out, Yeah, and Tom's in Bournemouth doing fuck all and his brother's doing heroin and selling his arse to pay for it at motorway service stations and I might just as well be doing the fucking same for all there is to do around here. But he said nothing, took some cake, knew that he had it all wrong anyhow. They hadn't had heroin, his grandma's generation, no, but they'd had a world war instead. He knew he really had nothing to tell her.

His grandma judged no one. He knew that. Anyone else might have been probing and demanding about when he was going to get a proper job, what he was going to do about it. But not his grandma who had seen everything and endured everything, suffered much and judged nothing.

Ah yes, his grandma was saying. Gone are the days when the estate used to employ half a dozen fulltime gardeners or more. Mind you, she chuckled, there were too bloomin' many of them, to be honest. The Tilley brothers and Jacob who couldn't even bend over. He used to spend hours inventing long-handled tools that he could use to save his back. None of them ever worked, of course. Oh we did laugh, Jack and me. Jack had this wonderful laugh.

There was a pause. There was no awkwardness. Grandma had fallen silent for a moment to remember her dead husband whom she had never stopped loving all the years he had been gone. It was as if her love for him was still the same as it had been when she was a girl of nineteen and first married to him. When he died her love didn't die but, mysteriously, like Jack himself, it stopped growing older. Her love had never grown old and tired and habitual, because her lover had never grown old and tired and habitual. John and Lewis waited, watching her lowered eyes soft and expressionless. Then she started again.

They'd all be sittin' up in the pottin' shed most of the day, she said, brewin' tea and readin' the *Picture Post* and when old Mr Sedley comes bumbling round they'd all be on their feet standing in a row, pretending they were talking to the seedlings!

His grandma chuckled, her head down. Lewis and his father exchanged looks. His father winked at him.

Oh dear, she said, and began to pour more tea, strong and aromatic, from the green pot. The cake was delicious. The clock ticked slowly on the mantelpiece, measuring time out far more slowly than in the world beyond. Even long silences in conversation didn't matter here. His grandma smiled round benevolently and on the walls were little framed prayers and blessings that Lewis knew off by heart, having stared at them so often during so many long sleepy Sunday afternoons.

And what about you, John, how are you keeping?

He deflected the question immediately.

Oh well, work's very busy at the moment, plenty of visitors an' all that, y'know. Yes, pretty steady work.

She nodded.

Had these investors in t'other night, big spread laid on for them an' all that.

91

Oh, investors, she said, repeating the word with reverence.

Yeah well, big money-men, y'know, wanting to see how we were getting on. Rumour has it that they may be opening another sort of farm – he snorted – farmstead or what have you, whatever you want to call it. Up our way, so they say.

Oh? said Grandma.

Yeah. They're looking up at Hound Wood for a site.

Hound Wood, she repeated. Ah well. She sipped her tea and looked out of the window. She remembered Hound Wood in springtime, and she and her sister in pinafores clutching fistfuls of cowslips gathered from the edge of the wood. She remembered walking there with Jack, kissing under the trees. Time ago. Ah well, she said again. Can't stand in the way of progress, I suppose.

Nor can you, said John Pike. Nor can you.

They talked on, of things in the village and of the weather and of Katy and Andy and the children and Lewis saw her eyes crinkle with delight at the very thought of them. Grandma's black cat Tinker came into the room unnoticed at first and slinked around Lewis's legs and miaowed once and looked up at him. He gave her a little pinch of cake which she rolled about between her front paws for a while before deciding that she did not like it. Then she looked up at him with her fathomless green eyes and fixed him and he was obliged to uncross his legs and put his plate down and prepare his lap for her comfort, having really no choice at all in the matter. Tinker jumped up and approved the standard of comfort she found there and turned about once and then curled up and began to purr. Lewis stroked her.

I don't suppose you've seen much of the new vicar, have you, John?

John grinned at her broadly. Not in church I haven't, ma, not since Christmas.

Oh John, she said reproachfully.

But mind you, he added, scratching his head, we see him down the pub sometimes, don't we Lewis?

Do you?

Well, he pops in for a pint on occasions. Just to keep in with people like, I suppose, and I'm sure he means well by it, but to be perfectly honest . . . well, there's not many churchgoers down there. Not with the Mabey brothers down there anyhow!

I don't see why he shouldn't go for a pint, same as any other man, said Grandma in his defence.

I don't like it, said Lewis quietly.

Grandma laughed. Oh Lewis, I never thought I'd hear you to be such an old stick-in-the-pie.

Well . . . said Lewis.

I think he's just trying to be modern and lively but I know some people don't like it and get all hot and bothered about it, said Grandma. Joan for one. She says to me the other day, Well he's a nice enough chap, but a bit of a funny one, to my way of thinking. I asked her what she meant and she said, Well, there doesn't seem to be much in what he *says*. Last Easter, she said, it was all very nice, but there didn't seem to be much to it. I said I thought he was doing his best, but you can't please everybody. Someone will always criticize. I'm sure he does very well for most of us.

She looked up at the clock on the mantelpiece. How soon hath time, the subtle thief of youth, Stol'n on his wing my three and twentieth year, she said.

John Pike had to put his tea down very rapidly so as not to spill it from laughing. Ma, you do come out with the oddest things.

She got slowly to her feet.

Do you know who that is? Lewis, do you know who that is?

Lewis shook his head. Why were people always asking him about poetry these days?

That's John Milton, that is. Now I remember learning that

in the village school. We all sat in rows and recited that until we could recite it standing on our heads. Mind you – she frowned at the carpet – I used to know another of his and that's clean gone to Putney on a pig.

Lewis looked at his father and they both tried not to laugh again. They thanked Grandma for the tea and cake.

Ah well, come again, my love, and you too, Lewis. Now you take care now and God bless. She squeezed Lewis's cheeks tightly and kissed him. I can hardly reach to do that any more. I shall have to stand on a stool soon.

She said that every time, and he loved her for it.

They waved goodbye as they walked down the tiny garden path and got back in the car and continued waving as they drove away.

She stood small and neat and white-haired and looked down the lane long after they had gone, her expression of cheeriness changed for something older and more troubled, lost in thought and perhaps even in prayer. The one quiet centre in all that rootless disquiet and turmoil and in all that imminent and omened outbreaking of blood and blood's rage and the shouldering of sorrow's burden.

19 The Hill

Later, Lewis looked at his watch and told his father he was going out for a bit.

Not takin' Allie, then?

He didn't look at him directly. Allie's eyes were round and pleading. He hated himself then. No, he said, I think she seems a bit tired today.

Ah, well, maybe she is, said his father. Vet's girl said she'd be a few weeks before she was as right as rain again.

Yeah, said Lewis, I reckon.

I won't be that long, he called from the back door.

He sat on the ancient hill beyond Hound Wood that was fringed on the north side with beech trees. He remembered the Poet saying that the hill was a tumulus and probably had been a pagan site of worship, and sometimes the Poet came up here on warm starlit nights and lay on top of the hill and communed with the ancestors. Even better, he said, was to lie all night on the long barrow up on the downs and to know that, but for a few shepherds, one was the first person to lie there since its bronze-age builders first came and built it and laid their revered dead or slain inside it in mystified and haunted remembrance, and watched the stars wheel changelessly about the pole and return and the seasons pass and return again the same in time and so knew that all things likewise must pass and come again and so were comforted. That little tribe haunted and weeping for its chieftain on the bare hillside.

But for now the summer sun shone down strongly on

Lewis Pike and the wind was as gentle as a flower and the whole valley lay beneath him, the little trickle of river with its Celtic name like the sound of water over pebbles itself, and the great bare shoulders of the downs, and the wooded valley below with only a glimpse of church steeple or thatched roof or whitewashed wall. He could barely breathe for love of it. Half a dozen gardeners in the old days, his grandmother had said, and God knows how many more labourers on the estate farms. They were poor then and died younger and had no televisions and ate bread with a scrape of butter or else with jam, but never with both. He had seen photographs of the harvest time when everyone worked, everyone. In the photographs the ranks of men and women stood in formal rows for the occasion, however their backs might ache and their palms blister and their heads thunder from bending and standing endlessly under the sun. The women wore long dresses and were bare armed and the men wore white shirts and waistcoats and baggy trousers and baggy flat caps. Behind them, the haywagon almost hidden under its load. All the village then in the fields.

He shuddered and stood abruptly and shook his head violently to clear away the thoughts that plagued him and walked rapidly down the hill as if to ease his aching heart with the violent coursing of his blood.

20   Jack and Rose (2)

It was the following Sunday after they had walked home beside the haycart. Rose was coming out of church with her mother and father and her sister Nora when she saw Jack Pike sitting on the church wall in his best Sunday suit. He was clutching his cap to his breast nervously and looking over his shoulder towards her.

As they approached the lychgate he sprang to his feet and came to meet them.

Morning, Mr Parsons, he said far too quickly, touching his hand to the cap that wasn't on his head. Morning, Mrs Parsons. I was wonderin' if I might . . . if I might . . .

Rose was pink with embarrassment and pride. She fixed her eyes steadily on the buttercups in the grass at her feet. Mrs Parsons smiled at Jack.

. . . if . . . I might . . . go out for a walk with . . . with Rose today.

Mr Parsons started fumbling in his pocket for his pipe. Mrs Parsons said, Well, Jack, I think that would be very nice, but we're on our way home to dinner now. You can come over this afternoon if you like.

Hmph, added Mr Parsons. Not before two, mind.

Jack arrived outside their house at twenty past one.

The house had been built only a few years earlier and was considered rather grand. Mr Parsons was a sheep farmer but Mrs Parsons had had an inheritance recently.

Jack sat in the field opposite, hidden by the hedge, and tore furiously at grass stems. Then he looked down and saw with horror that the grass had stained his fingernails green and he spent the next ten minutes furiously sucking them pink. When he stood up he found he had been sitting on the very edge of a fresh cowpat. He ran his fingers all over the seat of his trousers and decided that he had not made physical contact but was terrified none the less in case the odour had somehow impregnated his suit which he knew was fairly old and ripe already. He bent down and tried to sniff it. Yes, it would definitely benefit from having some fresh air wafted through it.

He took his jacket off and laid it carefully in grass free of cowpat and slipped his braces off his shoulders and held his trousers up by their waistband. Then billowing them in and out he started to jump up and down and dance and pirouette about in an attempt to generate the maximum possible airflow. He leapt and cavorted and then, pausing for breath with his trousers clutched loosely about his waist, he saw Mr Parsons only yards away from him leaning over the gate. He was smoking his pipe and regarding Jack's movements with the sheep farmer's typical lack of facial expression.

Jack was unable to move. He managed a sickly smile. At least half a minute seemed to pass in terrible silence. Then Mr Parsons removed his pipe from his mouth and looked down at it.

My wife won't let me smoke in the house, he said.

Jack's smile grew sicklier. It had just occurred to him that Mr Parsons might have been standing there for quite a while. He might have been standing there watching when he was bent double, trying to sniff the seat of his own trousers.

Another long silence.

This was terrible.

Well, said Mr Parsons at last, still wearing an unreadably blank expression. If that's how desperate you're feelin' you best come over to the house and see Rose.

*

Jack and Rose walked out for the first time that Sunday afternoon.

Jack felt like he'd been holding his breath all the time he was in the Parsons' house and it was such a posh house too, with fitted carpets and a huge radiogram in the front room and everything. Mr Parsons had offered him a whisky but he had said no.

Once they were out in the fields he felt more relaxed again and sneaked a sideways look at Rose. She was looking lovely. Her hair was long and brown and glossy in the sunlight and she wore a plain cotton dress that outlined her figure in such a way that made Jack swallow hard.

They wandered side by side down the lane and then over the stile to the stream.

So, she said, suddenly bold, what are you doing, taking me out for a walk when I heard you were seeing a lot of Jeanie Weathered?

Jack didn't look her in the eye.

No I'm not, he said. Least not any more. That was ... that was a few weeks back now. That was just bein' friendly.

Just being friendly, she repeated carefully.

Yes.

So – what's this, then? Just being friendly too?

He looked at her with an expression that was almost pained.

She walked on ahead of him, swaying her hips victoriously and calling back over her shoulder, A girl just likes to know where she stands, that's all, and then she turned away again so that her long hair swung across her back and he couldn't take his eyes off her even as he ran to catch up with her and nearly tripped over a tree root from not looking where he was going.

They walked on in silence again.

Anyway, he said at last to break the silence. The hay's all in now.

Is it? she said.

Aye. Finished just last night.

That's good going, she said. Usually it takes to the end of August, doesn't it?

Varies a lot, he said. We started on the top field mid June. It's been a good year. The watermeadows especially. We haven't fitted it all in the barn even this year. Had to build a rick down by the church.

You built a rick?

Well, he admitted, all of us together. Dad's an old hand and Grandfather, he got all het up about it and said it was like when he was a boy building ricks, though he said even in them days young lads used to go out and set fire to them. He said he wanted to go up the ladder and all but Dad wouldn't let him. He was furious!

They laughed. Rose thought that Jack had a wonderful laugh.

Do you want to see it? he said suddenly.

What? Oh, the rick. Well yes, all right then.

They walked over to the church and he proudly showed her the rick behind. It looked just like a stack of hay to her, with a thatched roof.

The secret's to build the top as steep as possible, Jack explained. To let the rain run off.

I see, she said. She gave it a shove. Quite good, she declared. Very solid. She turned and leaned her back against it and closed her eyes and raised her face up to the sun. She opened her eyes again when she felt his lips on hers. She hesitated for just a moment and then pushed him off.

Jack, she said.

He grinned, already emboldened by that moment of hesitation on her part, that brief moment when she seemed to return his kiss, and by the rather half-hearted way she protested against it.

He wondered whether to say I beg your pardon but then thought, No, bugger it and took her hand instead and walked her back to the riverbank. Behind a curtain of willow he slipped an arm round her and pulled her close to him and kissed her again. This time she didn't protest so much and closed her eyes.

Later he walked her home and beside a hedge he stretched up and picked her a wild rose, one of the year's last, squeezing through the stalk with forefinger and thumbnail.

Here you are, he said. A rose for Rose.

She took it from him.

Rose, he said. Rosie. Can I call you Rosie?

She smiled. If you like.

Have you any other names?

Elizabeth.

That's nice too. Lizzie. Beth. No, Rosie's best.

What about you?

No, he said.

Just Jack?

Just Jack. Jack Pike.

She looked around. She found some scabious growing in the grass and picked a single flower.

Here you are, Just Jack, she said. A flower for Jack Pike.

He took it uncertainly. You can't give me flowers, he said. Girls don't give men flowers.

Why not? she said.

It's not . . . it's not the right way round, he said.

Why not? How do you know I'm not one of these new liberated women?

Oh corks, he said, I hope not.

Why?

Cos . . . you'd 'ave to cut off all your hair and . . . and . . . you've got such lovely hair.

She reached up and kissed him on the cheek. You charmer, she said.

All right then, he said, slipping the flower casually into his pocket. I'll keep on to it.

That's right, she said. You do that.

That night he removed the flower with utmost care from his pocket and pressed it between the leaves of a pocket Bible.

He slept with the Bible under his pillow.

The next morning his brothers teased him without mercy. And he had a lot of brothers. They said they'd seen him out walking with Rose Parsons and they bet that she had grass stains on her elbows and he on his knees. But Jack didn't care. He just laughed and said they were jealous.

21 Mary (2)

Lewis came to the Poet's cottage and peered cautiously round the corner but Mary spotted him immediately and beckoned him over. She was crunching into a red apple and as he came close he saw in the sunlight little flecks of foaming apple juice fly out and when she smiled at him there were little bubbles of apple juice around her mouth which she wiped away with her finger.

Have a bite, she said, passing the apple to him, laughing. Just call me Eve. She sat down.

He grinned and took the apple and took a deep bite. It tasted good. He handed it back to her.

How's your finger? he asked.

Hm?

The wasp sting.

Oh that. She was curiously touched that he even remembered. Oh, it's gone now. She looked at him sideways. He didn't see.

Sit down, she said. My husband's out on one of his jaunts. Though I secretly suspect that he just finds a shady corner somewhere and flops down for a snooze.

She tucked up her feet and hugged her knees.

He's very keen on idleness. He says it's very important for poets to be idlers and wanderers and just to spend whole days at a time daydreaming and doing nothing in particular. He always quotes that line of Yeats's, 'I who have always hated work . . .' and makes no secret of feeling the same. She laughed. Oh well, he may be right, I don't understand it. I can see what he means when he says he can only write well after a good night's sleep, when his imagination has been recharged with dreaming. He says that a single line of poetry may come only after hours and hours of dreaming sleep. I don't know. It all sounds like a very complex argument in favour of a prolonged afternoon nap to me. She shaded her eyes and giggled at Lewis.

He thought he would feel embarrassed to find her just on her own again, but it was fine really. She talked so much more when Gerald wasn't here and he liked the way she talked about him. It wasn't unkind but it was sort of teasing. She laughed at him, and it was true, there was something funny about Gerald. But she still liked him. He could tell that. She talked about him as if he was lazy or like a little boy or full of mad ideas that never came to anything, but she still liked him. Loved him, he supposed.

So, she said, what have you been up to lately?

That was another thing. Mary always asked him about himself. Gerald never did that. Poets are like that I suppose, he thought.

Oh not much, he said, plucking up grass stems. Collected Allie the other day.

Is she all right?

Think so, said Lewis. Collar comes off tomorrow.

Oh poor thing, said Mary. That's to stop her scratching?

He nodded.

They hate that sort of thing, don't they? They *know* it makes them look undignified, especially in front of other dogs.

I've kept her away from other dogs deliberately this week, said Lewis.

She looked at him. That's very considerate of you.

He shrugged. She hates it, he said. It's bad enough for her in front of cows and stuff.

Mary smiled. They know, don't they? she said. They have such natural dignity.

He nodded.

They must think we human beings behave in a *frightfully* undignified way at times. And there's nothing so unnatural and undignified for them as having to wear a contraption like a collar. It must be like, I don't know – it's like men on holiday who, she giggled, wear beige socks with their sandals.

Lewis grinned. Yeah. Sort of, he added laconically.

Or, I don't know – wearing socks at all in summer seems odd to me. Not necessary at all.

I just wear boots, said Lewis.

Exactly. Mind you, I suppose we don't really need to wear anything at all on hot days.

Well . . . he said.

I often wear nothing else under my dress.

She looked at him slyly. He looked at the grass.

Oh Lewis, I'm sorry, she said. Am I embarrassing you?

He looked up, grinned. No, he said.

Tell you what, she said. Surely time for a cup of tea?

Oh, yes please, said Lewis. I'm that thirsty.

Tea coming up, she said, standing in a single swift movement that delighted him. It made him think of an animal grace, of a deer leaping a high fence delicately, from standing.

Pint or gallon? she asked.

Gallon please, he said solemnly. Twelve sugars.

She laughed and went inside.

He lay back on the grass and rested his head in his hands. This was all right.

She came back with two mugs of tea. Couldn't find the gallon mugs, she said. Will this do?

He took a mug from her. It'll do, he said.

She lay down on her stomach facing him. *Nothing else under my dress*. From the way her dress lay over her bum he thought she wasn't wearing anything else today. The thought dizzied him, the blood raced in his head. Perhaps this could get embarrassing after all, he thought, yet almost chuckling to himself, changing his position and lying on his stomach on the grass like her, flattening himself into the lawn, hoping she wouldn't have noticed anything. His throat was dry.

Good tea, he said.

Thank you. She brushed her long hair away from her face.

He plucked up a grass stem and began to chew on it.

What is it about chewing grass? she said.

He shrugged. Cheaper than chewing gum.

She liked that, smiled. He was surprised at himself. Yes, it wasn't a bad little joke. It was easy to joke when you felt this happy.

She plucked a blade of grass and did likewise. Then screwed up her face and stopped. Ugh, she said. Really bitter.

Too dark green, he said. The darker green it is, the more bitter. You want a pale bit.

Aha, she said. You're a connoisseur.

I certainly am.

She put on a funny voice. A Connoisseur of Fine Grasses and Sedges from Around the World.

She was such fun, he'd never realized before. Such a mad sense of humour. He felt so happy. He knew he'd remember this afternoon at some later time and not believe he'd felt so happy then.

She said, My husband would no doubt have some terrifically complex and elaborate theory about why we like to eat grass, which he would expound at great length to anyone who cared to listen. I can just imagine it: something to do with trying to recapture our primal innocence, in the Garden of Eden. Our original herbivorous innocence, before we became meateaters and bloodshedders. Like Nebuchadnezzar.

Dad says we never were vegetarians or nothing like that, said Lewis. Says how can we be, we must have always eaten meat and stuff, cos look at these. He pointed to his teeth. We always were meateaters and bloodshedders as you say.

What do you mean?

These two, he said, touching his forefinger to his incisors. Pointy teeth, aren't they? Predator's teeth. For eating meat.

She ran her tongue over her teeth and found them and said, My God, I'd never really thought of that before.

He grinned. Delighted to have told her something she didn't know, shown her something new.

Pointy teeth, she said again and smiled. Well, well. Still, it doesn't mean we can't eat grass as *well*.

Oh no, he agreed. You just have to find the right sort. It's not the blade you chew on anyhow, it's the stem. You want one with a good juicy stem. Um . . .

They both started to hunt around. She found one and picked it. Here we are, she said. This looks like a good one.

It was mad. Here they were, lying here, talking about eating grass. He couldn't believe it.

She chewed meditatively on a stem, her eyes half-closed. Mm, she said. Rather a good one, this. Warm, full-bodied, with a distinct bouquet of . . . of . . . She waved her hand about, searching for the right word.

Grass, he said.

Oregano, she insisted. And perhaps almonds.

Tah! He laughed.

Here, she said, taking the stem from her mouth. Try it.

He tentatively reached out and took the stem wet with her saliva and put it in his mouth and chewed. Mm, he said. It's good.

It is, she said. Must be a rare vintage. We'll never find another one like it.

Have to split it, he agreed. Half each.

Afraid so.

He reached up and took the stem from his mouth but she said No and he hesitated.

Then she wriggled forward toward him face to face and said, No hands allowed. Tug of war. Whoever gets the longest piece is the winner.

He understood. Clamped his teeth down hard on the end of the stem.

Her face now so close, only inches away. He could feel her warm breath on his face, see her wide eyes. She closed her teeth on the other end of the stem. Now pull, she said.

He jerked his head back swiftly and she was left with nothing but a scraping of grass behind her teeth.

Hey, not fair, she said, sliding the grass out on her tongue and wiping it away with her finger. You've played this game before.

Played for England, he said. Under-16s Grass-Pulling Trophy.

Right, she said. Half each.

And suddenly she closed her mouth over half the stem so that their lips brushed each other and he saw deep into her blue eyes and it was as if they were kissing and then she bit through the stem and took half with her.

She laughed and lay back on the grass with a hand behind her head so that her dress was tight across her small breasts and she turned her head towards him and said, What larks, eh? What larks!

He grinned. She was mad.

I don't know, she said, looking skyward again. Then softly she added, Shocking behaviour. And he ached with desire.

Then a voice hallooed from the side of the cottage and the Poet had returned.

22   Gerald and Mary (2)

He was dressed as usual in bottlegreen corduroys and a tweed jacket with no shirt. His thin chest was very white and his belly sagged like a loose sail. He beamed at them as if momentarily forgetful of who they were. He got a deck-chair out of the garden room and came and joined them under the cherry tree.

Tea? Mary asked him.

Oh yes please, darling.

Lewis scrambled to his feet. I'll get it, he said.

Are you sure?

Yeah, go on, he said.

Oh well, that's jolly good of you, Lewis, said Gerald. Milk, no sugar, if you please. And mind the kettle, it's a bugger! he called after him. Likes to dribble boiling water on you!

That was the last kettle, murmured Mary.

Heh? said Gerald.

In the kitchen he could hardly think straight. One step at a time, he concentrated on filling the kettle, plugging it in, finding the milk, the teabags . . . His hands were shaking and his breathing was shallow and broken. All he could think about was what might have happened if Gerald had not returned at that moment. Standing staring at the slowly boiling kettle, all he could see was a picture of him leaning over and kissing her, of her turning to him surprised and delighted and smiling, her raising one knee, her dress sliding up her brown thigh . . .

When he returned with tea Gerald was laughing and rubbing his hands together with delight, evidently regaling Mary with the events of the afternoon. It seemed that he had not been for a walk after all, but on a whim, passing the church noticeboard, had decided to spend the afternoon up at Wardour House, at Mrs Armitage's famous harvest festival meeting.

The first of many, I hope, chuckled Gerald. Seems like she's planned a whole series of 'em. And she is *full* of ideas of course, being the breathtakingly bossy cow that she is. So bloody abrasive too. You could tell, you could *feel* that she was putting people's backs up straight away, when she started on about how dismal traditional harvest festivals could be with just a few manky old pumpkins and a tin of pineapple chunks on the altar steps and tea in a tatty village hall. Even in the countryside! she said. Surrounded as we are by the abundance of Nature! She actually said that, flinging her arms wide and crushing the front row of people to death with her mighty breasts.

Lewis and Mary were both laughing now.

Old Joanie and Mrs Whitaker were at the back of the room muttering to themselves about how it wasn't right, she had no right to talk like that, they remembered some very nice festivals in the past, etcetera, etcetera, and I leaned over to them and whispered, Ladies, you have my full support, which made them look all sheepish and giggly.

But of course old Barmitage just sails on regardless like the bloody Queen Mary with a full head of steam, wide-bottomed and spewing guff from all four funnels. Was the Queen Mary four funnels?

Lewis shook his head.

Christ knows. Anyway the point holds. It's the right image. So the poor old dears relegated to the back, timid enough anyway at being up at Wardour House where Joanie was actually a maid when she was a girl, and them just about the only *real* locals there, they start mumbling away, but of course they're hopelessly outnumbered and outgunned and Barmitage carries all before her. Oh and there's Gavin our beloved vic of course, desperately trying to keep the peace. I like him but I still can't help thinking of him as a bit of a milksop. Who else? Oh, the usual crowd. The couple from Pound Cottage, him in a Norfolk jacket for fuck's sake, in *this* heat, and Mrs Brigadier, and our dear friend the lady novelist wreathed in smiles and batik scarves, wafting around like the fairy godmother and no doubt collecting lots of ideas for the next instalment of her multi-volume ongoing rural soap opera, *Life in a Lovely English Village* or whatever the fuck it's called.

Now then, darling, said Mary, laughing despite herself, do I detect a twinge of petulance in your voice?

A *twinge*? More than a fucking *twinge*, growled Gerald. Fucking barrel-loads of it . . . Firkins . . . Fucking great *hogsheads* of petulance!

He giggled to himself after this outburst and Lewis and Mary laughed with him. Lewis never realized that poets swore quite so much. He always imagined that they talked poetically all the time. But there was no denying it, Gerald could be a real laugh when he put on this act.

He was still burbling on about the lady novelist.

Do you know how many copies of her latest dollop of trex she sold? he demanded. Do you have any idea?

Lewis shook his head.

There was a pause.

No, well, neither do I as a matter of fact, but I'll tell you one thing, you can be sure that it sold a fuck sight more than *Lacunae*.

Lewis looked blank.

My latest collection, explained Gerald with exaggerated patience. *Lacunae*: Poems, 1984–1994. You haven't . . . ?

No, said Lewis.

Hm. Somehow I had a feeling you'd say that. He clasped

his hands as if in prayer and touched his fingertips to his lips. *Anyway*, he said after a sigh. The meeting.

It got worse. It turned out that Barmitage wasn't really there to *discuss ideas* at all, of course, she was just there to air *her* ideas, surprise surfuckingprise, and make sure we all agreed with her. And Jesus, does she have a lot of ideas. It seems that she wants to add *ceremony* and *ritual* to the occasion: she kept saying these words with a terrible emphasis while waving her flabby arms around. We must restore *ceremony* and *ritual* to rural life, she declared, like some benighted fucking sociologist or something, as if you can just come along and graft it on like a . . . a fucking rose cutting.

Actually Barmitage, I wanted to tell her, most people around here haven't got time to sit around on their fat arses agonizing about the absence of ceremony and ritual in modern rural life, they're too busy getting the kids off to school and worrying about paying the next fucking poll-tax bill. I tell you, that woman has no idea. Anyway, the two old dears had just gone silent by now and I could see Gavin the vic getting distinctly jumpy at the thought of what the tabloids would make of it, not to mention that slimeball media vicar from Essex – what's the cunt's name? – if ever it got out that there had been pseudo-pagan rituals reintroduced into the C of E down in darkest Wiltshire!

Gerald slurped his tea and went on. He's unstoppable, thought Lewis. It will never end.

Because that's what it was all coming to. La Barmitage has got it into her fat, addled head that we should resurrect the ceremony of Cutting the Neck of the Doll, you remember Gavin said in the pub about it? Sacrificing virgins on the altar and stuff. Not that she understands the first fucking thing about it, of course, whereas I must modestly own up to knowing a great deal about such things, having pored over Frazer since I was in short trousers.

Gerald cracked his fingers. Lewis loved the tone of irony

and self-mockery in his voice, and saw how it was that the Poet was still charming and Mary still loved him for all that he did little but lie around all day and drink cider and tea and talk. And talk.

Anyway – La Barmitage starts waxing lyrical about this *primeval ritual* of Cutting the Neck of the Doll, and how it represents the death of the old year and the corn god and the hoped-for rebirth of the new, and how we should enact this ridiculous ritual and make a doll from the last sheaf, and then process to the church on Harvest Sunday, and Gavin, who is getting twitchy now anyway, bless his heart, is the only one with the balls to stand up at this point and say that wheat doesn't actually get harvested in sheaves any more, and it would be a nightmare for a combine driver to have to leave just one little stand of wheat in the middle of the field, which is what La Barmitage was demanding. And she's completely nonplussed at this, the wind right out of her sails or the coke out of her boilers or whatever, and goes absolutely *purple*, with her whole fat face swollen up and about to burst like a ripe plum – and yet it was Gavin who was the only one to point all this out to her, probably the only one in the room even to know it. Not a real fucking farmer there, of course. Most of them probably still like to think it's done with a fucking sickle.

Gerald bowed his head into his chest and giggled his mad, hissing giggle through his teeth.

It gets worse, he gasped. After this objection and Barmitage finally just brushing it aside and saying she's sure it could all be *arranged* — yeah, I'd love to see Maurice's face when he's told he's got to steer the combine round a one foot square patch in the middle of the field — then it gets really priceless because the missis from Pound Cottage says only half jokingly that she hopes the harvest isn't too early this year because if it is most of them will be on holiday at the time! Can you befuckinglieve it? The rude and humble village folk will all be off in Chiantishire or the

113

fucking Algarve and there'll be no one around to Cut the Neck of the Doll! Priceless! Gerald almost choked with laughter. Priceless! Meaningless!

He got his breath back and wiped the tears away from the corners of his eyes. Oh dear, he said. Anyway – it's decided that with the weather we're having the harvest will be earlyish and they actually have the humility – a very rare occurrence with this lot, I can tell you – the *humility* to acknowledge that we don't *yet* control the weather, and the harvest will have to be done when the crop's ready and can't be delayed just because of some naff and bogus little ceremony dreamed up by the idle, underemployed mind of La Barmitage. So it's decided to ask one of the farmers and see if it can be *arranged* for the end of August, and anyone sunning their haut-bourgeois butts off in Tuscany, darling, will just have to miss the fucking thing!

Gerald drained his tea and smacked his mug down triumphantly. I know we're incomers ourselves, sweetheart, but *really*. Toe-curling embarrassment, I tell you. I know they're not *all* like that, but total wankers this afternoon.

Lewis felt quite exhausted after this dramatic mono-logue. He plucked at the grass and looked around and tried to absorb all that Gerald had said. Such a stream of stuff, of words. His grandmother always said that the newspapers were bad for you because they gave you mental indigestion, too much too quickly and no time to chew on it. And Lewis sometimes felt the same listening to Gerald. He needed time to sort it out. To Gerald, it was all a game. Cutting the Neck of the Doll. He'd have to ask Grandma about that.

He screwed up his courage suddenly and said, I heard the vicar say God's dead.

Gerald looked at him with interest. Is that a poem? he asked.

Lewis felt embarrassed. No, he laughed. I just said it.

But – hm. A perfect iambic tetrameter. *I heard the vicar say God's dead*. Y'know, that really could be the first line of a poem, by Larkin perhaps. When did he say that?

I think he was jokin', said Lewis. In church the other day.

Ha! laughed Gerald. Good on him. Good old Gavin. There's hope for him yet. All he needs to do now is to forsake the pale Galilean and discover the white goddess, and he'll be just fine. I must say, his main objection to La Barmitage was practical, not theological, so I was quite touched by his broadmindedness. He seemed quite prepared for them to resurrect the ritual and use the church for a service of blessing or whatever, sad and farcical though it all is. Good on him.

Anyone want some cake? Mary asked.

Gerald and Lewis both said yes and Mary went inside.

So what is this doll then? asked Lewis boldly, needing to know.

Hm?

The neck of the doll an' that.

Oh that. Well. Gerald steepled his fingers and took on an intent expression. It's not entirely a figment of La Barmitage's dreary imagination of course. You must know corn dollies?

Lewis nodded. He could see the dolly faded almost white with a scarlet ribbon about its neck that his grandmother kept over the kitchen door. He said as much to Gerald. Reminds me to duck me 'ead when I go through it, he grinned.

Well yes, said Gerald, though that's not its real meaning.

I know that, thought Lewis.

The twee little dolly favoured by old dears – *pace* your grandmama – is a survival of a rather more grim and ancient custom, and La Barmitage's thing about cutting the neck of the doll is an echo of it. God, I'd love to tell her that. I'd love to tell her just what that red ribbon signifies. But she's such a stupid bitch. The thing is, when our ancestors gathered in the harvest, millennia ago – their main concern was for the next harvest to work just as well as the last. Now in time the ritual came to involve saving the last sheaf,

115

fashioning it into a human figure, and then ritually slaying it and leaving it behind to rot in the field. But what you must realize is that originally our ancestors did it *for real*.

As those words impressed themselves upon him, Lewis Pike sank his shoulders and began to shake. He had an image of a rushing spiral of wind that was centred on him and himself caught there hunched over, or stuck like an animal on the wire.

Not all that long ago either, it seems. It was human sacrifice, plain and simple, to propitiate stroppy gods and ensure divine benevolence in a dark time. Of course, we don't hold much with human sacrifice nowadays, except to keep the economy sound, or on the high altar of capitalism, otherwise known as wars. And the Christians say we have had the one and only sacrifice to last for all time. So.

Lewis was shaking so much when Mary handed him a piece of cake that he could hardly take it from her. She pretended not to notice and sat down opposite him. She didn't know why he was shaking like that but she didn't need to know a reason. She wanted to take him in her arms and hug him so tightly that he couldn't shake. She thought with a faint smile that her husband probably wouldn't even notice if she did.

However, said Gerald. We will never quite let go of the idea. Even in our time, our secular chosen ones must die a violent, unnatural death: Lennon, Marilyn, Gandhi, JFK, the Blessed Diana. Quite a thought.

23 The Doll

When Lewis left Mary and Gerald he was still shaking and his stomach was cramped up and aching. He walked back towards the lane and then turned right and came to the wheatfield near the farm. He skirted the edge under the chestnut trees and then paused and picked a few stalks of wheat and twisted them into a loose torc and hooped it over his head and around his neck. He stepped carefully in amid the wheat and took his knife and was going to draw it clear across his throat but thought that his father would want to know what that cut was. So he drew it fiercely across the back of his neck beneath his shirt collar and felt the blood ooze from the cut and trickle down from the lower end of the cut and down his back. Then he lay down hidden among the wheat. Then he stopped shaking.

He came home with a bloodstained shirt and he sneaked into the house and upstairs and washed it in the basin and then craned his neck in the bathroom mirror and washed the cut across his neck as best he could. It was long but not too deep and already crusting over. It bled again when he washed it but stopped quickly when he staunched it with cottonwool. Cobwebs they used to use in the old days, he remembered his grandma saying. He found a whole jungle of cobwebs in the corner of the bathroom and took a clot of that ancient silk and laid it along the wound and held it in place with two wide plasters. It hurt now and he was reluctant to move his head. He glanced in the mirror and then looked quickly away like a dog reluctant to see its own image. He went downstairs and cooked his father supper.

Days passed. He practised ceaselessly with the crossbow and became a perfect shot. He went out and killed animals which he always took home to eat, to his father's pleasure and concern, and skinned and plucked them and gutted them and cooked them up. They ate a lot of rabbit and wood pigeon. He watched a lot of television, taking nothing in. Days passed.

24   The Town (2)

Then one Friday afternoon the phone went and Lewis answered it with reluctance.

Hiya Lew, said a voice. It's Tom.

Oh hi, Tom. What you doin'?

Just back from college. Off to sunny Spain next week actually but I'm staying at Steve's for a couple of days, fuck knows why. We're all out on the piss tonight, d'you wanna come?

Oh right. Um, well . . .

Ah, go on. Be a laugh. Or you got no dosh?

Um. Not really, said Lewis.

Ah sod that. We'll 'ave a few beers. C'mon.

So Lewis left a note for his father and caught the last bus into Salisbury that day and hung around by the riverside and then turned up at Steve's about seven.

Steve lived in a decaying block of flats off Exeter Street. Lewis walked up the urinous concrete stairwell to the first floor walkway and knocked on the yellow door. The front doors were alternately yellow and blue, the whole block. He wondered if any other colours were allowed.

Tom answered. Well, whatever, never mind, he sang in Lewis's face. Music thundered out of the sitting room behind. Tom sniffed and grinned. Come as you are, he said.

Lewis grinned back. What the fuck was he talking about?

Poor old Kurt, RIP, he said. If only it'd been Courtney what topped herself, hey? Come on in then, you old cunt.

Lewis followed him in and thought how much he missed Tom, wiry and shockhaired and a nonstop talker.

Except he made Lewis feel so stupid though he knew he didn't mean to.

Steve's in 'ere, he said.

Steve was lying on a thin mattress in the sitting room. Apart from that and the stereo, the room was bare.

Tom had to shout. Ask 'im what 'appened to all 'is stuff. Eh, Steve?

Steve just scowled at Tom.

Burgled wasn't 'e? said Tom cheerfully. By Lem and Danny.

Lewis didn't understand. I thought they were mates?

Junkies don't have *mates*, said Tom. Lem and Danny have expensive, er . . . *habits* to maintain. They got to find four hundred quid a week from somewhere. That right, Steve?

Steve ignored him.

He used to have blond hair but it was so unwashed that it looked mousy brown. His arms were white sticks and ropey with veins. Lewis was always a bit scared of Steve: his sharp face, his cold eyes. He never trusted him and he didn't know why Tom was here. He asked him in the kitchen.

Tom shrugged. Cheapest B&B in Salisbury. I'm not going back to Hicksville.

Lewis stared at him.

Oh come on, Lew, I go back odd days to see mum but I can't stand it there, I dunno how you do. What do you *do* all day there?

Lewis shrugged.

Exactly. I'd rather be in the big city, even kippin' on the floor with some arsehole junkie like Steve. Suits me. Anyhow I'm off to sunny Ibiza next week. Wanna cup of tea?

Later they went out to one of the big anonymous pubs favoured by under-age drinkers and drank export lager. When they'd had three pints each and were on their fourth Steve suddenly lurched to his feet and went over to the two girls sitting at the bar.

Hey Lise, he called out. Hiya girlie.

One of the girls turned and saw him and immediately covered her eyes with her hand. Steve went up to her and laid a hand on her shoulder.

Hey, join us for a drink.

Nah thanks, Steve, she said.

Ah c'mon, meet . . . meet Tom and this other bloke, he's just up for the night.

Lise was still looking doubtful when Tom appeared by Steve's side.

Delighted to meet you, he said. *Please* join us for a drink.

The two girls glanced at him.

Our evening just wouldn't be the same without you. Go on. We'll behave ourselves. Well, he added with a wink, mostly.

Lise and her friend exchanged glances and giggled and so joined them for a drink.

Lewis thought they were both quite pretty. Lise looked like she hadn't slept for a month but she had nice black frizzy hair, and her friend Trudy was quiet and blonde and had a wide friendly smile. Tom immediately seemed to get on with her very well. He started to tell her his favourite joke about Cinderella and the melon. It was pretty rude but somehow Tom made it sound hilariously witty.

Lise and Steve were talking with their heads close together when suddenly Lise lost her temper and rose up.

No way, Steve, you're fucking out of order! she yelled at him.

Steve looked up at her resentfully.

You're fuckin' screwed up you are. I'm fuckin' finished with it, I told you. I've had enough. I don't give a shit how you screw up your life but I'm not going to.

Steve stood up abruptly and looked round at them all. He put his hands in his jeans pockets and hunched his shoulders up. His shoulders were so thin.

I gotta split, he said. He looked like he was shaking.

One of the bar staff suddenly appeared beside them.

He was burly and balding and held a bar towel tightly in his fist.

You gotta problem here, folks?

Tom held his hands up in innocence. No, no problem mate.

The barman was staring at Steve. I know you, he said. I'm not havin' any junkies in this pub. Go on, 'op it.

What you on about? protested Steve.

I'm not arguing with you lot, now 'op it. I want you outside now.

Slowly and sulkily, they stood and moved to the door. Druggie scum, said the barman, collecting their glasses.

Outside in the street Steve shivered more than ever. I gotta split, he said again. Where you headin'?

Tom looked over at the two girls and then said, Maybe the Lizzie Gardens.

Might catch you later, said Steve and turned and walked away with a strange hurried jerky stride.

They watched him go and then Lise started sobbing.

Hey hey, said Tom, quickly putting an arm round her. It's all right, don't cry baby.

She buried her face in his shoulder. Trudy and Lewis looked at each other anxiously.

Lise stood back from Tom and wiped her eyes. That bastard, she said. Calls it 'just doin' 'im a favour'. What does he think I am, a fuckin' prostitute or something?

Tom took her hand gently. He's gone now, he said, that silly cunt. Come on, let's get some tinnies and go and sit in the Lizzie Gardens.

Trudy looked doubtful at first but Lise said, Oh come on, so they all headed for the riverside park stopping at the off-licence on the way to buy some Special Brew.

When they got to the gardens they sat under the tree at the very corner where the two rivers met and looked across at the placid cows kneedeep in the pasture beyond. They sat for an hour or more and drank and smoked. They were all fairly drunk after another can each and Lise rolled a joint and passed it round. Lewis wasn't used to dope and it made him feel sick and his fingertips tingled and he sweated and passed it on quickly.

Lise looked at him slyly and giggled.

You're no druggie, are you, darlin'?

He grinned sheepishly. Not exactly, he said.

Country bumpkin, she said.

That's me, he said. Oh ar.

She snuggled up close to him. She took a deep drag on the joint and said, You're nice.

Thank you, he said composedly. You're not bad yourself. He felt very grown up.

Next to them, Tom and Trudy were already kissing. Lewis was just leaning forward to kiss Lise when a voice called out, Hey, you cunts there!

It was Steve.

Oh fuckin' hell, said Lise, resting her head on Lewis's shoulder. He put his arm round her tentatively. He looked over at Tom who was staring foully at Steve's approach. Steve came over and squatted down with them.

Happy now? asked Tom.

Happy now, said Steve. You can't always get what you want . . . he sang softly. His eyes were quite unfocused. He gazed around. Well, whatever, never mind. He stared out over the river.

Look at the size of those fuckin' gardens he said. Look at those *houses*.

Yeah, said Tom. And that one's all for just one man.

Steve looked at him dumbly.

What you talkin' about?

That house. Ex-Prime Minister's, innit?

Steve looked across the river. Why?

Tom waved his cigarette knowingly. See the security cameras?

Steve gawped. Fuck me, he said. The Prime Minister's. We're that near to 'im.

Ex-Prime Minister's, said Tom. Yeah. He stubbed his cigarette out between the roots of the tree. That near. But still, he said savagely, *the other side of the fuckin' river.*

Steve stared at him, then at Lewis, then started to giggle. I'm goin' to go and see the cunt, he said.

Steve . . . said Lise warningly. Don't be a prat.

Steve grinned shakily. Who, me? he said. I'm goin' to go and visit the old cunt. Cheer 'im up a bit. What's 'is name?

He turned and started to wade into the river when two swans came floating by. Steve promptly forgot his planned assault on the house. He stood up to his thighs in the fast water.

Fuck me, he said. Swans.

Well observed, Stevie boy, said Tom. You could be the next David Attenborough.

Steve's mouth hung open and his fingertips trailed loosely in the water. Fuckin' swans, he slurred. Don't you just hate them? They look so fuckin' . . . arrogant. Swans are fuckin' Tories.

Lewis looked from Steve to the swans and back to Steve again and smiled. Lise saw him smiling and reached over and began to kiss him.

I fuckin' hate those bastards, said Steve. I'm goin' to rip their – hic – fuckin' heads off.

He started to wade towards them. They raised their heads and arched their wings and regarded him soundlessly, preparing to break his sticklike arms with a blow of their beaks.

Lewis pulled away from Lise. No, don't, he said.

Steve heard nothing. He was wading deeper when he caught his foot in a tangle of weed or maybe a submerged supermarket trolley and fell into the water. He floundered for a while and then crawled out on to the bank a few yards away, spluttering and hawking. I've got cholera now, he kept saying. I've got fuckin' cholera.

He flopped over wetly on to his back.

Totally headfucked, he said. Then lay still.

Silly cunt, said Tom. He turned to Lewis. He gets metha-
done on prescription and then just takes it on top of the
junk. He could 'ave been doin' anything tonight though.
Where did he get the money?

Lewis looked over at Steve. Poor sod, he said.

Wanker, said Lise. Now stop brooding and kiss me on the
mouth.

Later they went over to Steve.

Hey Steve, we're heading back. You comin'?

Steve didn't move.

You think he's all right? asked Lewis.

Fuckin' hope not, said Lise. Could be dead for all I care.

Some chance, said Tom. He scrutinized the body at his
feet. His breathing's fucked, he said. Least we can do is – he
bent down – turn the cunt over. He slid his hands under
Steve's torso and flopped him over on to his stomach. Don't
want him inhaling his own vomit.

Well, *I'm* not inhaling it for him, said Lise. They all
laughed.

Yeah well, said Tom. A true rock'n'roll death. Steve
would *die* for a rock'n'roll death.

He reached down and put his hand in Steve's soggy jeans
pocket and helped himself to his bunch of keys.

See you later alligator, he said. Come on then.

Back at the flat Lise lay on the mattress and beckoned Lewis
down beside her. Trudy and Tom went into the kitchen to
make coffee. The coffee never appeared.

Lise kissed Lewis hard. She took his hand and pressed it
against her breast. They were both breathing hard. They
started to undress.

Jesus, said Lise. What happened to the back of your neck?

Oh, said Lewis. Er . . . got caught on some barbed wire.

Looks horrible, she said.

Sorry, he said.

Never mind, she said. It's not the back of your neck I'm interested in.

She pulled his cock out and gripped it tightly. I want you, she said. She hitched her skirt up and knelt on all fours and raised her bum. She splayed her hands over her buttocks.

It's my time of the month, she said. But you can fuck me here. Fuck me here.

He tried. He gasped with frustration. She reached behind her and tried to excite him but nothing happened. She flopped down on her stomach and looked over her shoulder at him.

You a poof or something?

No, he said.

She regarded him for a moment and then smiled. No, I know you're not, she said. Come here and give me a cuddle.

So they lay all night side by side naked and when they awoke Tom was standing over them with an odd expression on his face.

Steve's in hospital, he said. He's in a coma.

Tom told the three of them that he'd handle it, that they needn't say they were with him in the park with Steve. Lise cried and cried, Trudy looked ashen. Tom said to Lewis, You might as well head out of town, cowboy. Some night out in the big city, eh?

Lewis said nothing.

Tom sang softly, *Life's a piece of shit / When you look at it . . .* Yeah, bummer, he said. I mean – he's a prat and all but – I've known him for five years or something. Maybe he had it coming to 'im but I still can't believe it really. He sighed. Anyhow.

How did it happen?

Fuck knows. He shrugged. A massive overdose of Daz Automatic. He laughed. Lewis realized he wasn't shocked that Tom was joking about it. He tried to understand.

Well, he said. I'm sorry.

Yeah, said Tom, me too. He looked at Lewis. You better get that bus back to Hicksville.

Yeah.

Tell you what. I'll send you a postcard from Ibiza anyhow, and next term you can come down to Bournemouth one night.

Lewis nodded. He felt a knot of fear at the very thought. He said nothing.

If I'm still there, added Tom. Bournemouth's OK. Good clubs. More e than h, he grinned.

Lewis nodded.

OK. So long then, Lew.

Bye then, Tom. See ya.

Yeah. You take care now.

Lewis turned to the two girls. Bye Trudy. Bye Lise.

Lise came over and hugged him tightly. She looked like she wanted to say something but she said nothing. She stood back and looked at him and then squeezed her eyes tight shut so the tears ran out over her face and then she looked at him again. Bye Lewis, she said.

25 Work

A few days later he got a scrawled note from Tom. Tom had been to Steve's funeral.

It was fuckin' awful, wrote Tom. The reverend gives us this extended drugs lecture, like *he* knows fuck all about it, talking about 'the evil men' who had trapped Steve into 'this half-life of drug addiction', which is total wank as we all know. Steve trapped himself. Still, at least we didn't get any religion. You never seem to nowadays which is something. Just this pep talk. Then at the wake afterwards there was an excellent catfight between Steve's mum and his dad's new girlfriend. She's about Steve's age and all. You should have been there. Girls fighting. Wahey. Schwing.

Anyhow me old china. Take care. Tom.

He got another letter the very same day.

You're popular, said his father. All these girlfriends.

It was the job centre. They wanted Lewis to come for an interview in two days' time or to telephone if not. His father was pleased. Now you bloody well make sure you go or I'll be that cross. D'you hear me, Lewis?

Lewis nodded.

He planned running away all that day. He would take his knife and his crossbow and knapsack with plastic bivvy bag and a toothbrush and he would just head out west towards Cornwall or maybe Wales. Like Gerald said. Up on the ox-drove, through Shaftesbury and on and on . . . Hunting for his supper or begging at farmhouse doors, otherwise talking to no one. He sat and thought it all through, his eyes unfocused, his mouth hanging open.

Then on the day his father gave him some money and in a trance he got the morning bus to Salisbury and walked through the backstreets to the riverside and went into the job centre and had his appointment. A middle-aged woman took him to one side although there were other desks all around and everybody in the room was listening to them or laughing at him and he clearly heard one young woman say, God what a dirty-looking bastard he is, and the whole room tittered at him. He disregarded them and tried to concentrate on what the woman was saying to him. His throat was dry and the air-conditioning hummed endlessly in the ceiling and he felt nauseous.

She was asking him what he was interested in.

He knew what he was supposed to do and say but he couldn't. He shrugged his shoulders and said, Dunno really.

Have you ever done any work before? Paid or voluntary work?

He hesitated. Done some gardenin', he said.

Gardening, right, she said with great energy. And would you be interested in doing something in that line permanently?

He nodded.

Because of course there are two very substantial garden centres here that take on a lot of staff, down on the Southampton Road. Would you be interested in that sort of thing?

Suppose so, he said. He pictured a huge warehouse with bright lights and people buying piles of stuff in trolleyloads. He'd never go there. No way.

She made some written notes and then asked, What else?

He shook his head dumbly.

Do you like animals?

He nodded.

A job in a pet shop perhaps?

Again he nodded.

Hm, she said and wrote something. Now, it says here that you like to be out of doors. Is that right?

Yes.

So would transport be a problem?

He didn't understand. Nothing was making sense. Nothing connected. He kept thinking back to Steve, to Mary, to his mother . . . Nothing here connected with that. He could hear a couple talking close behind him and he knew they were talking about him.

. . . he has such a lumpy head . . .

. . . like butter . . .

. . . he is so ugly . . .

. . . and evil too . . .

. . . I don't think he should be allowed in here . . .

. . . fucking cheek . . .

. . . smells like fish . .

The lights overhead were flickering and unbearable and the carpet beneath his feet was painful to his boots. He held the metal arms of his chair very tightly under clenched fingers and the cool steel felt good. I'll not fucking break, he swore. I'll not.

Lewis?

The woman was looking at him and smiling evilly. She wore big glasses that looked as if they were on upside-down and her mouth was pursed in a questioning little smile. He imagined reaching down and picking up his crossbow from under his chair. Holding it against her head and pulling the trigger, the bolt punching straight through the thin bone of her forehead and burying itself in the dark cave of her skull. Her look of shock, not understanding. Slumping forward, blood issuing forth over the desk, blotting out the notes and names and details and destroying it all. Then him reloading and turning and people cowering before him or huddling in doorways and alcoves before his absolute power. One by one he'd kill them, each one pleading silently. A neat execution, a bolt to each frail fore-head, walking through endless corridors bloody and pained under the lights until finally he was alone and stepped outside and was free.

Lewis, she said more sharply. I am asking you a question. Please try and pay attention. You do want to work, don't you?

Yes, he said far too loudly.

Right, she said. Well, transport. How easy would it be for you to get to work in Salisbury?

There's buses, he said.

Pretty few and far between, aren't they? Especially going-home time?

I could walk.

She laughed then. Rather a long way, she said. Must be a good ten miles.

He shrugged. Couldn't be bothered to argue with the bitch. Do what you fucking like with me, he thought. Do what you fucking well like. Put me in a can along with the slug pellets and sell me off the shelves of a fucking garden centre.

Ah well, she said. You can't be blamed for the skeleton bus services the villages get nowadays of course. We'll have to see when it happens. I mean, some of these jobs are quite well paid, especially on night shifts. You might even find that easier, come to think of it. Get the last bus in each day and go home first thing in the morning.

Yeah. Whatever, never mind.

Right then. She scribbled in a lot more details. Well, Lewis, thank you for coming along this morning. As I say, it's only a very informal little chat to see if we can put you together with the right sort of job. I would think you stand a good chance of getting something this summer.

Right, he said, standing up. Bye then.

And he went out of the room with his eyes fixed firmly downward, looking neither to left nor right where the people stood around in groups laughing at him and whistling and catcalling and chanting *cunt! cunt! cunt!* at him, and pulling bestial faces like cathedral gargoyles or animals in a zoo.

He left the building sickhearted and walked alongside the river northward to Old Sarum. The river was thick with newborn ducklings that seemed to have hatched in mayfly profusion this year, partly from the weather, although they were always well fed here too by the people going to Sainsbury's. When he felt better and his breathing had returned to normal he turned and headed back southwards and saw rearing over the buildings the grey gnomon of the spire in all its medieval mystery and perfection like a compass pointing towards the free and empty summer sky, as if to accompany some old map whose features have long since been erased by rain and time. Yet he went towards it with the usual pull of attraction wordlessly and without explanation if one had demanded it of him. He passed through the arch by the millrace and across the road alongside the river where a grey wagtail was bucking on the flat stones and stropping broken insects' wings from its beak. He glimpsed the watermeadows beyond and the cows there through the willows, but, unable to pass that way, he went into the street, and up the high street walking in the road to avoid the troupes of tourists, and went through the stone arch into Choristers' Green. People lay all over the close in the sunshine enjoying their lunch hours and the beautiful houses looked on imperturbable. He passed by the walking Magdalen that he liked, by some modern sculptor, and went in through the small door and pushed past the woman in the ticket office, saying that he was local. She tutted after him and rolled her eyes at the next visitor.

Inside the cathedral he cooled his hands on the columns of Purbeck marble and trod slowly down the aisles as he would tread through a wood, tracking animals. He gazed at the iron clock and he read the inscriptions on the walls and smelled the ancient air. He paused to listen to a guide talking about one of the stone knights recumbent on a tomb. He learnt that the knight's body had since been disinterred and a rat found in his skull, its body preserved by arsenic poisoning after having eaten the murdered knight's brain. The knight's wife went into a nunnery, brokenhearted, when he died.

He walked to the east end and stood and looked at the vast blue prisoners of conscience window. It was hard to make sense of, but beautiful, and he stood there a long time. He said some sort of prayer for Steve.

As he left the cathedral he laid his palm one last time against the Purbeck marble and gazed back, farsighted, up to the choir.

He had missed the second bus and the last one returned to the village at half past three. He could walk it in less time than that. He drank a bellyful of water from the cold tap in the toilets and then turned away and walked out of the cloisters, out of Harnham Gate and over old Harnham Bridge and up the Old Blandford Road a little way. Then he cut off to the right behind new housing and followed the track across bare fields and beside a single farmhouse until he met the oxdrove. Here he saw a hare, most beautiful and mysterious of creatures, lolloping along the track ahead of him, unhurried and unafraid, and he wished he had his crossbow with him. The hare went through a gateway into the grass field and hid.

He wished he could have brought Steve with him up here. Too late for that silly sod now. He had this idea of taking him by his white sticklike arm and slapping him and dragging him protesting off his mattress and bringing him up here. Just showing him stuff. He looked back towards the town and away again. But not now. Not now.

So he headed west along the oxdrove past the racecourse

and Hare Warren and either side of him the land fell away to the rivers Ebble and Nadder and the sky was vast overhead where the larks sang and the white clouds drifted. He walked on past where the downs to his right fell away steeply towards Compton Chamberlayne and the Nadder opened out into the Vale of Wardour and the Fovant badges lay hidden from him just over the edge of the downs beyond Chiselbury Camp. He wondered if the Wilkins brothers had been stationed here before they left for France and had helped to scour out those symbols in the short turf, or if anyone who worked there in the sunshine before they went to war had afterwards returned in different weather to the army hospital set up in Fovant at the foot of the downs, their limbs ragged and lungs torn, to lie there amid the coughing and see their own youth's glad confident handiwork up there on the downs through some grimed window.

And he crossed over Fifield Down and Prescombe Down and descended into the silent valley and came home.

26   John Pike (2)

His father asked him that evening how he had got on at the job centre. Lewis had already blotted it from his memory like a bad dream and had to think hard to recall it.

All right, he said.

He sensed his father's worry and out of pity, though also with pangs of fear at the very memory of it, he added, They said I might get something at one of the garden centres. On the ring road.

Oh really, said his father, full of enthusiasm. Well, that would be all right wouldn't it, hey? You'd be well set up there, hey? Out of doors a fair bit too, I expect, and I bet you know a darn sight more about gardenin' than most lads your age. Tell you what though, you'll 'ave to get that bloody moped of yours fixed at last. Hey?

Yeah, said Lewis.

And if it really doesn't want to go then I spose I can run you in every morning.

Dad, it's in the opposite direction.

Well it'd be bloody worth it, eh? How much d'you get paid then, not bad money I shouldn't reckon?

Lewis shrugged. I dunno. They said I'd get more on night shifts if I wanted.

Ah, said John Pike, screwing up his face doubtfully. Now I'd steer clear of that if I were you. Funny old routine that is, night shifts an' all, just not worth the gyp. Stuart's boy did nightshifts at a supermarket, shelf-stacking. Nearly drove 'im to suicide he said. Saw no daylight all winter. An' besides, he added jovially, who'd 'ave my bloomin' supper on the table when I get 'ome in the evenings?

Well, said Lewis. Maybe it's time you started learnin' to cook for yourself.

Ah. Now then, said his father. We can't all be wizards in the kitchen, can't all be Delia Bloody Smith and suchlike. My talents lie in other directions.

Yeah, said Lewis. Right.

Anyway, what delights 'ave we in store tonight?

Pizza.

That'll do, said John Pike. S'long as it's not veggie.

It's not veggie, said Lewis. It's got ground beef and pepperoni and stuff.

Sounds good, said John Pike. I'm goin' to wash me 'ands.

Lewis checked the pizza and heated up some baked beans. When his father returned he started again.

So, he said, sitting down to his semicircle of family-size pizza and cracking his knuckles. Garden centre, hey – sounds all right that does.

Yeah, said Lewis.

Maybe his father was right, maybe it would be all right. Be a laugh. Maybe it would all be all right.

The local paper carried the story about Steve's inquest. Lewis read it and said nothing. His father said, Poor sod. Why do they do it? It's these wretched dealers I blame. Lewis said nothing.

When he got a letter a week later from the job centre, it was to ask him to come not to a garden centre but to the big dairies building on the Wilton Road on Monday morning at 7 a.m. and to phone if he couldn't make it. For the rest of that week his fingers hovered at intervals over the telephone and his excuses became ever more outlandish and unnecessarily elaborate, like a bad liar's. His house had burnt down after a gas explosion. A horse had been startled by a car and fallen on top of him. His mother had died suddenly. Fuckin' joke *that* is, he grimaced, reeling from the thought as if from a blow to the head.

Then on Saturday morning he told his father the good news and his father was delighted. Well done boy, he said. No bloody night shifts either. I tell you, you'll be a darn sight 'appier getting out of the house and doin' some regular work *and* you'll 'ave some money in your pocket for a change.

Lewis nodded. Yeah.

Well look, 'ow is that moped of yours?

Lewis spent the rest of the weekend cleaning the little engine and starting it up until eventually it ran smooth and his father examined it and declared it as good as it would ever be. Get you there and back, he said. That's all that matters. And you never know, in only a month or two's time you'll most probbly have enough to buy a new bike, a 125 or something.

Yeah, said Lewis. That'd be good.

27 The Dairy

So on Monday morning he left the house at half past six on a beautiful morning with the sun up and his stomach clenched tight with fear and hatred and he drove to the dairies and reported to the desk at five to seven. He felt dizzy and could take nothing in. Stared stupidly.

Right, said the man there busily, shuffling invoices around on his desk. Ade'll show you round. Just a sec.

It took nearly twenty minutes for Ade to appear. He was about Lewis's age, sharpfaced and redhaired and freckled, in a white cotton overall and his hair covered in a white net cap.

Aha, he said. Another lamb to the slaughter. OK, follow me.

He followed him into a tiny room where Ade found a hat to fit him and arranged the netting round the bottom of his hair.

They go on like fuck about hygiene, said Ade. You have to wear one of these things all the time and look like a total knob or else. If they found a single pube in the milk they'd shut the whole fuckin' dairy down. Right, follow me.

The dairy was a series of huge warehouses but Lewis's job took him into only two of them. In one a conveyor belt brought plastic cartons of milk that he had to collect and rack up on wire trolleys. Then he had to push the laden trolleys through a curtain of wide plastic strips into a bigger warehouse and get the trolley ticked off before putting it on a ramp which lifted it up to the level of the loading bay. From here it was wheeled straight into the backs of waiting lorries and the trays of cartons were stacked up and driven away. Then he returned with the trolley and repeated the process.

The room with the conveyor belt was very cold and the second room humid and he could never accustom himself to the sudden change as he passed through from one to the other and his throat felt chilled each time. He needed to keep both hands on the big trolley. And each time he pushed through the curtain of plastic strips they fell back on him and knocked his hat off. Ade saw this happen and called out, I'll get you a hatpin or something. But he never did. So each time Lewis had to stop and reset his hat. Then he passed back through the strips. Then his hat was knocked off. Then he stopped to reset his hat. Then he . . .

The warmer room stank of milk. Sour milk and spilt milk and though the floor was mopped almost continuously it still stank from leaks and fallen cartons. Lewis never wanted to touch milk again. He was sickened by the memory of what his sister's flat smelt like. Surely it wasn't this bad? The soles of his boots were sticky and when he tentatively sniffed his fingers when no one was looking they smelt so sour and disgusting that he almost gagged.

The other workers there all hated the work too and said so often. When not moaning they made jokes. The one about the nun . . . the elastic band . . . the German with his dick on a barbecue . . . Helmet Coal . . . None of them talked directly to Lewis.

They stopped for lunch at twelve and everyone produced their sandwiches. Lewis hadn't thought to bring any so he went outside and pretended to fiddle with his moped. When he came back after half an hour they had started work already and some of them looked at him.

Finally he had the courage to ask Ade, Couldn't all this work be done by machine?

Don't you fuckin' start, he said. Put us all out of a job, you will. That's treason, that is.

Lewis grinned sheepishly.

Course it could be done by a fuckin' machine. And we'd all be out on our ears, wouldn't we? Now stop that treasonable bollocks and help me shift this trolley.

At three they finished. On the way home Lewis told himself perhaps it wasn't so bad after all. But when he arrived the next morning at seven o'clock and faced another eight hours of that – and another three days after that – and the weeks – with no end in sight, then he knew that it was bad. He didn't smile or talk to anyone all that second day. For lunch he drank water and ate some oatcakes sitting by his moped in the goods-in yard. No one noticed him.

In the afternoon he dropped a two-pint milk carton on the floor. His first. Everybody else dropped milk cartons all the time but he still felt bitterly ashamed. He stared down dumbly at the broken carton lying on its side with milk leaking from its tetrapak wound and before he knew what he was doing he had made a sign of the cross over it. Darren saw this and prodded Ade.

D'you see that?

Ade nodded.

Must be a fuckin' Catholic or something. Weird bloke. He doesn't say much, does he?

Ade shrugged.

'Ere. How do get a nun pregnant?

Ade shrugged.

Fuck her.

By Wednesday they were all talking about him. When he walked in he heard their voices quite distinctly. They made no secret of their intense hatred for him.

There's that cunt Lewis Pike, said one. He couldn't tell which, they didn't need to move their mouths, he saw.

We ought to chop him up and feed him through the milking machines, said a girl behind him. I'll bite his cock off and spit it out. I'll eat him alive.

The women all leered at him with gargoyle faces and horses' teeth and the men spat and ground their teeth at him. He bowed his head and worked on desperately, ignoring them.

There was no escape. Ade came over on his own and started being nice but Lewis knew it was all an act and made sure that he never turned his back on him in case Ade stabbed him. His skin twitched in the small of his back just where he would feel the knife entering deep into his kidneys.

Hiya Lewis, said Ade.

Lewis nodded. Ade would use a short stubby knife, he thought, and twist it. Tomorrow he resolved to bring in a knife of his own. To protect himself. He'd not go easily. He'd take a couple of the cunts down with him.

There's a, um, party on Friday night, Ade was saying. Get bladdered. Over at Waggs. I dunno if you want to come.

Not fuckin' likely, thought Lewis. I know what kind of party *that'll* be. A Harvest Party, and it'll be me up in the wicker man while you lot all drink and dance and fuck naked around me while I go up in flames. Oh yeah. You just want me there so you can kill me.

Ade shrugged. Oh well, it's up to you. If you want to – bring a few cans and that. We'll all be there.

Oh I bet you will, he thought, nodding to Ade. I bet you fuckin' will. He trembled violently and gripped the heavy trolley to steady himself.

In the afternoon he crashed his trolley down the ramp. He went over Kirsty's toe and left her clutching her foot in pain and then let his trolley thunder down the ramp and tip over at the bottom and break about a hundred cartons. Mr Dale came out of his office specially.

But what were you doing on the ramp anyway? he demanded of Lewis. He turned on Ade. He shouldn't have been on the ramp, he should be on the floor. On the push-ramp.

He was making no sense at all. Lewis wondered how Ade understood a word he was saying. I know, said Ade, looking stonily at Lewis. I don't know.

Nobody was making any sense at all.

Anyone would think you were trying to crash the trolley deliberately, said Mr Dale. You only have to push it *that* way, towards the doors. Not *too* much to ask, is it?

That old note of schoolroom sarcasm. Lewis idly wondered whether to jump at him and bite his face off. Tear his lips and fuckin' eyelids off. Or grab his thin hair and smash his head into the corner of that upturned trolley, the steel digging a big corner into his skull. Now that would hurt. A slick of blood on the floor like spilled oil. He bowed his head and said nothing.

Right. Get this lot cleaned up straight away and get on with your work. I don't want any more of this nonsense.

Lewis and Ade salvaged what cartons they could and dumped the rest and hosed away the fallen milk. Ade said nothing more to him. There was no more to be said. Ade was beginning to think he was pretty fucking retarded. A couple of pints short of a gallon, he said to Kirsty. She rolled her eyes.

When they had cleared up, Ade told Lewis to go and get washed in the lavs. Lewis went and found solitude there and lingered too long and then feared to return. In the cubicle there was an open window. It was small but he could do it. He lowered the toilet seat and stood on it and got one leg through. Then he hunched his head into his shoulders and prised himself through and drew the other leg after. He dropped to the ground and shook off his hat. He ran over to his moped with his keys already in his hand and started it up and rode away, not looking back, without a sound.

Back in the lanes riding home he whooped like an Indian brave returning on his pony laden with scalps and his head cleared. He still heard the voices but they were gentle and low and less threatening than foreboding. They told of what was to come and how he must be strong and brave because things would get worse before they got better and they must be this way. He rode on through the lanes with the pollen so thick between the high hedges that the air looked cloudy and yellow. He heard a voice saying that he must keep his secret safely, and that he had been chosen for something special, and that it would all begin to make sense to him towards the end. He mustn't worry about a thing. It was all taken care of.

But when his father came home that evening he told him nothing.

How was work today, then?

Fine, fine, said Lewis, stirring the baked beans. Quite a good laugh actually. He tried to laugh.

That's good, said his father settling down with the local paper. That's good, well it's something, isn't it? It's not a job you'll want all your life but it's work in the meantime, hey?

That's true, said Lewis.

His father grinned at a thought. And I'll 'ave to start chargin' you housekeeping, eh?

Lewis turned. I'd thought of that, he said. Why don't I just do a big shop once a week for us both and I pay for it?

His father considered. Yeah, OK, he said. That'll do.

And so Lewis kept up the pretence. He left for work the following morning on his moped at the same time and drove all the way into Salisbury. He took a duffel bag and a basket around the supermarket and filled the duffel bag with expensive stuff like smoked haddock fillets and bone-less chicken breasts and best sausages and gammon and in the basket he put bread and milk and apples which was all he paid for when he came to the checkout.

On Friday the job centre phoned.

The dairies tell us you left work early on Wednesday and that you haven't been back since?

Yes, said Lewis.

Is there a good reason for that?

Um, said Lewis. It's . . . I just didn't like it.

Well, you know we did try and find you a job that you were suited for.

Yeah, said Lewis.

You can't just say you don't like it just like that, you know. It'll mean you lose those three days pay for one thing.

Why?

They explained why. It made no sense. So what sort of thing *would* you like? Is there anything you'd be more interested in?

No, thought Lewis. Going back in time. Dying. Garden centre, he said. Something like that.

A job in a garden centre? repeated the woman.

Yeah, said Lewis in a bored voice.

Well, that's narrowing it down a bit isn't it? We'll try to look out for something like that and let you know. But you'll have to show a bit more willing.

Yeah, said Lewis.

On Saturday he went out early poaching and by the time he returned the job centre had phoned and his father, hungover, had answered it. And he was deeply shocked to hear that his son had just walked out of a good steady job, shocked and baffled, for John Pike was a man who loved to see a good job done, a clean shave, a proud small garden in the village, a well-laid hedge or the perfection of mortise and tenon, and he always took pride in whatever proper work anyone had given him.

He was standing at the top of the stairs redfaced with sleep and anger when Lewis returned.

I want a word with you, my lad, he said, coming down the stairs.

What? said Lewis dumping his jacket in the corner, already sulkily prepared.

Don't you *what* me, son. I had an interesting little chat with the job centre just now. They tell me you 'aven't been into that dairy since Wednesday. Well?

Lewis bowed his head.

They tell me you bunked off early on Wednesday and 'aven't been back there since. What's the problem, too much like hard work or summing for you, was it?

He hated that tone of sarcasm in his father's voice. It was all wrong.

'Ey?

I hated the job, that's all. It was awful.

His father raised his voice. It don't bloody matter whether you hated it or not, a job's a job these days and don't you bloody forget it!

Lewis looked away. Scraped his fingernails in a repetitive motion along the tabletop.

How dare you just walk out when they've found you a job! How dare you!

Lewis shrugged.

And another thing. Where's all this bloody food come from if you 'aven't got any money? Hey?

Lewis grinned, looking his father in the face. Comes from Sainsbury's.

And 'ow d'ye pay for it? Hey?

Still he grinned. Who's to say I did?

He father took one step toward him and struck him hard across the face with the flat of his hand. Lewis turned his head with the blow and stayed where he stood, not raising his hands or moving his feet, not speaking. His face began to burn red and flush with blood. There was an agonized silence and then he turned and made for the door.

Lewis, said his father softly, all anger gone.

Lewis didn't pause.

Lewis, he said again. Boy, I'm sorry, I . . .

Lewis opened the door and stepped outside.

I shouldn't 'ave. You shouldn't 'ave done that, but look, I'm sorry . . . I didn't mean to . . . His father held out his offending hand as if offering it in sacrifice.

Lewis walked steadily away. Up the broken stone steps

146

towards the gate. His eyes were blurred with tears and he stumbled on the top step.

Boy, said his father. He swallowed hard. Don't leave me. Don't leave me, boy.

Lewis said nothing but opened the gate and stepped outside. No, I'll not leave you, he thought. I'll not leave you.

29   Gerald and Mary (3)

He went to visit the Poet.

He could barely breathe for the turmoil in his heart. He could not understand in the least what had just happened but he knew that however long they lived now, something was gone between his father and him, the old simplicity was gone. There would be forgiveness but not forgetfulness of that moment of fury and hatred and shame and grief. These passions endure, like any form of energy. They mutate and adapt but they survive, come what may.

He thought about going to see Tom. But Tom was in Spain, wasn't he? Or back in Bournemouth. He couldn't face all that again. The town and the drugs and the wrecked girls. That was where they thought he should be. He couldn't understand it.

So he went out trembling to visit Gerald and Mary, hoping to find some peace.

And when he came round the side of the cottage and into the garden and saw Mary and the Poet there beneath the cherry tree he felt that it was all going to be all right. They were so . . . so *together*, Gerald and Mary, that was what he liked about being with them. They were so fucking middle class and leisurely and lived such nice lives. Everyone else seemed to live in such chaos, but here were husband and wife, just as before, under the cherry tree in the summer sunshine. That was what he liked in them, how he pictured them. In a sudden surge of emotion he thought how he loved them for it. Their humour and tolerance. They took life easy. They had enough money not to work much. They read books and talked a lot. They would always be here, just the same. He pictured them in forty or fifty years time, white-haired, wrinkled, looking so wise.

They both called out hello to him and seemed not to mind that he had come over so early. Perhaps they sensed his need. When he came closer he thought how good Mary was looking in a long pale blue dress patterned with small yellow flowers and her face sunburnt with a scatter of freckles across her nose and cheeks. She smiled broadly at him and her teeth looked so clean and white with her brown skin.

The Poet was lying back almost horizontal in a deckchair hung with cobwebs. He was barefoot but wore thick green corduroys and his tweed jacket and had a pipe clamped unlit between his teeth. Although he sat in the shade he wore a very tatty straw sunhat tilted down over his eyes. Mary sat on the grass beside him with her legs stretched out in front of her catching the sun, her dress hitched up to just above her knees. She leant forward and slipped her hands flat under her knees and looked up sideways at Lewis and smiled.

It's our gentleman caller, she said. And how are you today?

All right, he answered. He heard the catch in his own voice but wasn't sure they did. And he thought he saw a look of concern cross Mary's face. He wondered if his cheek was still burning red from where his father had struck him.

Gerald adjusted his hat. Ah, my dear fellow. My word, you look redfaced and hot. Have some shade. He gestured about him like an emperor over his small domain. Lewis sat crosslegged and chewed a grass stem. Mary caught his eye and raised a single eyebrow. He wished he could do that. He tried not to giggle. She was teasing him with the memory of last time.

So, and what have you been doing with yourself lately?

Lewis shrugged. That hated question. Not much.

149

And quite right too if I may say so, said the Poet, struggling upright in his deckchair and becoming suddenly impassioned the way he did. Being, not doing, is that it, eh?

Lewis grinned warily. Fuck knows, he thought. Well, whatever, never mind, as Tom would say.

We don't spend enough time just *being*, said Gerald, and far too much *doing*. Let alone *having*. We all know in our heart of hearts that *having* and *being* are two virtually exclusive activities, and yet the average good citizen still spends – what is the working day nowadays? Do remind me, five days a week? Forty hours a week or something ghastly – in the pursuit of *having*, in the toils and sad dreams of ownership and illusory security and possessions and status, with never a thought to the supremely urgent human task of simply *being*.

Never mind darling, said Mary soothingly, resting a hand on his knee. You are very successful at just being, not doing.

Gerald guffawed loudly. Oh my dear, he cried, do I detect a certain note of irony in your voice?

No, not at all, she protested. And gave Lewis a quick conspiratorial grin.

Lewis began to feel more sane. The agony of his father's hand on his cheek and of his father's contempt gusting in his face began to recede. Gerald talked on. Lewis and Mary exchanged many looks and smiles and glances, all of them composed of amusement and secrecy and affection for the nonstop talker in his deckchair and other feelings. The sun rose higher in the sky that grew deeper and deeper blue before it. When Lewis's attention returned Gerald was asking rhetorically, What is a village?

He spread his thin white hands and repeated, *What is a village?* Lewis wasn't sure whether this demanded an answer or not, but Gerald answered anyway.

It is something I have been giving a lot of thought to lately. I have even been toying with the idea of composing

150

some sort of late twentieth-century sister poem to Goldsmith's 'Sweet Auburn!' Because it seems to me that the village as we know it has all but disappeared in . . . well, in my lifetime, I should say, and I have not yet seen the passing of forty summers. Or do I mean fifty? Anyway: consider. The village is not *in essence* to be defined as a collection of cottages and a church, or as something between a hamlet and a town. These are the external details. The essence of a village was always that it was somewhere inhabited by people who worked on the land. Well, that agricultural, that *peasant* class – and I use that word with the greatest respect, Lewis, that old tough English peasantry that one still sees very clearly in Cobbett, in Hardy, perhaps even in *Lark Rise* . . . and a class which I imagine you are proud to consider yourself a member of, and one of the last – the English peasantry, whose demise began in Hardy's lifetime, and provides him with one of his greatest themes – has in our lifetime, or at least *my* lifetime, been all but annihilated. The peasant, the agricultural labourer, is now a rarity in the age of agribusinesses and chemical sprays. And so the village as a place inhabited by *peasants*, by people who stepped out of their cottage doors in the morning to work in the neighbouring fields and returned home in the evening, that place is no longer. The village is now what they call a dormitory suburb, inhabited by retired middle classes, or by commuting accountants and solicitors and allied besuited wankers. The *village*, that feature of the landscape for – what? 2000 years? 4000 years? Since the advent of neolithic farming, I suppose – has ceased to exist, since the Second World War at most. Now does that not strike you as significant?

Lewis looked clearly at Gerald and said nothing.

So what one really means by *the village* is the type of people that lived in it, not the fabric of the buildings. We have witnessed, virtually without comment, the extinction of an entire class of people. A class, if I may say so Lewis, of which you are one of the last proud representatives.

Lewis grinned through his teeth like a fox. He wondered if he should stand up and bow to the Poet's imaginary audience. Exhibit A: a peasant. His father would like that, would grimace. His stomach clenched. Then they were talking again.

But I mean, consider your case. A hundred years ago, you'd have simply followed your father on to the nearest farm. But nowadays . . .

Lewis saw Mary reach out and pinch her husband's foot in such a way that he stopped short.

Well, he said, yes, quite, I didn't mean to get personal there. Anyway, we're all layabouts here, eh? And he roared with laughter.

Lewis smiled.

Anyway, said Gerald, hitching himself up in his deck-chair. Fancy a spot of lunch? He turned to Mary. Darling?

Mary looked at him then at Lewis. Staying to lunch?

He shrugged. Why not? Then he added, Yes please.

So what can you do for us, darling? asked Gerald.

Salad, quiche. A scotch egg. It's too hot for much else, isn't it?

And a glass or two of . . .?

Mary smiled and rose to her feet again, with that smooth animal grace that so delighted Lewis.

Come on you, she said brusquely, not looking at him. You can give me a hand even if he won't.

Gerald waved a munificent hand towards his courtiers and sank down in his deckchair and tipped his hat forward over his eyes and gave himself up to reverie.

In the cool kitchen Mary laid out three white plates on the table and the heavy sound they made on the wood seemed full of significance to Lewis. He felt strangely happy now and very definitely hungry and also full of thoughts that didn't quite connect but surely would soon. He watched while Mary chopped up some spring onions and put them in a large wooden bowl. Then he blurted out without knowing why, Had a row with Dad this morning.

Mary looked round. Yeah?

Lewis nodded.

A bad one?

He shrugged. He didn't want to look her in the eye. Bad enough, he said.

Oh, Lewis, I'm sorry. I'm sure it'll blow over.

Yeah, he said.

They both stood there a little awkwardly for a moment. Then she reached out her hand and stroked his cheek where his father had hit him. But in defence of his father Lewis brushed her hand away, saying nothing. He didn't know why he had told her about it, but he felt better now he had. As for Mary, Lewis suddenly confiding in her like this made her feel wary and yet closer to him. She understood his defensiveness, didn't want pity to show on her face, patronizing and motherly, so she became brisk.

Ah well, she said. Here, handing him a bag of granary rolls from the breadbin. You can butter three of these for me. The butter's over there, look.

He did as he was told. While buttering away he found himself idly wishing she could be stung by another wasp this afternoon so that he would have to rub some cream into her finger like last time. And he would come back down from the bathroom and she would be standing there at the sink with her dress hitched up, sponging the front of it. Her legs bare to the hem of her . . . only she said she didn't always wear . . . He would bring the cream over to her and she would turn and smile and loop one leg around the back of his legs and . . .

I think that's probably enough butter now, don't you? she said, holding her head quizzically on one side.

He looked down. The butter was indeed spread fairly thickly. He looked up again. I like butter, he said.

Evidently.

He finished the other two rolls and put them on the plates, watching her as she tossed the salad and added capfuls of olive oil and tarragon vinegar and crushed garlic and some black pepper and some mixed herbs. She dipped her finger into the bowl and tasted it. Mm, she said. How do you like your salad dressing?

He shrugged.

She laughed. Daft question, she said. I don't suppose it's something you worry about too much.

All the time, he said. Lie awake at night worrying about salad dressing.

Idiot, she said. She carried on stirring. I always use about two-thirds oil. If not three quarters. Olive oil of course. Extra virgin. She dipped her finger in again. You have to do it by taste really though. Come here.

He came and stood beside her.

Taste, she said.

He hesitated.

It won't bite, she said with a certain kindly mockery in her eyes. It's only my finger. She held it out to him.

His heart was beating furiously. It felt like a heavy pendulum swaying inside his ribcage. What did she mean by it? He thought his grandma would have a word for women like her. Then again . . . it doesn't happen every day. He leaned forward and hesitating to take her finger in his mouth he licked a little drop of oil from the end of her finger with a rapid flick of his tongue.

Mm, she said in a musical way. Taste nice?

Yes, he said, unable to taste anything at all, not even registering.

OK, she said. That'll do.

She tossed the salad once more and then forked it out on to the plates along with the rolls and quiche and half a scotch egg for each man.

Don't you like scotch eggs? he asked her.

Oh, she said, scooping her hair out of her eyes. Only one left anyway.

Have half of it if you want, he said.

I don't mind, honestly, she said.

He stared at the half on his plate. She desperately wanted to ruffle his hair at that moment and kiss him lightly on the forehead. But no, she thought. Flirting with him is one thing, but being maternal at the same time would be getting just too complicated for the poor boy. Let's just keep this friendly and flirtatious.

Right, she said, and took the two other plates and led the way out into the garden, knowing that he was watching her closely, swaying her hips a little more than was strictly necessary, knowing that as she stepped from the kitchen into the garden, from gloom to bright sunlight, her dress would momentarily be translucent and he would see exactly what she was or wasn't wearing under her dress. You dreadful old tease, she scolded herself with a tiny smile, a wave running up her body like a hot hand, up her thighs, over her bum, over belly, over breasts . . .

But no cider? asked Gerald, snapping out of his reverie the moment the plate was laid on his lap.

Oh . . . said Mary half-turning back.

Lewis swiftly set his plate down in the grass. I'll get it, he said and marched back to the kitchen.

Bottle's in the fridge, called Mary. And three glasses from the cupboard over the sink.

The bottle of cider was cool in his hand. He hesitated to carry the three glasses with his fingers gripped inside them until he thought, Well I've just been *licking* her finger, and he shook his head with a baffled grin and carried the bottle out in one hand and the glasses clenched in the other.

Oh you're a honey, said Mary. You pour. You can have a bigger one than us.

Water droplets stood out on the bottle like beads of sweat. He poured the cider and they drank and ate their lunch. They ate slowly, it was so hot, and interrupted their eating with sighs of pleasure. At last they laid down their plates and Mary refilled their glasses. She drank most of hers in one draught and then said, I am *so* thirsty.

Gerald beamed. How about another bottle?

Darling, that was a litre, she protested mildly. Of farmhouse cider at 8 per cent.

Yes. And it's a very hot day, he said.

She blew out of her mouth, her hair wafting off her face in the draught of air, and then rose to go and get another bottle.

Not busy this afternoon, I take it?

No, said Lewis.

Well then, said Gerald. What else is there to do on a day like today but lie in the garden and drink cider? Tell me that it isn't the very apogee of the good life!

It is, said Lewis. The very *apogee*, he thought. Gerald was definitely mad but he liked the words he used.

Mary came back with a second bottle and gave Lewis a rueful look. His glass was still nearly full but Gerald drained his in a gulp and held it out to her. Please can I have some . . . more? he asked plaintively.

Mary refilled his glass to the brim and set the bottle down in the shade beside his chair.

Gerald began to talk again. He talked about the need of human beings to dull the pain of existence with drugs and he said that alcohol just happened to be the socially acceptable drug of our time. He thought that all drugs should be legalized. He himself had smoked pot and opium and taken acid. He had always wanted to take coke but had never been offered any. He asked Lewis if he had ever taken any of this wonderful e that everyone kept talking about. Lewis said not. He talked about Coleridge and De Quincey, Rossetti and Evelyn Waugh. (He leaned precariously sideways and seized the bottle by the neck and refilled his glass, giggling, Why thank you, I don't mind if I do). He quoted a line of Byron and a bit of Shakespeare and then with quite a thick slur to his voice he said he thought it about time for a quick forty winks. To ravel up the knitted sleeve of care, he said. To knit up the knitted . . . And he was fast asleep.

30   Mary (3)

Mary leaned over and rescued the cider bottle that he had dropped on to its side, glugging gently into the grass, and set it upright. There was only a swill of cider left in the bottom. She held the mouth of the bottle to her lips and took a swig. She passed it to Lewis. Here, she said. Finish that off, sweetness.

He drained it.

Come on then, she said scrambling to her feet. Let's leave this drunken old reprobate and do the washing-up.

They stacked up the plates and took them inside. She piled them on the kitchen table then she turned and took his hand in hers. Come on then, she said.

Feeling quite unreal, the blood thundering in his ears, he followed her upstairs. She held his hand close to her so that it brushed against her bum. She led him into the low-ceilinged bedroom, hot in the afternoon sunshine. She lay back on the double bed and pulled him on top of her. They began to kiss.

What about him? he said.

Don't worry about him, she said.

He kissed her deeply at first as he thought he should and she responded and then she pulled away and darted her tongue out at him in little lizard flicks. He tried to catch the tip of her tongue with his and missed. She grinned up at him.

Slow reactions, she said. It's all that cider. I hope you haven't had *too* much cider. And she slipped her hand down between them and rubbed the front of his jeans. No, not *too* much cider, she said and whispered closely in his ear, Nice and hard.

That made him even harder and he ground himself desperately against her. She reached down and pulled up her dress, right up over her breasts, leaving it loosely wrapped around her neck and shoulders. Then she pulled his shirt off and reached down and unbuckled his belt and undid his jeans and as he wriggled frantically out of them she slid her hand down and freed his cock and ran her fingers down the underside of his cock so that he buried his face in the bedclothes beside her head and gasped. Realizing from his shudders that this was not going to be the most prolonged session of lovemaking in the world, with the ghost of a secret smile to herself, she reached down and took his cock and guided it home. And almost immediately he came with deep shudders and she hugged him close with her heels in the small of his back and rubbed herself against him. When he relaxed he rested his head beside hers and said, I'm sorry, was that too quick?

Just a little bit, she said softly, stroking his hair. But who knows? We could make it last a bit longer next time, hey?

Next time, he thought deliriously, hardening again just at the thought. Did she mean they were going to do this again? And *again*?

She felt him hardening and slid her hand down between them and took his cock and rubbed it very slowly up and down her furrow. Mm, she said. You're insatiable, young man.

He felt a delicious mixture of embarrassment and lust. She was so nice. And so outspoken! He didn't feel nearly so embarrassed as he thought he would. He felt her fingers running ticklishly up and down his cock and around his balls and then he felt her running them up and down over her cunt and thought again happily how bad she was and didn't seem to care. She drew her fingers up to her mouth and turned to stare at him directly and he watched her bring her wet fingers to her mouth and lick them one by one, drawing them slowly out of her mouth so that her lips pouted around them and they shone still wet. Here, she said. And she pushed a finger gently between his lips and moved it rhythmically in and out. He sucked on it hard and then giggled.

What's the matter? she asked.

Seems the wrong way round, he said. I could get confused.

That's the fun of it, she said softly, confusing one thing with another. There's no knowing *what* we might end up doing to each other, is there?

She moved her hand down and dragged her wet fingertips over her nipples and arched her back a little, pressing them upwards against her own palms and looking up at him through half-closed eyes with a half smile, strands of hair plastered hot to her cheeks and forehead. And he thought at that moment that her expression, her face aglow with pure sexual pleasure, was the most beautiful sight he had ever seen, more beautiful than sunlight on the river or October light in the pine woods or any sunset over the darkening downs. He wished he had a camera to photograph just that, her face: lips apart, eyes half-closed, breathing deep.

She reached her hand round the back of his head and brought it down until he kissed her breasts and took her nipples between his lips and she arched her back harder against him and told him to bite harder, harder. At one moment he paused and wondered what time it was and could not help asking again, What about him?

And she said again, Oh don't worry about him, sweetness, and added with a wicked smile, He'd probably be quite happy to come up and watch anyway. Then seeing that he was truly shocked at this, she added casually, I'm only joking, although it was quite true that Gerald and Mary were happy to spectate at or participate in groups of three, four, whatever, when the fancy took them and the alcohol levels were right. But now Mary saw that all Lewis wanted was to be with her alone and make love to her alone and she scolded herself inwardly for not remembering that he was after all only seventeen and at an age when lust and love are hardly differentiated, that tumultuous, brief age of never-recaptured intensity before things stale.

So she added, No. He'll sleep for hours yet.

She lay back and stretched her arms out behind her head and sighed deeply. Lewis took this as a sign that the sweet half-hour was at an end and rolled off and lay beside her and then reached almost immediately for his clothes.

Hey, she said, turning swiftly on her side and laying her hand flat on his chest and pushing him back down on to the bed. What's the hurry? Had enough already?

He grinned without knowing what to say and scooped the hair from across his forehead and this made him look momentarily so ridiculously young and innocent that she wanted to straddle him there and then and fuck him until their sweat ran together, and their cries, and the whole valley knew that they were up here in this sunlit bedroom, fucking, she and this sweet lustful sad-eyed seventeen-year-old boy. And she did straddle him and rubbed her cunt against his skinny chest for a time while he held his head back and mouth open, not believing this was happening. She raised his hands up to stroke her breasts. Then she covered his face with kisses and worked her way down, his ears, his neck, left a trail of hot kisses down his chest and circled his nipples with her lips. He twitched beneath her.

That feel nice?

He nodded.

She leaned up and whispered in his ear, Now you know why men have nipples, and he giggled and turned his head away from her and her shameless mouth.

She kissed her way down over his belly and ran her tongue lightly in and out of his belly button and then ran her flattened tongue up and down the underside of his cock, lying erect on his belly. He gasped and shivered. He never realized a girl could do this to you *after* you had come. Then she ringed her fingers around his scrotum at the base and squeezed and with her other hand squeezed very tightly around the base of his cock and at the same time licked her lips wet and lowered her mouth over his cock and moved her head up and down over him very slowly, making sure her long hair fell down just so that it tickled his balls and thighs with each movement. His back arched and his feet stretched out from the bed arched and taut. He wanted to lift his head up and watch what she was doing to him but at first he didn't dare. Then at last he summoned the courage and the sight of it almost made him come at once. She felt it close and stopped sucking and squeezed hard on his cock and balls and looked up at him and smiled,

Not so fast, young man. I haven't finished with you by a long chalk.

But she knew he couldn't last out much longer so she turned and straddled him and took his cock and he slipped in so easily, inside her wet cunt, and gave a little groan of pleasure that she should be so wet for him.

Now you lie still and don't move, she ordered him. I'm fucking you this time.

And she raised and lowered herself on him so slowly that he could hardly breathe.

You've got to make the moment last, she sang. My husband swears by reciting Milton, she said softly. The least sexy of all the great English poets, he says, and just ideal for delaying the moment of ejaculation.

He wondered at her that she could talk so evenly like this while fucking, until she gradually began to speed up her rhythm and arch her back and he saw her reach her hand down around his cock and frig herself at the same time and the sight made him come inside her. As he came, she fell forward still frigging herself and rubbing herself up and down him whimpering *yes, oh yes*, and he thought this meant she had come too and that was probably a good thing.

She lay on top of him and he shifted under her as if to pull out but she tapped him on the lips with her finger and murmured, Why so fast, my lover? I like feeling you inside me, all wet and juicy.

He managed to look her very briefly in the eyes.

Simultaneous climax, she whispered. Only the second time and we get there together. *Come together* . . . and she sank her head and laughed. Her hair tickled his face. He licked the ends of it. They lay there together for a long time.

They dressed each other and Lewis was amazed at how little shame he felt at her seeing his skinny white body. She danced her fingers lightly over his ribs.

You need to eat more, she said.

It's true, he thought. I do. I must. And a knot of fear tightened in his stomach.

As they walked back across the lawn towards the sleeping Poet, Mary whispered to him, I'm still wet.

He didn't look at her, didn't or couldn't even quite understand what she was saying. She saw his embarrassment and loved him a little for it so she laid her hand on his shoulder to halt him for a moment and bent down her mouth close to his ear and said very slowly and clearly, I still have your come running down my thighs. What a pity you can't kneel down in front of me right now and lick it off.

He was so startled then that he did look at her and saw her laughing eyes and the unimagined mix of kindness and lust there towards him. He felt like he had once felt when he heard some music in church, or like he sometimes felt when watching the sunset from the hills, an impossible desire, a desire to laugh and cry, to laugh and cry at one moment, as if that unreal hybrid sound could be the only response that made sense of it all, to the question without an answer, the mystery and the meaning in one moment, laughter and tears in one breath.

She saw all this conflict of emotions in the battleground of his young face and was even a little afraid of the intensity that she saw there. So she laid her hand sexlessly and firmly in the small of his back and guided him over to the shade and awakened her husband.

Aha, said Gerald, awaking when she rapped him on his bony knees. Yes, he said, taking off his hat and running his hand back through his hair and replacing his hat again carefully. Yes, he said, and then continued into his monologue as if there had been no interruption.

The aesthetic and the erotic, said the Poet. I sometimes feel that as I get older, it is to these two things, these two fields of human experience alone that I shall confine myself. Here, perhaps, are the most sublime moments to be found. The central mystery of Beauty.

He steepled his hands. Then his voice became less musing, more brusque.

Of course, old age is a bummer anyway. But we all get old, we all have our tragic history to live out. For I have no doubt that getting older is a *tragedy*, or – let us be precise – a sad story, not strictly a tragedy; unless one argues that youthfulness is essentially noble, and any decline therefrom partakes of the essential nature of a tragic fall from nobility – which is arguable.

Lewis looked at Mary. She seemed to be asleep. He wanted to lie down and sleep beside her, one arm across her belly, one arm cradling her head.

Oh, old buffers tell you that they are quite happy being old: less sex drive, more time to do the crossword, less general anxiety, not giving a toss what people think of you, all that cal. But are you telling me that if they could be twenty again they'd say no? Like fuck they would. No – we all grow old and we all have a sad story to tell, or to live.

Gerald went on to talk about television and journalism and what he called mass culture, and other things.

Lewis did fall asleep, and awoke to the sound of tea being poured into mugs. They sat on the lawn and had tea. Mary asked Lewis what he had planned for next week. He shrugged. Not a lot, he said. She caught his eye and grinned wickedly. Oh well, she said. I'm sure you'll find something to keep you occupied.

He flashed a smile back at her then looked down quickly in obscure shame. Surely it wasn't right, with Gerald sitting here and everything. But she had said not to worry about him, even that he wouldn't necessarily mind. Surely it wasn't right.

After tea he said goodbye and walked round the side of the cottage to the gate. Mary followed him. He closed the gate between them. She reached out and pulled him close to her and gave him a long slow kiss, her tongue lingering over his lips.

Come again soon, she whispered.

He nodded.

And I'm sure it'll be all right, she said. Do come again some time.

Yeah, he said. OK. Bye then.

Bye bye, Lewis.

She wanted to watch his skinny figure go back down the track to the lane and remember him by that but she denied herself and went back to the garden to sit with her husband.

And Lewis walked home hopelessly in love, full of love and empty of hope, beating the hedgerow nettles with a stick and flicking the heads of hedge parsley and chervil until the flowers flew in clouds about his head and humming odd lines of songs he had heard on the radio whose names he didn't even know.

His father was in the garden among the runner beans when he returned from Mary.

'Allo there, he called.

Hiya, said Lewis. He went over to him and stood. His father went on working. Then he produced a giant runner bean. Look at that, he said. Too bloomin' stringy already though.

Yeah, said Lewis. I reckon.

There was a pause.

Ought to take Allie for a walk.

Oh right, said John Pike. Righty-ho.

OK, said Lewis and turned away.

It was going to be all right.

He took Allie and sneaked his crossbow out in a rucksack. Out in the hot fields he lined up birds in his sights a number of times and also a couple of rabbits and in the river even a trout lazing half under the bridge, head into the current. But he killed nothing. He even sighted on a dragonfly perched on a bulrush and thought to pin its meshed outspread wings with a perfect bolt. But he killed nothing.

Come on, Allie, he said and stowed away the crossbow and walked up the track between the high hedges. Summer was already turning rank and all the leaves were dulled with a fine dust. He stroked the back of his hand underneath a nettle and stung himself. He paused to lick it and shook it cool in the air and someone's voice somewhere said, You are a strange boy. But the air was growing humid, the weather must break before long. Everything was building up to it, he could feel it. Allie sniffed in the hedgerows but could smell little, snuffled up dust, turned away in disgust. And Lewis wondered that any animals should survive after so many days without rain and the earth baked so hard. But he knew that they would survive, survivors all, in their wholly different world.

All that summer the sun had shone. The streams shrivelled to nothing and the river ran shallow over the chalkbeds and the bare fields crusted over and it was unimaginable that the winterbournes should ever run again. Small birds sat openmouthed and second or third broods died in their nests. Lewis wondered if more didn't die now in this summer holocaust than on the bitterest February nights. Certainly lots of hedgehogs died, and badgers, outstretched and bloated under hedgerows. Foxes survived. Drinking the blood of their prey, they survived and Lewis loved them for it.

Mary sat all evening in the garden with her husband and was thoughtful and anxious and she wondered. She felt she would need to be careful in ways she had not before suspected. Oh, it was fun, they were two very nice fucks, just what she expected from a boy Lewis's age, though she smiled softly to herself and thought how much more erotic it had been just playing the hose over each other that time, or nibbling grass stems, with all the possibilities ahead of them, all imagined intimacies still in the future and unexplored. The anticipation was always the most erotic thing, and she remembered her husband saying that the erotic was always about being unfulfilled to some extent. When it came to the fucking – well, that was good too, nice, close. Less selfish somehow. Her pleasure then was to a large extent in seeing his pleasure, his sheer excitement, his disbelieving face, feeling his hot gasps on her cheek.

What are you smiling so much about, cat that got the cream? drawled her husband, tickling her ear.

Oh, nothing, she said, still smiling.

She resolved to be vigilant with herself, never to be selfish. Almost to imagine that she was the seducing older man and Lewis the virginal young girl. He was so young and – breakable. She wondered at him, a seventeen-year-old boy, ill-educated and obscure and resolutely from a small country, that he should seem at times and without a word of explanation to bear all the sorrows of the world on his thin shoulders and yet not appear ridiculous. Almost as if he didn't know it himself. For she knew teenagers well enough, was one herself only a few years back, and knew how this illusion was common among them, giving those seven years all their irrecoverable drama and a certain spuriousness and yet making us all but fated descendants of our younger selves. But about Lewis Pike she felt little or nothing was spurious, no playacting there before parents or peers, and the burden he bore did indeed, for no reason that she could fathom, seem to be the bitter truth.

She asked herself if she could somehow save him? And she felt like a parent with a son or daughter going to destruction, who might watch and love but cannot save. So those around Lewis, she thought, his father and his grandmother and Gerald and I, and others more distant who still in their various ways care for him, can watch him and love him but no more.

31   Jack and Rose (3)

On the last Sunday in August Jack Pike went over to the Parsons' house and asked Mr Parsons if he could marry his daughter. Mr Parsons sucked his pipe for a bit and then said he didn't see why not. And then they had a long conversation about football.

Afterwards he and Rose went out for a walk even though it was raining. They kissed a lot and the rain ran down their faces and mingled between their lips. Jack tried to undo Rose's dress but she wouldn't let him.

Oh come on, Rosie, we're practically married now.

Practically, she said. But not quite.

But I'm dying for it!

You just wait, she murmured with a smile that made his dreams feverish with lust for the next four months. She kissed him and nibbled his ear. You just wait till our wedding night, she murmured.

He said goodbye to her at her front door and then he ran all the way home at top speed but he was so happy that when he got home he couldn't stop running so he ran on another five miles all the way to Tisbury and then all the way back. His brothers teased him obscenely for looking so flushed and exhausted and said that Rose Parsons would wear a certain part of him away completely but when he told them why it really was they paraded him all round the farm on their shoulders and then dropped him in a dewpond.

The next day the whole village knew that Jack Pike had got engaged to Rose Parsons and then run all the way to

Tisbury and back because he was so excited. It became one of the favourite stories in the village.

On the following Friday, Germany invaded Poland.

On Saturday plans were begun for evacuating children from target areas.

On Sunday Rose listened to the wireless with her parents after ten o'clock matins and heard the Prime Minister say that Britain was now at war with Germany.

32   The White Horse (3)

On Sunday his father drove him up to the pub for lunch and they each had a Cheddar ploughman's and drank beer. The car park was overflowing and the pub garden filled with visitors from the town. They sat inside in the tiny local bar. The Mabey brothers were both there and after a while Tom dropped in as well. Then Gavin the vicar came in with his bicycle clips still around his trouser bottoms and he perched on a barstool and sipped his pint.

What's all this I hear about some new-look harvest festival, then? John Pike asked him in a friendly hectoring tone. He put on an extra broad accent. We don't loike change around these parts ye know, Reveren'. We don't loike change at all!

Gavin grinned and set his pint down.

Usual story, he said. I thought I'd moaned about it to you before. Some of the incomers – is that a derogatory term, *incomers*? I never quite know.

John Pike shrugged. Don't see why.

Dave Mabey said too loudly, Only if y'are one!

OK then, said Gavin, and whispered, The *incomers*, have got this idea about reviving an old harvest festival ritual. No, *custom* is a better word. Some local custom. Don't want people to get the wrong idea.

Though they'll always have a bloody good try, said John Pike. Scusin' my French.

Yes, well, said Gavin, sipping his pint. That's the trouble. Have to tread so – damn carefully. You know what it's like.

They all nodded.

Now, I wouldn't say this village is exactly on the verge of civil war . . .

They all grinned.

Oh not at all, said John Pike. I don't think there's hardly any bad feeling in the village, not as compared to some others I could mention. Friend of mine, Will, who works with me, tells me they've had some terrible trouble down his way this summer. They were lettin' sheep in to graze in the churchyard till some of the old dears said they didn't think it was right.

The *locals* said that? asked Gavin.

Oh aye. Well, you can see why, it's their old Ps that are buried there an' all.

Gavin nodded slowly.

An' then the incomers kicks up a fuss and says it's *traditional* to see sheep grazin' in the churchyard, it's what country life is all about, and they tells *them* to stop being so fussy. Ruddy cheek!

Gavin smiled.

It's not *their* parents and grandparents is havin' their graves covered in sheep muck and what 'ave you. Who the 'ell made *them* such experts on what's traditional anyhow?

They read it in a book, said Gavin with an ironic twang to his voice that Lewis rather liked. He looked at him again. Maybe he wasn't so bad, the vicar.

Which brings me back to the harvest festival, said Gavin. That's all out of a book too. Mrs Armitage . . .

Dave Mabey snorted. What still owes me a tenner for strimmin' 'er edge two months back, he said. Does too.

Gavin flattened out his hands as if in apology. Mrs Armitage has an idea that we should save the last sheaf of the harvested wheat — or *stand*, I think she keeps calling it, now she's learned that there aren't such things as sheaves any more . . .

They all roared with laughter. Appreciated that, the vicar slagging off one of his own flock, eh?

Oh I mustn't be too rude, said Gavin.

And why not? chuckled Gary Mabey.

Hm. Well, anyway, said Gavin. We shall have to see. I think we're still trying to persuade Phil Evans if he'll leave a corner of the field over the stream uncut or unharvested or whatever you say. Then Mrs Armitage and her cronies will go down there on Sunday at dawn and pick the last of the wheat and make it into a big corn dolly and bring it into the church for the Harvest Service. Something along those lines.

Well, there's nothing new about a corn dolly, said John Pike.

Oh I know, said Gavin. It's just that Mrs Armitage said that she wanted us to place the corn dolly on the altar steps at the climax of the service, and then cut its head off with a scythe.

There was a stunned silence. For reasons none of them could quite name, this idea made them all feel slightly sick. At last John Pike murmured, I think she means a sickle.

Gavin nodded to him. You tell her, he said.

She's barking.

She's . . . eccentric, admitted Gavin.

So – what's going to happen?

Well – I may be a soft touch some of the time, if only to try and keep people happy, but there's no way I was having that. So I explained to her very politely that there was no way we could have some primitive re-enactment of a blood sacrifice on Harvest Festival Sunday in *my* church. Very patiently, I explained to her that there has been one sacrifice for all time and there'll never be a need for another. Couple of thousand years ago. Place called Calvary.

Gavin half-expected downcast faces and awkward silences at this sudden, rude intrusion of religion, but he had spoken in a tone just sarcastic enough, albeit gentle, for them to take it as a sly joke, and they nodded in appreciation.

Good point, Vicar, said John Pike with a grin.

Sound theology, said Gavin. Anyway. He stood up and drained his pint and felt deeply happy. My wife will have the roast on the table and I can't be late for *that* now, can I?

They all shook their heads in sympathy.

So. See you all around.

Bye then, Vicar.

Bye.

They nodded wryly after his exit.

He's a good old bloke really, our vic.

Yeah, said Dave Mabey. He's all right he is.

The Mabey brothers bought another pint each and then Dave whispered something to Gary. Gary whispered back harshly and then said out loud, Oh yeah. And in case anyone's interested in a bit of a gamble, it is just possible that there may be a, er . . . He hesitated and Lewis looked at him curiously. Gary resumed. Over in John Cox's barn next Friday night after-hours, he said. If you 'appen to be walkin' past then it's just possible you might hear a couple of dogs 'avin' a right old barney.

John Pike harrumphed loudly.

You comin', John? taunted Dave Mabey.

No I don't think I am, to tell you the truth, Dave, said John Pike. Don't much interest me that sort of thing, to tell you the truth. He set his pint down firmly and looked at the Mabey brothers. Not exactly much of a *sport*, is it?

'S entirely natural, protested Gary Mabey. These dogs are trained to be fighters, they're born to it. They *enjoy* it for Christ's sake.

What, with a back leg 'angin' off or their neck 'angin' open?

Now now, gentlemen, said Derek from behind the bar, let's be having no raised voices this Sunday lunchtime.

Not raising my voice, Derek, said John Pike evenly. Just putting my view.

Well . . . said Derek, and then stopped as two visitors came in.

They were both dressed alike, the two men in perhaps their mid thirties. They wore little round spectacles and polo shirts and sweaters loosely over their shoulders and baggy shorts and deck shoes and Lewis marvelled how brown their legs were. He knew these were the sort who worked in offices, in London even. How did their legs get so brown?

They ordered their smoked trout ploughman's and bought gin and tonics and went back outside.

Well, John, said Gary more calmly. I don't want to fall out with you over it. Everyone's entitled to their opinion.

Fair enough, said John Pike. Only don't expect me to come.

Gary lit up a cigarette. T'other dog's comin' up from London so it should be a good one anyway, he added, it being a matter of pride that he should get the last word in. John Pike understood and said no more.

On the way back to the car they met George walking over to the pub.

'Ullo, George, said John Pike.

Ah John, said George coming over to them. Just the man I wanted to see. I wonder if I could have a quick word?

Course, George.

Um . . . George thumbed away towards the pub. Lewis froze. They were going to talk about him. About Mary. About the crossbow. About . . .

His father and George stood at the entrance to the pub and talked for two or three minutes and then John Pike came back over looking redfaced.

What's the matter? What did he want? asked Lewis far too rapidly.

Get in the car, said John Pike. That bloody old fool.

They hadn't been talking about Lewis at all.

That bloody old fool, said John Pike revving the car violently. Bloody cheek.

What about?

Oh I dunno, all about some old boy called John Cobden who left some money 'for the poor of this parish', yonks ago. You'll 'ave seen his board up in church.

And Lewis remembered the wormeaten board on the church wall that told that in 1823 John Cobden of this parish had left the sum of £50, the interest to be distributed by the churchwardens to the poor of the parish annually.

Not many poor left in this parish except us, son, said John Pike with a savagery that Lewis had rarely heard before. He thought immediately of the job at the dairy he had left and of his father hitting him and felt hollow with guilt and quite worthless. If only . . . if only he could *do something* . . . to redeem . . . But at least this time his father was not angry with him.

Nope, said his father. Not many poor left, y'see. Bloody yuppies and what have you. Bloody retired folk on their fat pensions. Bloody Brigadier Hoare, oh yeah, he really looks like he needs a fuckin' charity blanket or two come the winter, awful draughty up in the old Rectory.

Well.

He slewed the car around a sharp bend and gravel spat out into the hedgerow. He was driving far too fast.

Old George can stuff his fuckin' blankets up his arse.

The car lurched to a halt outside their house.

His father very rarely said *fuckin'* in that way. It was normally just *bloody*. Lewis knew he must be angry. And he felt the worst of things, pity, for his own father, who only a few years since had been a man who knew everything and could do anything, almost godlike, the centre of his world, his hero. And now he saw him humiliated. Humiliated from humiliation to humiliation. Father and son went into the house.

33 Gerald and Mary (4)

He wanted desperately to go and see Mary that afternoon, but somehow he felt that this would be to betray his father and he must wait until tomorrow when his father was at work. So instead he took Allie and went for a walk, although he didn't feel like walking far, and lay down on the edge of the hill and left Allie to look puzzled and sniff about. He lay on his back and wondered and wished that, just for a moment, just for a few blissful hours, he could stop all his thoughts and think of nothing. That was why people drank, he knew. They drank, they took drugs, and though the law was against it, nobody really in their heart of hearts blamed them. He lay for two hours with his heart and brain in riot.

And all that night he dreamt of Mary, confused and jealous dreams in which he found her half-undressed and smiling and coming towards him with outstretched arms, only to turn away and begin to kiss some other man, her husband or some other shadowy figure. In one dream Lewis waited for her on the edge of a dark wood with his crossbow in his hand, looking out over the fields for her coming. And when he heard a movement in the woods behind he was afraid and turned and fired his crossbow and then realized with relief that it was only a deer. But when he went to see if he had killed the deer he found that it was not a deer at all that he had killed, for he found his crossbow bolt buried in a treetrunk, pinning to it a long slim severed hand that he knew was Mary's.

And he awoke crying.

*

All day Monday he thought of Mary and could make no sense of what he felt. It all seemed wrong, all the wrong way round. They had been to bed together and yet he felt he hardly knew her. That couldn't be right. He wanted to know everything about her and felt that he never would. She would laugh and tell him little and turn away, not under-standing. It all meant so little to her, he knew with a knot of panic and fear inside him. Any time she could say that it was fun for a short while but now they must stop. She could find some other man or *boy* to . . . fuck, any time. If that was all she wanted. The cold bitch.

His daydreams had for some time been as vivid as his nightdreams or nightmares. He stood or sat and stared and before his blank eyes everything passed with terrible vivid-ness. Mary flirting with other men. Mary having all that time, all those hours when he was not there, to do as she wished, to talk or . . . And her husband there, sleeping, not minding, not caring. She could be doing anything, seeing anyone.

He sat motionless for two hours or more, not stirring a muscle, his throat burned dry, seeing everything pass in dumb show before his eyes.

Then he took his crossbow and went out with Allie but could find nothing. The birds were all deep in the woods cowering from the heat, the animals in their burrows. Butterflies, though, were everywhere, peacocks and marbled whites and painted ladies. He brushed through the buddleia by the railway line and they rose and flew in clouds about his head and he watched them go and dance, so careless and shortlived, until raising his eyes too high he was blinded by the sun.

He returned and stowed away his crossbow and fed Allie. He could eat no lunch. His stomach felt as if it were held in a vice or a claw. He drank a pint of water and then splashed cold water on his face and went out walking again. There was nothing else he could do but walk.

In the fields they were harvesting already and it was not yet August. By mid August they would be finished, too early, leaving the rest of the month and all of September eventless and empty of all but the long slow dying of the summer. And the wheat was too dry and a poor harvest and the pasture even worse for lack of rain. From the eastern counties the news was worse, the farmers watering their fields under the vast Norfolk and Lincolnshire skies and still the beet leaves shrivelling and the great trees shedding their leaves early so as to save the trunk at least, and the smaller trees in the hedgerows dying stunted and greying with bare bleached branches like trees under a sun far hotter than the English sun was ever meant to be.

They forecast rain soon, saying the weather must break. Lewis had no faith in forecasts. He gawped openmouthed at the yellow combine harvesters lumbering through the dry air and wheatdust and pictured some raindance or some ritual to restore the rain to the parched earth, though too late now for this year, this harvest. Like at Stonehenge or something. The Poet would know all about raindances.

Gerald was in the garden but there was no sign of Mary. He didn't even mention where she was. She might be anywhere, doing anything. Gerald motioned Lewis to sit down and began to talk. Lewis heard nothing.

After some time had passed, Mary returned, gliding through the side gate with a handful of hedge parsley and willowherb and scentless mayweed. She smiled at Lewis and went inside.

I'll just find a vase for these, she called.

The Poet settled back in his deckchair. Time for a cup of tea, I think.

Should I . . .? began Lewis.

Mary's voice called out from the kitchen, Lewis! Come and help me with the tea, there's a love!

He scrambled to his feet and went inside.

Mary laid her hands on his shoulders and pulled him

179

towards her and began to kiss him. Still kissing, they moved deeper into the kitchen out of view of Gerald in the garden.

She reached out a hand and pulled a kitchen chair out from the table. Her hands on his shoulders pressed him to sit down and then she drew up her long dress about her thighs and straddled him. She began to kiss him again, harder.

But . . . he said, pulling back from her, isn't this a bit . . . ?

Risky? she said, her face serious and urgent. Yeah. Makes it more exciting.

She crushed her mouth against his and held him close to her. She unbuttoned her dress and let it fall down around her waist, and she unbuttoned his jeans and unzipped them and pulled his cock free. She straddled him and drew him into her. Lewis sat gasping with desire and disbelief and her long hair fell down either side of his upturned face and tickled him and he half-closed his eyes while she laid her arms over his shoulders and gently rode him. As they moved slowly up and down she caressed herself and then shuddered as the waves of pleasure began to break over her.

Ten minutes later they carried the tea things out to Gerald who awoke delighted.

On Tuesday they made love in the bedroom again, for two long lazy hours while Gerald slept off his lunch.

On Wednesday she said she wouldn't be able to for the next few days, but she sat him on the kitchen table and sucked his cock until he came while he closed his eyes and softly stroked her hair. Afterwards she had him taste her mouth with long kisses.

34   The Deer

He returned home to find his father already back from work and with him, another woman. His father was standing in front of the fireplace and Lewis knew immediately by his stance that there was some awkward news to impart, some great change to be announced, and he felt that same panic again that he felt whenever changes came to threaten his peace. His father stood with his shoulders a little hunched as if preparing to box, although with a kind, wary smile on his face, and his hands thrust deep into his pockets. Lewis looked from his father to the woman. At first he could see nothing but a blank, nothing but for the fact that this was some woman he had never met before and already never wanted to meet again. She sat in the armchair where his mother used to sit, especially that time she was really ill, with that tartan rug over her skinny knees, watching television, when her whole arm would shake with the effort when she brought a cup to her lips. This was the armchair in which some other woman was now sitting. Lewis bowed his head as if from a physical blow. His eyes followed repeatedly the spiral pattern in the carpet.

Ah Lewis, said his father. Ahem. Um, there's someone I want you to meet. This is Patricia.

Hello Lewis! she said brightly. Pleased to meet you.

He did not look up. Hello, he said, so quietly that he barely heard it himself.

Well, she said, laying her hands on her thighs and looking up helplessly at John Pike.

He nodded reassuringly at her and smiled.

181

So she had a name. Patricia. Lewis glanced quickly up and saw everything about her with the eyes of a six-year-old, clinical and unforgiving and without comprehension: the red hair, the mole, the pointed chin. But he didn't look her in the eyes.

I'm going upstairs, he said.

He shut the door of his bedroom. He lay on the bed and reached under it and pulled out the crossbow. He polished the sharpened bolts that he kept taped to the stock and he oiled and polished the bow with a soft cloth. Then he stood at the window and sighted it on various objects near and far, and thought he hit every one with perfect accuracy.

He must have fallen asleep because his father had to call up the stairs twice before he heard him.

We're just poppin' out to get some fish and chips. What do you want?

Lewis heard him groggily but didn't answer.

Cod an' chips all right?

After a pause he called back, Yeah.

Okeydoke then. Won't be long.

When he heard the car pull away down the lane he rolled off the bed and stowed the crossbow in a rucksack and said goodbye to Allie in the kitchen and went out.

He walked up the lane and along the track under the row of sweet chestnuts and was covered in thunderbugs. He walked under the louring summer sky and knew that the weather must break tonight. The thunderbugs settled on his bare arms and on the sleeves and shoulders of his shirt and sweat coursed down his temples and down the back of his neck. He walked fast in the humid evening air and the rucksack was sticky against his back. The thunderbugs were everywhere in pointless profusion. They caught in the hairs on his arm and crawled there as if damaged or they drowned in the sweat on his forehead. He wiped them and the sweat away and walked on, his face streaked with sweat and flies, and he thought of Jesus walking the long white roads in the wilderness with flies about his face and his robe clinging to the sweat on his back with all the desert world about him and only Calvary ahead.

It was getting darker already, several weeks now past the longest day and many flowers over for another year and all the colours of the land shrinking to the beautiful and unusable spectrum of smokegrey and brown and gold and on into night. In many of the hedgerows there seemed to be little left already but umbellifers and bindweed although all the fruits and seeds were quietly growing out of those deaths, the sloes as hard as stones and the hazelnuts pale green and half hidden. Something was gone though, the arrogance of summer, the nettles blackstalked and rank and the horsechestnut leaves already yellowing and falling.

Emerging from the track out into the parkland he saw a deer at the edge of the wood grazing. He froze. The deer had not seen him and the silent wind was towards him from the animal. The deer waggled her ears against the flies and stopped chewing. She looked in his direction. She was small, maybe no more than forty pounds. She looked away again. He stepped back, agonizingly slowly, and lowered the rucksack from his back. He drew the crossbow out, drew back the ratchet, fitted a bolt. He moved close to a wide sweet chestnut and peered round the side. The deer was gone. He emerged from behind the tree, too carelessly. The deer had only moved on a few yards, but this time she saw him, a dark shape moving against the paler grass and with a single bound she was back over the barbed wire and into the wood. Lewis heard the footfalls die away into the heart of the wood. He went and retrieved his rucksack.

He scouted along the edge of the wood to where the deer had leapt but could find no sandy hairs on the wire, only a tuft of sheep's wool. Yet he felt some strange strength or promise in the air and ducked under the wire and went into the wood.

It was the worst time of day for human eyes, in daylight

the best after the birds'. But he walked on into the wood along the track that even after the weeks of drought remained muddy and pocked with hoof marks. He found one track that changed from the neat closed cleaves to the splayed cleaves of the running deer but he doubted it was the deer he had just seen. He walked on down the track with less care until rounding a corner he saw before his disbelieving eyes a deer only yards from the track in a bed of bracken with its eyes wide open yet lying couchant, asleep. He raised his crossbow at once and sighted it between its eyes but he had no hope of being able to shoot this animal in its sleep and prehistoric dreams of fawns and predators. He walked on and, looking back from some way ahead, he saw the deer still sitting there as still as a statue in the twilight, unmoving and unmoved when all the other deer were feeding, as if this were some omen or an animal set apart from the rest by a curse or by its own inscrutable volition, offering itself carelessly to any hunter that should pass by but knowing itself eerily protected by its own impassivity, its unnatural fearlessness. Nothing would touch it, not a lion, not a man. Lewis went on.

And then he saw up ahead as he emerged from the wood westward, another deer out on the edge of the field, framed dark against the field's greater light. Three deer in one night, and with such little effort. This time the deer was feeding delicately between its outstretched forelegs, dipping its head to the dry grass and then raising it again to chew and look around, or to stop chewing and listen moment-arily. Lewis came nearer to it with painstaking slowness, again drawing the crossbow from his rucksack. He crouched and laid the rucksack on the ground and came still closer. The wind was changeable and almost against him now but still it seemed the deer had sensed nothing. He was as close as he dared to be and he raised the crossbow and sighted it on the animal's head. His finger tightened on the trigger. At that moment the deer knew by one of its other senses that it was being watched and looked up directly at Lewis so that when he fired the bolt struck the deer between the eyes. A blunter bolt might have glanced off the hard bone there but the sharpened bolt bit deep and entered cleanly. The deer felt the bolt as a bang in its brain and leapt backwards, stunned, and turned, preparing to run, when its legs buckled under it and it staggered to the right and fell dead.

Lewis could not believe it. He had never killed a deer before, but he reckoned he could butcher it well enough to take back some meat in his rucksack. He walked over to the deer and took its back hooves so small and delicate and leaned backwards against it and dragged it into the cover of the wood. There he took his big-bladed folding knife from his rucksack and clamped it open. He stood astride the deer and held one hind leg upright and crouched and stuck the knife deep into its belly. Then he began to draw it along towards the ribs, saw side first, sawing up and down. It was hard. When he struck liver and spleen a glove of blood welled up over his hand. Then he cut further and a heap of guts began to slither out and with them a purplish sac that he didn't understand until he saw the long white legs inside it and recognized the foetus of an unborn fawn. He dropped the handle and leapt away with a cry. He dropped his knife and leaned against a tree and vomited against it. He held his bloody hand up to his mouth to wipe away the vomit and saliva and left his mouth rimmed with blood. He stumbled away until he found a shallow puddle at the edge of the track and washed his hands and face repeatedly in the muddy water and scrubbed ferociously at his tear-stained face with wet gritty hands. He returned and found his crossbow and washed his knife in the puddle and stowed both back in his rucksack. He looked back at the dis-embowelled deer and cursed himself for his weakness and then he thought, It isn't the animals we should be killing.

35 The Barrow

He ran out of the wood and continued to run all the way up the track and over the stile and through the furze until he came to the downs. He had run for two miles mostly uphill and felt no tiredness. He was desperately hungry but his mind was free and whirling.

He walked for a long time along the crest of the downs until he saw away to his left the long barrow that Gerald was always talking about. He walked over to it and climbed over the barbed-wire fence that surrounded it. Gerald would often come up here, he had told Lewis, and strip naked and lie on his back on top of the barrow and look up at the stars. When the dew settled on his skin and he started to shiver he would dance on top of the barrow and wave his arms about. To the music that we each have in our heads, if only we would listen, said Gerald. And he would often mention the Powys brothers. Lewis didn't know who they were. Maybe they lived round here somewhere or maybe they were old friends of Gerald's.

Lewis stripped his shirt off over his head and then kicked his boots off and his jeans and underpants and lay naked on the barrow. The coarse grass prickled in his sweaty back and the scab wound in his neck. The sky was a clear bowl of stars, a cavern roof of jewels, and he named the stars and constellations that he knew, one by one, as he named the flowers.

There was the Plough and from there he found the North Star, the handle of the Little Bear. He found Cassiopeia easily and from there the trail of Perseus down the sky to the treetops northeastward. In the space between he watched the Perseids appear mysteriously from their single point as if newborn and as if emblems and mysteries put there to be learned from on rare summer nights and fly away and die in the dark spaces apart. He found the galaxy Andromeda and overhead the most beautiful Vega in Lyra, star of summer, and from there the great summer triangle of Vega and Altair and Deneb.

The cooling and dampening grass all around him gave off a sweet scent and his back tickled terribly from the grass stalks and sweat and yet not to scratch it was the greater pleasure. The nearest sound was an owl in the trees and the occasional sheep beyond. He ran his hand down his belly and stroked his cock. It was already stiff. He masturbated slowly, wishing Mary was with him now, wishing he was fucking her here. And yet whatever position he could imagine with her he would never have a clear view of the whole starry sky as he had now. He felt a sensation of delirious loneliness that was almost insufferably bitter and sweet and he came gasping and taut between tears and laughter with no space between the stars or between the stars and him and he the only person left alive on earth and imbued with godlike power.

Afterwards he rolled on to his belly and rubbed himself dry on the grass. Then he lay back and looked up at the stars for a long time. Then he collected his clothes and boots and, holding them in his hands he lay on his stomach and shuffled head first under the barbed wire. He walked back down the hill and along the track and did not dress again until he came to the stile into the lane.

36 The Village

There was no point returning home, there was no hope of
sleeping that night. Before passing his house he took his
boots off again and walked barefoot. He went down into the
village.

One or two lights were left on in people's porches but
otherwise the village was dark and silent. He sat on the
churchyard wall and stowed his boots behind it. Opposite
him was the row of old estate cottages. In one of them his –
now which was it? – his great-grandfather was born, or
even great-great . . . A bawling bundle that weighed 10lbs,
so his father said, and grew to be six foot four and the tallest
man in the village. But he died young. People did in those
days. It was no picnic. Now the cottage he was born in had
been knocked together with next door's and had a new
kitchen built on the back, and so it was all the way along.
People needed more room nowadays for all their things. Yet
the cottages were still pretty, Lewis had to admit, prettier
than their house. He thought of those ugly grey pebbledash
walls right on the lane always splashed with mud in winter
or with shit when the cows went by for milking. And he
looked at the cottages opposite, the middle one only occupied at weekends, and they were so pretty in their weather-
faded Chilmark stone and their lichened roofs and small
whiteframed windows. Their gardens were immaculate.
Maurice looked after most of them. Hollyhocks, mar-
guerites, a few last roses. Lewis felt a strange surge of anger.
The yuppies lived in that end one. He could just picture
them rushing home after their day's work in the town in

their flash new cars – they had one each – knocking over Allie as they came. And rushing inside past the hollyhocks and the dying roses with a portable phone clamped to their ears as they fumbled for their doorkeys.

He slipped from the wall and walked down to the end cottage. There were no lights on but the curtains were drawn upstairs. They were in bed fast asleep. He clenched and unclenched his fists. He wished he had his crossbow with him. He could put a bolt straight through a bedroom window. He went over to their Audi and broke off the windscreen wipers.

He stepped over the side gate in a single scissor movement and crept up the side of the cottage into the back garden. It sloped steeply, you could step from the lawn straight on to the roof of the kitchen and then in at the bathroom window. That was closed but the next one along was open. That was their bedroom, that was where they were sleeping. If he listened hard he thought he could hear snoring. He needed a piss so he pissed in their barbecue set mounted in a polished block of Purbeck marble. He wished he could shit on it too but he couldn't do a shit. He hadn't eaten enough.

He would smash the bathroom window and climb in. The husband would come and investigate, that cunt, wearing pyjamas. Lewis would grab a heavy wooden drawer from the bathroom cupboard and smash it down on his head. As he lay there gurgling in his own blood Lewis would bring the drawer down again and again on his pulpy face until he was dead.

She would be screaming by now. He would race along to her room and find her there with a look of horror on her face – in a nightie, a short white nightie. Brown suntanned thighs. That blonde bitch. He would smack her hard in the mouth, so she fell sideways across the bed. No no, she was pleading. He turned her on her back, ripped her nightie off and pulled her legs apart, stuffed his huge cock in her, and she came when he came, weeping and moaning, her legs tight around him . . .

Then he thought of Mary and of someone else doing all those things in Gerald's house. To Gerald. To Mary. And he hated himself then. He went quickly away, not caring if he was heard now, making no attempt to hide the noise as he climbed back over the gate and went back to get his boots. Not caring if anyone heard him, thinking that probably he deserved to be heard and get caught, and punished for all the terrible things he had done to the couple, those poor people who went rushing everywhere and never stopped to speak to anyone and looked so tired and had maybe more money but less time than him and had never even learned the names of the flowers.

Mary lay awake much of the night too and thought about Lewis. She tried not to, to start some dream, to keep her eyes closed long enough to sleep, but it was no use. She lay awake and stared up at the ceiling. She lay beside her heavily snoring husband and thought of Lewis and his sweet lost eyes. It had been so erotic, if irresponsible, those days of pure flirtation, before the real thing had happened. She supposed it was now an affair and hated the word. That afternoon of sucking on the same grass stalk had been so simple and sensual, and it should have stayed like that. Now they had started fucking it seemed to bring more complexities or even responsibilities. And she didn't want to be responsible. She didn't want to be responsible for Lewis Pike.

She was his first, she thought. And he was getting better, there was no denying it. He was useless at talking, it was true, but weren't most of them? But he learned fast. She smiled softly in the darkness when she recalled saying to him, We don't have to just gallop straight for the finishing line, you know. He had stared at her. She stroked his hair and said, We can take little detours along the way, scenic routes. We needn't just hurtle down the motorway. And he smiled that sweet smile made up equally of lust and curiosity and bashfulness. Then she showed him what she meant.

She didn't feel guilty, not really. They were both enjoying it, every minute. But she could not avoid the thought that, sooner or later, it must come to an end. Maybe just a summer thing, a mad summer, midsummer thing, that should be left out to die in winter. And she was anxious about how Lewis would take that. She hoped it might be only a matter of time before he met a girl his own age. Then she thought, What? Round here? In this village? There are no girls his own age *left* around here.

37   The White Horse (4)

On Friday night John Pike said he was going to the pub with Patricia, did he want to come too?

He said no almost immediately, but then he paused and said yes he would. He didn't know why. Half to be there just to annoy those two lovebirds, his father and that damp-eyed, redhaired old slapper, and half because he thought that if his father *was* going to get together with her, he supposed he would have to learn to rub along with the old slag. He felt quite proud of himself at the maturity of this thought. How very *grown-up*, he thought sarcastically. How very *mature*.

They picked Patricia up from her new redbrick house down the A30. Lewis sat in the back. Patricia turned in the passenger seat and smiled deliberately at him.

Hello Lewis, she said.

Hello, he said. Old slapper, he thought.

The pub was crowded, mostly with locals. The air was filled with cigarette smoke and the treacly smell of spilled beer. Men looked redfaced from the sun and sweaty and leaned at the bar brandishing twenty-pound notes and ordering huge rounds. Wives and girlfriends sat back and drank halves. There were even some children there. Phil Evans was there, saying he had finished his harvesting, hadn't finished this early in his life, not even in '76, although, he added, I've left a small corner for the vicar.

Oh aye, said John Pike to him. For this harvest festival.

Phil grinned. Vicar told me he wanted it or rather his *people* wanted a stand left in the middle of the field so it'd be *symbolic*. Symbollocks more like. I told him straight, Vicar, no offence or nothin', but if you think I'm goin' to drive my bloody combine round and round in circles just so as to leave an uncut stand in the middle, well you've got another think comin'!

What'd he say?

Oh he's all right, the vic. Bit wet behind the ears and I know he tries to please all the people all the time, I s'pose that's 'is job, but you can't do it, can you?

John Pike shook his head. No, indeed not.

Anyhow, no, he takes it very well, does his sort of sheepish grin and says, Phil, never you worry. You know very well whose idea it is, don't you? So I tip him the nod and the wink and tell him I have my suspicions, and he whispers, *So don't blame me!* Anyhow.

So what's to happen then, Phil?

Oh, I'm just leavin' 'em a corner down by the stream like the vic suggested, just by the footbridge to the church, so when they want to they can just pop over and make that life-size corn dolly of theirs or whatever the 'ell it is, though God only knows how they're going to cut it or whatever.

With a golden sickle! someone suggested.

While reciting the Lord's Prayer backwards!

And dancin' round in a fuckin' circle and burnin' their brassières! roared Dave Mabey, which nobody quite understood but laughed at anyway.

They drank a lot of beer, six or seven pints, and his father had a few whisky chasers. Lewis was surprised and expected him to drink less in front of Patricia or for her to say something but she drank nearly as much herself. Lewis hoped there were no police around tonight. Only last week someone from this pub got done driving home to Blandford. Lewis reckoned Patricia might be all right. She smoked too. She offered him one and he took it and smoked it heavily and felt sick and high and jittery.

Then toward closing time a whole group of people began to shuffle out of the bar with low murmurs.

Where they all off to?

Up the barn, the old dog fight, remember? said Dave Mabey.

Oh bloody hell, said John Pike.

I'll go, said Lewis.

You wanna go? said his father to him, looking drunk and bleary and yet severe.

Lewis shrugged. May as well.

It'll be the last time you'll want to go and see a thing like that, my boy, said his father. He drained his pint. C'mon then. Teach you a thing or two.

Patricia put her hand on his arm. John, she said.

You don't have to come, love, he said to her. We won't be gone long. She looked from him to Lewis and back again. She saw their expressions. I'll come, she said.

38   The Dog Fight

In the farmyard there were several cars drawn up and Lewis saw the Mabey brothers standing talking to two other men. The men had close-cropped hair and wore leather jackets and they leaned back on their car. It was a brand new 4x4, shiny red, S-reg. John Pike saw him looking at it.

Yeah, he said, there's plenty of money in this old game, son. Easy to make money in this world if you don't care how.

And even as he spoke they saw the shorter man hand a wad of notes over to Dave Mabey who stuffed them in the pocket of his camouflage jacket. The back windows of the 4x4 were obscured with blankets. That was where they had their dog. People said it was a Rottweiler.

They went into the barn. It was harshly lit. In the middle was a fenced area only a few feet square and already it was crowded round with people. Nearly all men, thought Lewis. Patricia must be almost the only woman here. She hung back, not wanting to see anything but not wanting to leave them here either.

At one end of the ring sat an extraordinary figure. On this hot summer night in a crowded sweaty barn, a very fat man with sleek black hair and a blank white puffy face sat on a high stool behind a desk. He was incongruously dressed in a white shirt and dark tie and a pinstripe suit buttoned up, and a dark overcoat on top of that. In spite of all his clothes Lewis saw that he did not sweat at all nor did he talk to anyone. He sat and regarded everyone with equal contempt and never spoke a word. On his desk he had a big notebook. John Pike saw Lewis scrutinizing this figure.

The bookie, he said, but with a passion that spoke much more.

The man was taking bets. Men approached him and murmured which dog they favoured and passed notes over to him. He regarded them blankly and then recorded their bet and took the notes. Instead of putting them into a cashbox, he simply stuffed them into the left pocket of his overcoat, as if the money was his already. Lewis could see even from where he stood that the pocket was bulging with notes. In all this press and commotion it wouldn't have been difficult, surely, to pass by and pinch a few notes off him? But no one tried.

The excitement was building to a pitch of intensity. All around them men were talking dogs. The Rottweiler was from south London where it had fought four fights this year and killed every time. This was the first time it had been out of London and some thought the travelling might have affected it, but others said that being cooped up like that all this while would only have made it fiercer. And several sneered at the very name of Rottweiler and said it was just a big poncy London dog and that a terrier would win every time.

And against the Rottweiler was indeed a mongrel terrier, certainly part bull terrier, that belonged to a Wiltshire man from a village up on the plain. Apparently the owner wouldn't say how old it was but some people had seen it before and said that although it was good it was getting on. Could be six or seven, although of course very experienced and had killed more dogs than you've had hot dinners, let alone badgers. Pride dictated that most of the money went on the Wiltshire dog but people were uneasy and several kept going to the barn door to eye the gleaming 4×4 as if they might surmise through the veil of blankets the quality of the dog within.

Amid all this hubbub the man in the dark overcoat sat impassive. Lewis looked back at him repeatedly, fascinated.

He sat on his high stool like a judge pronouncing execution or like the recording angel impassively noting down the sins of all the world, neither smiling nor frowning. Lewis felt there was some central mystery about this man that he could not identify. He had drunk enough to be bold enough to approach him and ask him a question. But before he could frame it right the noise levels dropped suddenly and two men appeared with a brisk air by the side of the ring. They released a perky Jack Russell which ran around and wagged its tail and looked well pleased with itself. The other carried a heavy burden in a canvas sack. Lewis saw that he held it carefully and also wore motorbike gauntlets. He held the sack over the ringside and shook it violently by the corners. A badger tumbled out.

A little warm-up! he roared.

The terrier was on the badger immediately, clamped to its throat before the animal had time for its eyes to adjust to the light. The badger on its back scrabbled desperately for the terrier's belly with its massive digging claws but the terrier knew better than to get disembowelled that easily and swung sideways and hung on there out of the wild animal's range. Then it was just a matter of time. A minute later the badger was suffocated.

Bring on the dogs! someone shouted.

People generally were unimpressed.

Oh very good sport, said one sarcastically.

The terrier was collected by its owner and fussed over. The badger was seized by the hind leg and slung back into the sack. Lewis watched hypnotized. He wondered where the badger had come from, how long it had been in the sack, how old it was. He wondered what the point of it was. This killing.

And then two dogs were brought in from either end of the barn. They smelled each other immediately and their handlers leaned back hard against their collars to restrain them. Both were muzzled.

Lewis feared the worst immediately. The terrier was

brutally built, compact bone and muscle with terrific jaws almost grotesquely overdeveloped by his owner's relentless exercises. Such a dog, he knew, could hang from a rope or bar by its own clamped jaws for hours. But it looked too old. A terrier's power is so much in its speed and suppleness and this dog's back legs looked almost stiff. And its hide was an incredible tapestry of scars. It had no ears left. They were probably lost in fights, although he knew some owners chopped them for the dog's sake.

The Rottweiler on the other hand was huge and sleek. If it had really been through four fights this year it appeared to have sustained no serious injuries. It must be only two years old and the bunched muscles on its neck and shoulders as it pulled against its handler were those of a young bull. Lewis thought if he had any money he would put it on the Rottweiler. But then he thought – No. I'd put it on the terrier. I'd put it on the terrier and lose it.

The dogs were now at opposite corners. The spectators had fallen silent. The judge at his table watched without feeling, his eyes black in a dough-white face, waiting for the bloodshed to begin.

Which it did almost immediately. Without delay, the dogs were unmuzzled and released and let fly at each other. In sudden collision the Rottweiler seized the terrier and flung it scrabbling into the corner. No one was even sure where the Rottweiler had sunk its teeth in until they saw the blood begin to seep from a crimson gash in the terrier's left shoulder. The Rottweiler had known what to do, gone in low despite its size so that the terrier could not easily get to its throat. In the far corner Lewis saw the two men from London turn to each other and nod.

The Rottweiler was already on the terrier which kept its back to the fence and they tore furiously at each other, bloodymuzzled and bloodyheaded.

At that moment John Pike lurched to the side of the ring and cried out, This is barbaric!

People turned to stare at him, even from the spectacle of killing before them.

This is horrible! he pleaded. You can't do this!

The rage welled up in their faces. Instantly several men surrounded him and started shoving him away. One raised his fist as if to punch him. And then Patricia was at his side and coaxing him away, just as Dave Mabey eyed the disturbance with undisguised contempt and called over, Get 'im out of 'ere!

Yeah go on, piss off mate, added several other voices.

And, bitterly humiliated, John Pike turned away to leave. He looked back once at Lewis.

I've had enough, he said, challenging his son directly.

I want to stay, said Lewis quietly.

John Pike sneered at him. And you call yourself a dog-lover, he said. You an' Allie.

Lewis looked down. I want to see it.

Suit yourself, said John Pike. You can walk home.

Together he and Patricia left with shoulders bowed.

The fight had progressed. Blood was everywhere, both dogs slithering in it, and neither looked to be winning. The terrier's hide, previously a dirty white, was now pink and red, but it couldn't be all his blood. And looking hard at the Rottweiler Lewis saw that its black coat was glossy with blood over its head and neck and its ear was badly torn. The dogs scrabbled about and snapped and tore at each other but neither could get a deathhold. The terrier managed to seize the Rottweiler's already injured ear and with a terrible howl the bigger dog tore away, wheeling in a frenzied semi-circle and flicking blood in an arc as it did so. Several spectators were spotted with blood and Lewis saw with something like horror that the judge's impassive white face was spotted with a single blob of blood. No one else paid any attention but Lewis watched spellbound as for some seconds the judge or recording angel did not react. Then very slowly he reached down into his left pocket and drew out a banknote and with it he wiped the blood carefully away and then he crumpled the banknote up in his fleshy hand and dropped it at arm's length on the floor. Through all this strange performance the man did not change his expression from utter blankness or stir one muscle more than he needed. He is the devil, thought Lewis.

Then the fight became an atrocity. Spectators murmured queasily. With a single snap of his jaws the Rottweiler seemed to bite the terrier's hind paw clean off and yet in doing so he exposed his neck and, seeming not to notice the wound, the terrier curled round with sudden youthful lithe-ness and sank its jaws deep into the Rottweiler's throat. The Rottweiler foamed at the mouth and grew frantic. It was in a deathhold.

All over now, said a man next to Lewis quietly. One minute till final whistle.

The two dogs sank down exhausted to await the end, the terrier clamped to the Rottweiler's windpipe like some night-mare experiment or some bloodboltered succubus. From both dogs' muzzles frothed blood and spume. A peaceful-ness descended on the crowd, the quiet of catharsis. The locals began to scent a victory.

But it was not to be. The terrier had lost too much blood and was faint and even as it held on, its eyes roving around the crowd blurred and its amputated foot leaked gore steadily, until at last the strength of its jaws was gone. The Rottweiler gave a desperate shake and the terrier lost its grip.

Christ, said the man beside Lewis. They're both catfood now.

The Rottweiler turned and closed its jaws on the terrier's neck and broke it.

The terrier was dead but the Rottweiler also seemed to be dying. It was on its side and struggling for breath.

Anyone give it the kiss of life? called out one wag.

Its handlers appeared and collared it and half-walked, half-dragged it away. There was no need to muzzle it.

Arguments broke out.

That dog's virtually dead, said many. It was a draw. They hinted that they wanted their stake back.

The judge eyed them all equally and said nothing. After a long time he said simply, The Rottweiler won, and picked up his notebook. A few people collected winnings off him, visitors. Then he went away.

People returned to their cars and went home. A few returned richer to the city. The 4x4 pulled out of the farmyard with its dying burden and roared away. Some men went home from the fight and awoke their wives and surprised them with urgent sex. Lewis set off across the fields.

39 The Night

He was very drunk and full of thought. He paused at stiles to look at the stars. He forded the river several times unnecessarily until his boots were heavy with water and he took them off and walked barefoot, heedless of thistles. He passed close by a herd of sleeping cows and they didn't know he was there and he stood by them and listened in wonderment to their sleeping breath, like great breathing boulders. They smelled warm and rich and sweet and he thought of lying down there with them to sleep. Mad cows, they said nowadays. Everything diseased, not to be trusted. They knew nothing. He walked on.

He wanted to visit Mary, tap on her window, slip into bed. He saw a fox up ahead and froze. The fox stopped and stared directly at him, front paw raised, seeming unafraid. Lewis knew his scent had carried already but he clamped his arms to his sides all the same and prayed for the fox not to move. The fox moved its nose in a little arc in the air and then turned and trotted away.

After an hour or two of wandering he came back to the garden. He lay for a while on his back and thought over the evening. The dog fight was foul. There was no fierce beauty in it nor even sense of exhilarating loss. It was merely manmade, and therefore ugly.

Then he went to the bottom of the garden and ran the tap by the shed. The cold water streamed on to the broken paving stones and flowed across into the vegetable beds. He turned the tap off and knelt and scooped up a handful of wet earth from the bed. He turned and looked at his ghostly reflection lit by the moon in the cobwebbed window of the shed. Carefully he laid wide streaks of mud the length of his face, wide badger stripes over his muzzle and his cheeks. He studied his reflection again and then took more mud and larded his hair straight back, flat to his scalp.

Then he undressed completely and ran the tap again and took great handfuls of mud and coated himself with it from the neck downwards. He studied himself in the window one last time and then he reeled away.

He danced and flung his arms wide under the moon and then got down on all fours and snuffled and rolled. He raced across to the barbed wire and got over into the field beyond and danced more wildly there. He rolled in sorrel and the brown seeds stuck to his sweaty skin and thistles hurt him and fresh cowshit stained his flank. Breathless and filthy, he flung himself about and threw back his head and laughed. He held his own hands to his throat and half throttled himself and he went to the hedge and dragged himself along against the blackthorn until his back was a pattern of scratches and needle-thin weals of blood. And back in his own garden he was torn among roses, agonizingly slow, muttering kinds of prayer with his head thrown back and his eyes sightless under the summer moon.

Later that night, after he had washed himself down at the basin in the bathroom and cleaned away the last splashes of mud from the tiles, he lay in bed on his back with his skin itching and stinging and fantasized.

He was naked and mounted astride a great black bull. The bunched and corded muscles of its neck were like steel hawsers and the bull was uncontrollable and it bellowed and sweated blood which dyed his thighs crimson. The bull bucked under him and he clasped it tighter and together they thundered through the village and through hedgerows and over cars and nothing could stop them. The bull's horns were twisted like barley sugar and yet thick and knotted, bright gold as if painted and wickedly curved, garlanded with flowers, and around his own neck he wore a garland made of ears of wheat.

The bull beneath him roared and bellowed and its belly was like a barrel of bronze echoing with its brazen call. All the village heard and attended them as they thundered down the street and Lewis saw old Jo and the Mabey brothers who were white with terror and his father and, standing in an upright coffin patiently as if on sentry duty, his grandmother, smiling serenely and nodding her head. He looked away from her in obscure shame. In the distance he could see Gerald and Mary standing arm in arm on a little round green hill like characters in a children's storybook. And up ahead there were far more people, crowds of people he had never seen before, blocking the road completely, as if gathered for some great event. The bull roared beneath him and he roared too and brandished the huge knife he carried. Then from his arms sprang golden flames and the flames grew around his head like a crown and flickered over his thighs and fluttered from his ankles like wings. The crowd ahead parted in terror before him and he rode on through them.

40 Grandma (2)

On Sunday they were all to meet at his grandma's for tea: his father and Patricia, him, Katy, Andy and the two boys. Lewis was dreading it. He told his father he would walk over and see him there.

Well, don't you be late now, said his father. You know how much Ma loves to see us all together. You be on time and no sloping off early neither.

Yeah yeah, said Lewis.

He walked across country to his grandma's, arriving at the back garden from across the watermeadows and between the watercress beds. He skirted round to the front and saw that there were no cars there yet. The others hadn't arrived. He hesitated to go in for he had an image of his grandmother lying dead in an open coffin on the dining-room table with her mouth full of flies. He hung around at the garden wall for a few minutes until he heard the door open and his grandmother saying, Well, come on in then, Lewis, don't just stand around catching cold.

Hello, Grandma, he said, smiling weakly.

He followed her into the tiny sitting room and they sat down. He looked around. How on earth was everybody going to fit in here? He recoiled at the thought. He might even be expected to have a baby on his knee or something.

Are we going to be sitting outside? he asked.

Oh, I think we'll have to, don't you? she said. Or it would be a real tin of sardines.

He grinned. Yeah.

Would you like an orange squash? You look ever so hot. I suppose you walked?

Lewis nodded.

I don't know, I don't know where you get your energy from. Mind you, when I was your age – still, I mustn't go on. Did you say you'd like an orange squash?

Yes please, he said.

He would have been very happy for her to go on but he didn't like to say so. He knew that when Katy got here she would start to roll her eyes at him across the room when Grandma started to go on like that about the old days, and he would have to roll his eyes back at her conspiratorially, although secretly he liked to listen to her. Orange squash on the other hand he didn't like at all, but it was the only thing Grandma ever offered him and he was thirsty. He would have preferred water but Grandma seemed to think that drinking water was bad for you. She said it gave you a runny nose or something. So he accepted the orange squash. He hated the stuff really but it was one of the things he always associated with Grandma, like banana sandwiches, and really dull dry biscuits, and those funny little doily things on the backs of armchairs that you never saw anywhere else.

There you are, my pet, she said, handing him the glass.

Again, typical Grandma. He could have drunk a pint or two of the stuff, he was so thirsty, but just as Grandma could not countenance tea in mugs but only in tiny little china cups, so now she brought him an orange squash in what looked like a sherry schooner.

Oh, thanks a lot, Grandma, he said.

He could have swallowed it in one gulp but instead he sipped it appreciatively and thought that he'd have to go to the toilet soon and drink straight from the tap.

His grandmother asked him how he was and he replied cheerfully. She talked a lot about the weather. How early the harvest was this year!

That gave him a chance to ask, Oh Grandma, you know this corn dolly thing they're doing for the Harvest Festival this year?

Yes I do, she said darkly, and I don't like it one bit. Not that it's got anything to do with my not liking the incomers or anything like that. Live and let live is what I say. Incomers have always been the more get-up-and-go types and thank heavens for it. Some of the folk around here, they wouldn't do nothin' if it wasn't for a few bossy types gettin' on their high horses about it.

Lewis grinned.

No, said Grandma, but this harvest dolly thing is too much. Not right, to my way of thinkin'.

So . . . you didn't ever have this corn dolly when you were a girl?

Of course we 'ad, look, I've one over there, said Grandma indignantly, pointing at the lintel. But I've always thought of it as something to make you mind your head. She chuckled. Oh, she went on, I suppose when I was a girl they were still made out of the last straw or whatever, I really don't remember. But we didn't mean nothin' by it.

So it must be a very old thing then, said Lewis. Like a ritual. Like Stonehenge.

There was a note of urgent curiosity in his voice that alarmed her. She spoke carefully. She set her teacup down and settled herself back in her armchair and clasped her fingers together in her lap.

Well, she said, now I suppose it must be. But you know, Lewis, just because a thing is old, like, that doesn't mean to say there has to be much good in it. People seem to think that straight away nowadays. Why do you think it was left off in the first place?

He bowed his head and said nothing.

I dare say it *is* old, she said. Just like Stonehenge. But people nowadays – I don't know. They want to bring back all these queer old things, all these longhaired types up at

Stonehenge every summer, causing the police a lot of work, so I'm told, and what do they really want out of it? It isn't right, you know. And even this dolly nonsense for harvest, and all this talk of cutting its neck. Well, it doesn't sound very Christian now, does it? If I was the vicar – well, it's not for me to say, I know, and he does a very good job. But I'd have been a bit firmer on it all. Mind you, he was quite right, of course, he said no they couldn't be doing all this nonsense of cutting its neck, not in *his* church, and he upped and told them quite plainly why.

Grandma spoke still more slowly and waggled her index finger at him.

The sacrifice has been made, she said. Once and for all. Our dear Lord Jesus was the sacrifice, and all this stuff with corn dollies and suchlike nonsense – well really, what are they thinkin' of? It's barbaric, isn't it? It's like savages!

Lewis smiled. He had a sudden image of Mrs Armitage and her friends daubed in mud like him last night and whooping around in Phil Evans's field.

There now, said Grandma. I do believe I hear a car.

Lewis's stomach churned within him. They would all be here now. The children and his sister and Andy. He moved over to the chair in the corner and sat with his back square to the wall. He wouldn't have to say anything if he didn't want to.

It was his sister and Andy and the two boys. They all came bustling in, talking and laughing, and saying hello to Lewis. Grandma went out to the kitchen and opened the back door and they all carried chairs out into the garden. A minute later John Pike and Patricia arrived too and the garden seemed filled with people. Lewis stood awkwardly with his hands bunched up in his pockets.

Come and sit here, Lewis, said Katy, there's plenty of room for you.

He squeezed in on the end of the garden bench and sat well back so as not to be noticed. He barely took in the small talk until Andy started telling them tall stories about his family back in Yorkshire.

He said that his family was run by women, very matri-archal, and that the practice was to have men 'brought in' from outside, like bulls, to avoid in-breeding. Andy spoke with a wide-eyed expression that challenged you to dis-believe him.

Oh Andy, said Katy, you do make things up. You're dreadful about your family.

No, honestly, said Andy. Then there was Auntie Vi who suffered from some strange and unmentionable deformity and they were worried she was never going to find a husband at all, not even in Yorkshire. They tried to put her together with a wealthy sheep farmer who was over eighty but he'd have none of it so she was dispatched to the Fens where she found herself a halfwit called Norman who worked as a fruitpicker.

Didn't know they grew much fruit in the Fens, said John Pike.

Well, said Andy, maybe that just proves he was a halfwit. Anyway, they had no children, needless to say. Then there was Auntie Maj, she really *was* mad, she gassed herself in the end. And Auntie Minnie who pasted everything into a scrapbook . . .

Andy made everyone laugh so effortlessly. He was always the life and soul of the party. Katy whooped with laughter though she must have heard him tell all these stories before. That's what marriage is like, thought Lewis. I will never get married. He thought about Mary.

Grandma and Patricia reappeared, wheeling a trolley with a great plateful of scones and a Victoria sponge cake and a teapot and cups and milk and sugar. There now, she said, everybody just help themselves.

Lewis paid little attention to the conversation until he heard his grandma saying, Didn't you, Lewis?

He looked up startled. Um . . . what?

Everyone laughed.

Old Jack-go-to-bed-at-noon, said his grandma in mock scolding tones. You walked here, didn't you, dear?

Everyone was looking at him. Everyone was munching disgusting cake and salivating in streams and grinning evilly and looking at him.

Yes, he said, I walked.

You're mad, said Katy. It must be *miles*.

He shrugged. Oh yeah, at least three, he thought sarcastically, you fat cow with your disgusting fat lardy childbearing arse that you shit children out of that wobbles when you walk down to the *shops* to buy more fucking *cake* and *milk*. He felt like giggling hysterically.

Well, why not? said Andy. It's a nice day for it.

Hm, said Katy, picking crumbs off her plate. I suppose.

It was a struggle then for Lewis not to get up and run to the end of the garden and over the fence and away. How he wished he could fly. In dreams he would sit at tea parties or gatherings of people, often in church, and sometimes he would snap and, driven purely by desire for escape or loneliness, he would rise up slowly above the heads of all the other people and float free away. Sometimes they would reach up and grab his ankles, snarling at him like big cats, clawing his flesh, trying to drag him down. But he always managed to kick free in the end. Then he would float high above the ground, maybe naked, and look down on them as they looked up at him openmouthed and disbelieving and frightened by what they didn't understand. He didn't hate them then but he didn't want to be among them any more. He kicked his legs out and flew away. Often higher still, into the mountains amid snow and ice and eternal sunshine where his cry like a bird echoed off the mile-high cliffs of ice and was lost forever.

41   The Trap (2)

August passed and seemed cooler than June. There was a lot of cloud and some rain. He went out all day and again in the evenings and often at night and he found himself looking forward to winter again. But he tried hard not to think of the future but to live in the sheer animal present. Tom phoned him once from Bournemouth and said why didn't he come down that weekend as there was a party and sure to be some tottie, but Lewis made his excuses. Instead he visited Mary whenever he could and they made love in the bedroom or kitchen or the sitting room. One afternoon he lay on his back in the garden and she straddled him and he came just as Gerald hallooed from round the corner of the cottage. Whether he noticed anything or not, he never said.

That evening he stood heartsick and restless and felt sure that with the summer gone Mary would say that they should stop seeing each other like this. It was just a summer thing. The hot weather. He could almost hear her saying it and he was sure she had hinted it once or twice. But again he tried not to think of it. To live in the present.

That evening after he thought that the Poet must surely realize, he stood at the railway crossing. It was a Sunday evening. The bells of the church carried across the fields and the cows were moving slowly westward in the long grass. This was a favourite place of his, an unfrequented chalk track between the fields leading nowhere in particular and always lonely, suddenly bisected by the railway line and the brutal rush of the London to Exeter Intercity. He loved to stand here and see the train return to London after the weekend and luxuriate in the thought that while those pale people behind the glass would awake in London tomorrow, after their weekend in their cottage or sailing or walking on Dartmoor, he would wake up and still be here, always here. He thought the faces must look from the window as they passed and see him standing there by the blackthorn and shiver as though they had seen a ghost.

He saw and half-hated the cityfaced commuters and week-enders on the Intercity passing by, white faces or blank faces and glazed eyes like ghost figures themselves, unreal people looking out, not understanding and without belief, upon the country to which they belong, as has been said, only by proxy.

He stood on that lonely crossing like an outcast from his tribe and felt very superior. And yet though Lewis might well feel this, there was another more strange and bitter truth that he ignored: for he himself was no less an exile from nature's kingdom than they, however he might not think it, he being human and not animal and so never to find simple animal peace, but always a wanderer, born into the world an orphan without any map or compass for a guide to shelter's door.

On Thursday night he was caught poaching.

Mr Van der Veen returning home from Waterloo by way of Tisbury where he had left his car, looked proudly out upon his estate as he passed by it and saw a torchlight flickering over his river. He promptly dialled up Harry on his mobile and Harry answered in his keeper's cottage. Right away, Mr Veen, he said. And five minutes later Harry was parking his Land Rover beside the river and calling out, Come on then, Lewis Pike, let's be 'avin' you, it's no use you runnin' away. And Lewis was caught redhanded, up to his thighs in the river with a torch, gaffing trout.

You young idiot, said Harry affably. What you doin' that for?

Lewis shrugged.

You won't get no more gardening work in the gardens there, now will you?

S'pose not. Don't get much anyhow.

He took him back to his cottage and made him a cup of tea and rang back Mr Van der Veen.

It's a local lad, Mr Veen. I know who he is. Fact, he's worked in the gardens before now. What do you want I should do with 'im, give 'im a clip round the ear and send him scootin'?

Mr Van der Veen didn't like the sound of a clip round the ear. He asked Harry if he thought he could trust the boy to go now if he promised to come up to the house one day soon for a talk with him.

Right ho, Mr Veen, said Harry. I'll make sure he does.

Harry gave Lewis what-for and told him those trout were raised and stocked in that river and however Lewis might not like the idea, rich chaps coming down from London for a day's fishing were all that kept Harry in a job.

See?

Lewis hung his head. Yeah, he said.

Even trout ticklin''s illegal now, said Harry. He could see from Lewis's face that he thought he must be joking. It bloody well is, he said.

Lewis shook his head. It meant nothing to him. He wanted to laugh. They had passed a law, down in London, against him tickling trout! How . . . ? Who . . . ? It was meaningless.

But he couldn't bear the thought of seeing Mr Van der Veen.

It would take forever to crunch up the gravel pathway to the house. When he came round the corner into view of the house he'd want to run away again. When he'd gardened up here, he realized, he'd avoided looking directly at the house. The portico alone seemed bigger than his own house. Fluted ionic columns and sash windows and thirty-eight

213

bedrooms upstairs. And four thousand acres of Wiltshire. Mr Van der Veen was very rich.

Lewis didn't know much about him but he seemed well liked enough. He'd been there seven years now, which was longer than most since old Mr Sedley had died, and he kept himself to himself. The big house was strictly off limits nowadays to villagers – no more summer fêtes on the lawn – and there were often comings and goings there at the weekend and big parties to which nobody locally was invited. On the other hand, Mr Van der Veen wrote cheques willingly enough for repairs to the church, was generous with his money, could afford to be. Mr Van der Veen and his 4000 acres, half of it downland under the plough, not even worked by anyone local but only occasionally ploughed and sown and sprayed and reaped, by contract farmers brought in from outside, their vast machines crawling on the lonely downs. Then there were the woods where men – Lewis had spied on them – in wanky clothes paid a thousand pounds *a day* to shoot. Then there were the fishing rights on a mile or so of prime trout stream. Meanwhile the old people like Phil Evans farmed their 150 acres and got poorer yearly. And at the bottom of the heap: the Pikes. Redundant, superfluous, as comically antiquated as a blunderbuss, to be hung up on a rusting hook in the barn wall along with the sickles and scythes.

All the rest of the week he was very frightened.

His head was spinning. He had to get away. He ran down to the stream and washed his hands and face and rinsed his mouth and spat and hawked out the sour taste so violently that he almost retched. He crouched on all fours like an animal and saw his broken reflection fleetingly in the surface of the water. What have I done? he wondered. What should I do? He had to get away. He went deep into the woods and climbed a great oak tree slowly and laboriously. Looking up, he caught flakes of bark or lichen in his eyes and tears streamed down his face. Only because of the bark or lichen. The saltwater tickled his cheeks and where tears gathered at the corners of his mouth and he shook them away. At last he lay back on a thick branch with his face in a shard of sunshine and wished he could fly and tried to stop his trembling. Overhead the vast blue sky was clean and empty and silent. He wished he was a bird. He wished he was a silent white bird far away and for ever.

He wanted so much, so much to . . . to . . . but always here, his beloved country, and yet . . . not . . . Everything is changed and lost in time. Rootless and restless, Time the passagebird, Time the swallow . . . For Time was over Tollard Royal and was wheeling over Win Green and over Chase Woods and over Gallows Hill and was a restless bird over Swallowcliffe Down and he heard its cry and felt his longing for all that was now lost to him. With his head against the hard bark he heard a bird's cry return an echo in the bone cave of his skull, he saw in a cave's maddened shadows old gods and heroes, bloodstained bulls led to the sacrifice, harvest home and horses thunderous.

His dreams got worse, they came in the daytime now. At least he thought it was the daytime, he never knew.

He stood at the railway crossing again, waiting for some figure to appear, a guide or guardian, he thought. He heard a train in the far distance approaching slowly. It rounded a corner and he saw it coming on. He debated with himself whether he was supposed to lie down in front of it. But no, that was not it. He stood back and let the train pass. It passed slowly, the many ghostwhite faces pressed to the glass looking at him. It was autumn and as the train went by it whipped up dead leaves in its wake and they flew about as if in slow torment until they settled again as before. The people were wanting him to go with them on the train but he could not and would not go with them. The train vanished down the track and he turned and went away down the dark lane alone, leaving behind him for ever that intersection of track and track, that sacral place, and his eyes followed the chalk track up to the downs beyond, made originally by deer passing through the young beech woods when the glaciers first retreated. Deer had decided its path. Then men came and made the track their own. They owned the forests and cut them down, not understanding finally that they only followed in the footsteps of the generations of deer that had gone before them. But when the brief human flower was blown or that meteor had passed and died in the dark sky, then the animals would return to the track and the young beech woods grow again. So Lewis turned from the railtrack and walked up to the hills alone until he realized that a crowd was following him after all, silent and whitefaced under the moon. So he led them up into the dark hills and they came after him, following the fallen spots of blood that he left in the dust as he passed.

42   Jack and Rose (4)

They were married in January, emerging from the church into a bitter east wind that froze the smiles permanently on their faces. Everyone said it was a lovely wedding. They had a two-day honeymoon, then at six o'clock on Tuesday Jack was back at work on the farm being ragged about how sleepless he looked. And he did.

In May, Rose's period was a day late. Then two days late. Then a week . . . She was pregnant. They moved into a separate cottage in the village that they rented off old Mr Sedley. The war was unreal and far away but months passed and after the lull suddenly it seemed closer. News from the cities was terrible, of bombing and fires and death, still unreal but not so far away. For a while the brothers seemed exempt from conscription because they were farmers but they felt guilty anyway and near the end of 1940 Jack and his older brother Ronald went to fight.

He said goodbye to Rose on a windy autumn day. She held her apron over her face with cupped hands but he pulled them gently away and kissed her. She said very little and when she hugged him he thought their bones would break. He told her not to worry. Ron and I will make it through, he said. They were being driven into Salisbury to catch the train and the car was waiting. Don't cry, he said. I'll soon be back. She watched the car go round the corner and out of sight.

And he was soon back. Two months later he was allowed leave to see his newborn son. They called him John. John

217

Pike. He was born with a fine head of hair and blacksmith's bellows for lungs and weighed nearly nine pounds. For a moment, holding him in his arms with Rose lying beside him looking on, he considered deserting. For a wild moment he saw himself and Rose and the baby, their son, taking off in a gipsy caravan, to . . . to Wales . . . or up north some-where. But then he handed the baby back to her. There you go, he said. Mother knows best.

Two days later he was back in barracks drinking scalding tea and smoking forty Woodbines a day and blacking his boots and drilling endlessly and learning how to unjam a Bren gun.

It seemed to last for months rather than weeks. And there were continual rumours: they were to be shipped to North Africa . . . to Turkey . . . to Russia . . . (Russia! spat Jimmy Tucker. It'll be the fuckin' moon next!) When the marching orders finally came through it was a relief. They were going out east. India, everyone said. The Germans are going to march down through Afghanistan and we're going to kick seven different kinds of shit out of them at the Khyber Pass.

Instead they went to Singapore. And it seemed like no sooner had they stepped off the ship than they surrendered. In fact there were two weeks of furious fighting but at last sixty thousand Allied troops surrendered and among them were Jack and Ronald Pike. They were marched to Changi jail and then worked in teams at the docks unloading ship-ments of cement. The two brothers were put in separate teams. They never saw each other again.

A few weeks later Jack and a couple of hundred other POWs were marched up country. After weeks of lugging 100-pound cement bags on nothing but a beaker of boiled rice a day they were already weak from fatigue. One of them, a big laughing Aussie called Dick, fell by the side of the road. A Japanese guard stood over him and screamed a single word. Dick rolled on his side and started to get up but it was too late. The guard bayoneted him through the side of his ribs into his heart.

It was the first time Jack had ever seen a man killed, despite the fighting he had been through.

When they had marched for seven days up country they stopped and had to clear the forest. Then they had to build quarters for the guards and then quarters for themselves. Then they were locked up for two days.

They were let out again to begin repairs on the road and to build a new one through the jungle towards a river to the east. Four men died during that day. They had to dig a trench to bury them in.

Jack Pike worked hard. He stopped thinking, stopped remembering. He never thought of Rose or the village or his brothers or parents or the Horseshoe. He lived entirely in the present and survived. He had a penknife hidden in his boot. It was of no use as a weapon but he had used it to dig insects' eggs out of the soles of his feet and he knew that as long as he kept his secret penknife safe and inviolate from the Japanese then he would survive. When they had inspection or punishment beatings he always managed to conceal the penknife somewhere, in the sand under his toes or in his mouth or rectum. Anywhere it wouldn't be found.

Weeks and months passed and few of them weighed more than six stone and fewer than a half of them were still alive. The Japanese were angry that progress on the road was so slow and beat them more often. One day, for some offence, real or imagined, they dragged a chap called Phillips out into the square and put a sack over him and tied it around his ankles. Then they beat him to the ground and kicked the sack for a quarter of an hour. Then they ordered Jack and another man to remove the sack and carry Phillips out into the jungle and bury him.

The sack was warm and soaked with blood. The other man vomited. A guard struck him and screamed. He couldn't move. Hurriedly Jack pulled the sack off. Part of Phillips's face came with it. Phillips looked like he had been painted all over with red paint. Jack seized him under the arms. The other man didn't move. The Japanese walked round him ready to strike again.

For God's sake, man, hissed Jack.

The other man picked Phillips up by his ankles and together they carried him out of the camp and buried him. Afterwards neither of them could speak to each other or even look at each other.

But killing the workers didn't make the work go any quicker. In exasperation the Japanese marched in a column of Chinese civilians of all ages and added them to the work-force. Between them, they somehow got the road built.

Then the Chinese tried to run away one night. They had heard a rumour that now the road was built the Japanese would kill them all. But the guards were alerted and pursued them into the jungle. All night long Jack lay on the ground in the hut and heard the sound of machine-gun fire and screaming women and children.

In the morning they had to dig a big trench for more than a hundred dead Chinese.

Then one day an aeroplane flew overhead and dropped leaflets in English saying that the war was over and help was on its way. They also dropped Atrabine tablets for malaria, but too late for most of them. The Japanese angrily confiscated them.

They seemed to be in a panic and started loading up their trucks. Then a squadron of guards came over and ordered Jack and the rest of them to march. There were eighteen of them left. They marched into the jungle ahead of the guards. They were ordered to stand in a line and then lie down on the ground. Then the guards bayoneted them.

There were a few screams, a few attempts to crawl away, but not many. Jack was bayoneted through the ribs. As the guard raised his rifle for a second thrust it seemed he had ample time to reflect. Perhaps it was better this way. It could never have been the same again, even if he had survived and gone back to her. It could never have been the same as it was at first, not now, not after all this. There would have been too much between them, too many nightmares and silences. She would never have understood. He thought that maybe it was better this way, and that probably they were happier together for those few short months than most people are in their whole lives.

The guards began to drag the corpses towards a gulch but then the sergeant shouted to leave them where they were.

As Jack's body was being dragged by his ankles across the forest floor his Bible had fallen out of his top pocket. It lay there undisturbed for days and weeks, rained on and sun dried, the leather slowly fading and cracking, the India-paper rotting, a dried flower pressed between the pages.

43 Gerald and Mary (5)

Mary greeted him differently, as he always knew she would one day. So the day had come. She looked him in the eye, yes, but she smiled too much.

Hello, she said. Come on into the garden. We've got some exciting news.

They sat and Gerald talked and he had difficulty taking everything in because the voices were so damn loud now.

Well, we poets can't look a gift horse in the mouth, Gerald was saying. Nor should we stoop to using worn-out clichés. He smiled wryly. Oh, we have loved it here, haven't we, darling?

Mary nodded and looked at Lewis. He stared at her.

But I admit that to be by the sea would be quite something, in the very heart of Hardy country. And so near to Tyneham too. Do you know Tyneham?

Lewis didn't respond.

The real-life deserted village, deserted since the war when the military took it over, with the promise to hand it back after the war. Never did, of course. Still an army range now. Still, what do you expect from paid killers? Good manners?

Gerald snorted and laughed savagely.

Anyway – a cottage in Lulworth, rent-free for at least a year. Dear George. It's not an offer we can refuse, is it, darling?

No, said Mary, taking his hand. We'll miss it here very much, but life goes on. It's not something we can turn down.

And who knows? said Gerald. I feel a certain confidence

that it will be there, by the sea, always so inspiring, the great mother of us all, that I will compose my poetic masterpiece on the modern-day Deserted Village: the village as microcosm of a wider dysfunction, emblematic of all that is wrong with our culture. Surrounded by streams of information and data, dwarfed by grain mountains and wine lakes, and yet all of us tormented by the most terrible, nameless ignorance and hunger. As I see it . . .

Lewis's attention wandered. When Mary got up to make the tea Gerald was saying, Autumn is the most beautiful and melancholy of seasons, and maybe the right time for moving on. People talk of springtime wanderlust, but I somehow think that autumnal wanderlust is more . . . more *honest*. Gerald drew on his pipe. All to do with death, of course, what poetry isn't? In autumn, death is all around, but he comes in the guise of a friend. Like some slim dark-eyed boy standing in the woods, more Puck than the Grim Reaper, beckoning to you, waiting so patiently for you. Some boy with brown gentle eyes and raggedy old clothes patchworked out of fallen leaves. And you go with him peacably enough into the darkening wood. Oh, you may glance back to the summer meadows, but you know there's no going back there now, that's over and done. The harvest's in. You must follow the brown-eyed boy down into the dark wood and onwards.

Of course we lack a real mythology of death now, don't we?

Lewis nodded.

Nowadays. Nobody believes the old stuff but there's no room or time for the new. Mind you, we lack so many mythologies now, don't we? We lack pretty well everything that might make any sense of it all. Except maybe love.

Lewis looked up.

We expect love to do all the hard work, to answer all our needs, to help us through. The love of other human beings. Gerald sighed. I think we overburden love.

223

Mary returned with the tea.

Lewis's attention was gone. A few minutes later he stumbled to his feet and muttered that he had to go. Mary came with him to the gate.

We're not going just yet, she said gently. And anyway, it's only – what? Forty miles away or so. We're popping down at the weekend to have a look around, it's no distance. You'll have to come down and see us. As often as you like.

Lewis smiled. All he knew was that she was stealing away again, without warning, like a thief in the night.

He ran dazed past the village shop and although he was passing by so quickly and no doors or windows of the shop were open, he quite clearly heard old Mrs Martin say, There goes Lewis Pike, he's a funny one.

Not right in the head, they do say, said Mrs . . .

Not insane, *inmad*, said Mrs Martin.

They laughed together evilly.

Lewis stopped his ears and ran on but still he heard them.

Terrible things.

Mother. Father . . .

44   The Dream on the Hill

Walking through the village absentmindedly a week or so later with his plan growing in his mind like a rare orchid, he met Mary sitting on the churchyard wall, swinging her legs.

Morning, he said.

Afternoon, she said. She nodded across the road. Waiting for the shop to open, she said. Need some stamps. She sighed. Hopeless really. We go on about village shops closing down and complaining about it and yet how often do we actually go there? And when we do, all we buy is one measly little book of second-class stamps.

Lewis nodded. Baked beans at 60p a tin, he said.

And sell-by date 1982 on them, said Mary. They both giggled.

Mind you, said Lewis, I'm that leery I wouldn't say no.

Leery?

Hungry, said Lewis self-consciously. I dunno, it's one of Gran's words.

Oh right, said Mary. Only I thought you meant leery as in lecherous. She looked up at him from under her fringe.

Lewis watched his own bootcap kicking at the church-yard wall. Shut up, he said gently, grinning.

Mary leaned back a little, stretched her legs out in front of her, grazed her palms over the warm lichen growing on the wall. So she said. You're *hungry*.

Just a bit.

I know, she said. Let's have a picnic.

What – from the shop?

Mmm – not unless you fancy fifteen-year-old baked beans.

And catfood, he said.

And second-class stamps as a garnish.

Well, he said. No, I don't think so.

OK, she said. Let's go back and see what we've got in the fridge.

What about your stamps?

Oh, bugger the stamps. They can wait till tomorrow.

Mrs Percy, just at that moment opening the shop, saw them heading off together and tutted disapprovingly.

She found all kinds of stuff in the fridge, salads and a lattice pie and some bread rolls and a couple of cans of beer, and packed them all in a bag.

Here, she said. Do your manly duty and carry.

Where's . . .? Lewis never knew what to call him.

Oh he's off in Bristol today, discussing a plan with some producer to do a radio programme. *Landscape and Poetry* or something. Too much like work for his liking but still, it brings in the money.

She asked where they should have their picnic and he led her out of the cottage and just along the edge of Hound Wood to the southern side to his favourite spot where they could lie and look out over the whole valley.

Good choice, said Mary.

They spread out the rug and lay down and ate their picnic. They didn't say much. There was no need. But when they had finished Lewis said, So. You went down to see your new place then?

Oh, this weekend? Yes, yes we did. Well, she said, modifying her enthusiasm carefully, though they had in fact both thought the cottage with its sea views absolutely beautiful, It was *OK*, she said. I mean, it'll do for now. And as Gerry says, you can't turn it down, not a free offer like that. The only alternative was six months in Marrakesh. Morocco. Lewis looked blank. Which would have been a *bit* far, she said.

Lewis tore his gaze away and stared out over the valley. They said nothing. Then Mary leant over and cupped his chin in her hand and turned his head and kissed him. They kissed for a while and then she slid her hand down and under his T-shirt and tickled his stomach but he pulled away and sat crosslegged with his arms bowed about his knees and again stared out over the valley wordlessly.

Eventually Mary said, Lewis, it's not the end of the world. Although he was thinking of just such an end even as she said it, and all the valley before him drowned for ever under a wave of water a mile high, thundering in from some global catastrophe, a silent and inexorable wall of water as black as rainwet flint. He shook his head and pulled up a grass stem and put it in his mouth and lay back and found his head nestling in Mary's lap and stared up at the sky. He felt unaccountably tired. Mary stroked her fingers through his hair and he closed his eyes and fell asleep.

Lewis! the voices were calling him now. Lewis! Shaking him.

Lewis! It was Mary, shaking him awake.

He felt quite calm. You were shaking like a rabbit, said Mary. What on earth were you dreaming about?

He felt still dreamy and confident and so he told her.

About how he'd dreamt that Mr Van der Veen was in fact the devil. The church bells calling. De Veen, de *Vil*, de Veen, de *vil*. About how he'd shot him in the chest, Mr Van der Veen staggering backwards.

He didn't tell her though of how he'd then walked back into the village reloading the crossbow and pointed it down and fired and reloaded and fired again and then walked on quite beyond pain or the government of pain for he walked unhindered by the bolt that had split his big toe from the rest or the second bolt that had entered perfectly and pierced his foot through and stuck out from his boot firmly situated and secure and then he fired a bolt through

227

the palm of his left hand and it exited clean and lost itself in the neighbouring hedge against his wishes for he wished to see the bolt stuck through his hand like a nail so the second bolt he pressed through his hand and then he tried to do the same to his right hand and though beyond pain and the urgent ordinances of pain and quite bewildered with grief he could no more put a bolt through his right hand than he could weep, so he knelt in silent frustration on the lane's tarmac and upended a bolt and pressed his palm on and over it, his flesh breaking around and down it.

But he told Mary how he dreamt he'd shot a bolt through the glass window of the village shop and then entered and shot an angry Mrs Percy high in the chest, then to the church and shot the verger in the upper arm and as he turned to run he shot him in the back and the verger continued to run and then he slowed and he ran nearer to him and still he ran slowly so he shot him in the head and he fell.

And he killed Mrs Gregory. She spoke to him, her lips moved but no words sounded, his ears heard only a song of blood and ash. And also in the village that day he killed Mrs Teller and Julie Murphy and her little girl and he killed the angry dog and he killed Mr Sims and he killed old Mrs Martin and he killed Mr . . . and Mr . . . and Mrs . . .

At last he returned to the church and he raised his bow and shot the stained-glass pelican through the very heart as it fed its children blood from its own breast and the pelican had flown in the form of many shards of pink and crimson glass. It was like jigsaw pieces scattered in darkness, mysteriously illuminated to form a perfect picture unforeseen. It all made sense. Then he knew what he must do.

It's very vivid, she said. Then after a long silence she asked, Is that how you feel? About everyone in the village, I mean?

He shrugged. No. I dunno. Sometimes. I don't *hate* them.

You'll grow out of it, she said, and then loathed her

words immediately. I didn't mean to be patronizing, I'm sorry, she said. It's just . . . you know, growing up and all that. It's hard for anyone.

Yeah, he said.

Harder for some than others, maybe, but . . .

Yeah, he said again. Right.

Things will get better, she said. I promise.

Yeah?

Yes, she said.

He laid his head on her shoulder and after a while he said softly, I love you.

There was no hesitation, no pause. I love you too, she said.

He pulled back and looked her in the eye and she looked back and he saw that now, at last, she was telling the truth and not just trying to comfort him about things getting better. She loved him. The circle was complete, the story finished.

They looked at each other, unflinching, and then, simultaneously, they both smiled.

Maybe we shouldn't go, Mary said to her husband that evening.

What? Oh darling, you do change your mind rather. What's got into you now?

Mary sighed. Oh, I don't know. It's just . . . I mean, we love it here, don't we? The village and everything. We're just getting to know the way it works and who everyone is. And then we go and move.

Gerald sighed too. I know, I know. He fiddled with his pipe. In some ways I agree with you. There is something special about this place. He gazed out of the window. Then again, we can't say no to George's offer of a freebie. We actually can't *afford* to.

Then . . . said Mary. Then . . . there's Lewis.

She was expecting puzzlement, incomprehension, or

maybe even a long peroration from her husband on the vexed subject of Lewis. But instead there was a prolonged, uncharacteristic silence. Finally Gerald said, slowly and gently, Ah yes. Lewis.

He sucked his pipe stem, looked out of the window again, and then said, What do you want us to do, take him with us? Like a pet guinea-pig? He shook his head. There is nothing we can do about Lewis. He spoke not with his usual ironic twang but with an odd tenderness. He took Mary's hand and stroked the back of it. We've done all we can for him. He paused and then added, Some of us more than others.

Mary looked away and then back, straight into his soft brown spaniel eyes.

He can come and visit us if he likes.

And you and I know that he never will, said Mary.

Gerald nodded. We do. He stretched his long lank body out almost horizontal and then snapped upright with surprising alacrity and stood. You know, I had thought that when I'd completed my poetic masterwork I'd give him a bell and ask if it would be OK to dedicate it to him.

Mary looked up at him and smiled.

Or better still, he went on, it'd be worth popping back here in person and asking him, just to see the look on his face: incredulity? Delight? What do you think?

Mary shook her head, still smiling at the thought.

But then again, I thought: no. There would be something, I fear, almost . . . *vulgar* in it. He hitched his shoulders back. They say there is a splinter of ice at the heart of every writer. But somehow . . . it's not like me to be affected by qualms, but . . . he chuckled, and then grew serious again. Well, it would seem wrong. Better for us simply to keep silent. Attend in silence his silent passing. The last of the tribe.

Don't put it like that, said Mary. Sounds . . . morbid.

Far to the west over Cranborne Chase and beyond over Blackmoor Vale the sun was setting and all around them it burnished the sitting room with a dusty golden light. Gerald reached down and took Mary's hand.

Come on, he said. Let's go for an amble down the lane.

And they walked out and down the darkening lane beneath the towering summer hedgerows, the Poet talking, not oratorical now but murmurous, pensive, his arm circling his wife's waist, their heads bowed together, and Mary listening, half-listening to his dream of words, the setting sun still warm on her cheek, her heart so full of wonder at the indissoluble marriage of beauty and loss.

45 The Harvest

He was lying late in bed that morning when his father came in and said he had just had a call from Mr Van der Veen. His father wasn't cross at all. Seemed to think it was quite funny.

You, out gaffin' trout, he said. A Pike to your marrow-bones you are, boy. All the same, he said that Lewis would have to go up and see Mr Van der Veen this afternoon, he couldn't keep putting it off. It was only good manners. And Lewis nodded and said OK.

He rose and dressed swiftly. He brushed his hair. This time he would do it all properly. This time he would be brave and not run away. He would see things through to their end.

After all, such an ending as he had dreamt was so predictable, everything tending towards it, and he rejected it. (He could smile now because he was strong and had wisdom.) No, it was him . . . himself, *him*. And it all made sense: Mr Van der Veen was on to him and would not give up, and Mary loved him. He had heard what he came for. It was the end now. He didn't need to hear any more.

Nor would he go the way of Mrs Martin, sad and old and brokenhearted. That's what women do, he thought: they live on sadly. Men won't take it. That sad woman's life.

His father was out in the garden. He could hear him mowing the lawn, sneezing. He smiled to himself then because he knew that he was no longer dreaming and that this was now real. He wished his father well.

He took his crossbow and bolts and loaded a single bolt

into it and he crossed himself as he did so, marvelling that the crossbow should be in the shape of a cross, the wood taut as if it shared the racked pain of a man's body stretched like a kite on a tree. He smoothed his fingers over its spine and its outstretched arms and murmured to it and he crept downstairs.

Allie lay on the carpet before the oven. She raised her head and looked at him happily and her tail thumped the ground.

Hey girl, he said softly. You come with me too, yeah?

He walked back down the lane, looking neither to the left nor right, neither happy nor sad now, but his eyes fixed on the road ahead, neither to the left, knowing the fields still lay there wet with dew, nor to the right, to the woods where he'd roamed since he was a small boy, knowing he'd not go there again.

Coming near to the church he realized that the bells were real. They were summoning people to the field behind the church where he saw a group already standing about the last of the wheat. The field where Jack Pike and his brothers once built their hayrick, another summer, years ago. He saw Mrs Armitage there, armed with a scythe, and he smiled. The village ladies were gathered in a horseshoe shape about the last stand of wheat. The lay preacher hovered uncertainly on the edge of the group and wished Gavin would get here soon. Mrs Armitage was intoning one of her own compositions. Lewis smiled softly and went round to the south side of the church. He pushed gently on the door. There was no one inside. The service was not for nearly an hour yet. He stepped into the cool quiet there and closed the door.

John Pike came in from the garden blear-eyed and running his hand ruefully through his grey curls. As soon as he stepped into the sitting room and saw Allie his head

233

cleared. Allie was laid out on the hearth as if for some ceremony, on her side with a crossbow bolt buried deep in the back of her skull.

Oh no, oh no, my boy, my boy! cried out John Pike, and hearing the terror in his own voice served only to heighten his anguish. He held his hands out towards her as if pleading for answer and fell to his knees and his head dropped on to his chest. Oh no, oh no, my boy, he wept. Not you as well, not you too.

In Dorset that day, having again visited the cottage that they were to live in, walking on the beach with her husband, Mary felt indefinably restless and unhappy and at one point she gave a gasp of pain and clutched herself. What is it, darling? asked Gerald anxiously, looking up and down the beach to see if anyone else could help. After a few moments Mary stood up straight again. No, it's all right, she said. It was nothing. It's passed. It's all right now.

In the village the people returned from the field with the last of the wheat raggedly cut and twisted into a garland that they looped over the head of a huge corn dolly that Mrs Armitage had been making for the past month. And when they entered the church carrying the corn dolly before them they found Lewis Pike on the altar steps, his neck strangely crooked, fantastically garlanded with ears of wheat, cradled among the fruit like a sleeping child.

Gavin was late for the harvest service, having been at early communion six miles away and got stuck behind a baler. By the time he arrived for the service the police car was already there and he saw the strips of fluorescent yellow tape dividing the village and he knew that the terrible and worst had happened. Mrs Armitage and the others were crying. He parked by the churchyard wall and asked a policeman what was going on.

Are you the vicar? asked the policeman.

Gavin could have sworn at him. He indicated his dog-collar and said yes. The policeman said that it appeared a young man had killed himself in the church that morning. Gavin asked if they knew who it was yet. The policeman told him. Gavin asked if he could go into the church. The policeman said no. Gavin could see people looking over and beginning to approach him, and for the moment he wanted nothing more than to run and hide and pray alone, in that church that housed so many dead or in its stone garden that sheltered so many more, to pray for this one small death among so many.

Then he saw John Pike himself coming down the lane at a shambling run and though he knew all his pastoral duties demanded that he stay here, he needed some short time away, alone.

Can I go round into the churchyard? he asked.

Yes, where it isn't taped off, said the policeman.

Gavin escaped round the back of the church and breathed steadily.

The late summer air was thick with the fumes of grass although most of the flowers were past their best now and dying. Swifts razed low hawking at hurtless flies and their screams were as old as the world and like weapons and quite without end and he bowed his head to their screams and gripped the headstone broken by frost and scabbed with lichen. Then his hands grew strong on the headstone and he felt strangely strong and sure as never before, and he raised his head and he prayed for Lewis Pike and for John Pike and for all the world and for all the living and the dead.

faber and faber

Amongst Women
John McGahern

Winner of the Irish Times–Aer Lingus Irish Literature Prize for Fiction 1990
Shortlisted for the Booker Prize 1990

Moran is an old Republican whose life was transformed for ever by his days of glory as a guerrilla leader in the War of Independence. Now, in old age, living out in the country, Moran is still fighting – with his family, his friends, even himself – in a poignant struggle to come to terms with the past.

'A masterpiece.' John Banville

'Though it bears no trace of strain, no whiff of midnight oil, it is obviously the product of much loving labour. It is compact but not dense, spare yet rich, and brimming with tension.' *Observer*

faber and faber

Birds of America
Lorrie Moore

Winner of the Irish Times International Fiction Prize 1999

Lorrie Moore's dazzling collection is remarkable for its range, emotional force and dark humour, and for the sheer beauty and power of its language. **Birds of America** unfolds a brilliant series of portraits of the young, the hip, the lost, the unsettled and the unhinged of modern-day America.

'The best American writer of her generation.'
Nick Hornby, *Sunday Times*

'Terse, witty, sprung with jaunty despair – Lorrie Moore is to the short story what Dorothy Parker was to the epigram.'
Harpers and Queen

faber and faber

The Buddha of Suburbia
Hanif Kureishi

Winner of the Whitbread First Novel Award

'Fizzing with energy, bubbling with warmth, salty, satirical and very, very funny.' *Daily Mail*

'A first novel to cherish because it is so splendidly itself.' *Financial Times*

'Funny, perceptive and moving, it should be read by anyone who enjoys the very best of contemporary writing.' *Evening Standard*

'One of the best comic novels of growing up, and one of the sharpest satires on race relations in this country that I've ever read.' *Independent on Sunday*

'It is a wonderful novel. I doubt I will read a funnier or one with more heart, this year, possibly this decade.' Angela Carter, *Guardian*

'This is exactly the novel one hoped Hanif Kureishi would write: utterly irreverent and wildly improper, but also genuinely touching and truthful. And very funny indeed.' Salman Rushdie

faber and faber

Jack Maggs
Peter Carey

Jack Maggs, raised and deported as a criminal, has returned
from Australia in secret and at great risk. What does he
want after all these years, and why is he so interested in
the comings and goings at a plush townhouse in Great
Queen Street? And why is Jack himself an object of such
interest to Tobias Oates, celebrated author, amateur hypno-
tist and fellow-burglar – in this case of people's minds, of
their histories and inner phantoms?

'A master of storytelling . . . Vivid, exact, unexpected
images and language match the quick, witty intelligence
flickering through this novel, and make it a triumph of
ebullient indictment, humane insight and creative
generosity.' *Sunday Times*

'When you have a Peter Carey novel open in front of you,
dinner and doorbell count for nothing . . . For its scope and
intelligence, the whole story is so compulsive that readers
will leave skidmarks on the pages.' *Evening Standard*

'Future reprints of **Oscar and Lucinda** may well bear the
legend "by the author of **Jack Maggs**".' *London Review of
Books*

faber and faber

The Lord of the Flies
William Golding

Winner of the Nobel Prize for Literature

A plane crashes on an uninhabited island and the only survivors, a group of schoolboys, assemble on the beach and
wait to be rescued. By day they inhabit a land of bright, fantastic birds and dark blue seas, but at night their dreams are
haunted by the image of a terrifying beast.

In this his first novel, William Golding gave the traditional
adventure story an ironic, devastating twist. The boys' delicate sense of order fades, and their childish fears are transformed into something deeper and more primitive. Their
games take on a horrible significance, and before long the
well-behaved party of schoolboys has turned into a tribe of
faceless, murderous savages.

First published in 1954, **Lord of the Flies** is now recognised
as a classic, one of the most celebrated of all modern
novels.

'It begins like a Ballantyne yarn, but ends grimly otherwise.
Beautifully written, tragic and provocative.' E. M. Forster

'Beautiful and desperate . . . something quite out of the
ordinary.' Stevie Smith

faber and faber

Oscar and Lucinda
Peter Carey

Winner of the 1988 Booker Prize
Also a major film starring Ralph Fiennes and Cate Blanchett

Daring, original, intense and bizarre, **Oscar and Lucinda** is a
brilliant achievement – a moving love story and an historical
tour de force that is also powerfully contemporary.

'**Oscar and Lucinda** is a little like the best Australian
movie ever made, except that it is a magnificent novel in
its own right – Carey's finest achievement to date.'
Peter Porter, *Daily Telegraph*

'A novel of extraordinary richness, complexity and
strength . . . It fills me with a wild, savage envy, and no
novelist could say fairer than that.' Angela Carter, *Guardian*

faber and faber

Our Fathers
Andrew O'Hagan

Shortlisted for the Booker Prize 1999

Jamie returns to Scotland with his grandfather, the legendary social reformer Hugh Bawn, now living out his last days on the eighteenth floor of a high-rise. The young man is faced with the unquiet story of a country he thought he had left behind and now he listens to the voices of ghosts, and what they say about his own life. It is a story of love and landscape, of nationality and strong drink, of Catholic faith and the end of the old Left. Jamie Bawn's journey home will leave him changed beyond words – beyond the words that darkened his childhood.

'By any standards **Our Fathers** is a powerful novel. As a first novel, it is very remarkable indeed.' *Independent*

'I have scarcely read so silvery beautiful a style when it comes to Scots landscape, nor one so tender when it comes to matters of life and death.' Candia McWilliam, *Financial Times*

'The tang of truth, the irreducible core of humanity lies like a shock in the shuddering heart of this great fiction debut.' *Scotland on Sunday*

'A beautiful, elegiac work . . . required reading for everyone.' Ian Rankin, *Evening Standard*

faber and faber

The Poisonwood Bible
Barbara Kingsolver

Shortlisted for the Orange Prize

Told by the wife and four daughters of Nathan Price, a fierce evangelical Baptist who takes his family and mission to the Belgian Congo in 1959, **The Poisonwood Bible** is the story of one family's tragic undoing and remarkable reconstruction over the course of three decades in post-colonial Africa. They carry with them all they believe they will need from home, but soon find that all of it – from garden seeds to Scripture – is calamitously transformed on African soil.

'There are few ambitious, successful and beautiful novels. Lucky for us we have one now in **The Poisonwood Bible**.' Jane Smiley

'**The Poisonwood Bible** shows what happens when one of the most talented writers of our generation comes to maturity . . . [It] ranks with the most ambitious works of post-colonial literature and it should at last establish Kingsolver's reputation in Europe as one of America's most gifted novelists.' *Independent on Sunday*

'Brilliant. Now, that is no sort of measured critical reaction but it is how I feel I must begin – with a one-word shout of praise for this superb epic novel.' Margaret Forster, *Literary Review*

faber and faber

Red Earth and Pouring Rain
Vikram Chandra

'Chandra is imagining and writing with such originality and intensity as to be not merely drawing on myth but making it.' *Sunday Times*

'Makes its British counterparts look like apologetic throat-clearings.' Adam Thorpe

faber and faber

The Remains of the Day
Kazuo Ishiguro

Winner of the Booker Prize

In the summer of 1956, Stevens, the ageing butler of Darlington Hall, embarks upon a leisurely motoring holiday that will take him deep into the English countryside and into his past . . .

A haunting tale of lost causes and a lost love, **The Remains of the Day** contains Ishiguro's now celebrated evocation of life between the wars in a Great English House – within those walls can be heard ever more distinct echoes of the violent upheavals spreading across Europe.

'A remarkable, strange and moving book.' *Independent*

'**The Remains of the Day** is a triumph . . . This wholly convincing portrait of a human life unweaving before your eyes is inventive and absorbing, by turns funny, absurd, and ultimately very moving.' *Sunday Times*

'**The Remains of the Day** is a dream of a book: a beguiling comedy of manners that evolves almost magically into a profound and heart-rending study of personality, class and culture.' *New York Times Book Review*

faber and faber

The Unbearable Lightness of Being
Milan Kundera

'A dark and brilliant achievement.' Ian McEwan

The Unbearable Lightness of Being is a story of irreconcil-
able love and infidelities in which Milan Kundera addresses
himself to the nature of twentieth-century 'Being', offering a
wide range of brilliant and amusing philosophical specula-
tions. First published in 1984, Kundera's masterly novel
encompasses the extremes of comedy and tragedy and
was at once hailed by critics as a contemporary classic.

'There are novels that are tragic, or entertaining, and this
one is both. There are very few that give a fresh perspec-
tive on existence, and force the reader to reassess his own
life and attitudes.' Victoria Glendinning, *Sunday Times*

Please send me

title	ISBN	Price
_____ The New York Trilogy *Paul Auster*	15223 6	£6.99
_____ Jack Maggs *Peter Carey*	19377 3	£6.99
_____ Oscar and Lucinda *Peter Carey*	15304 6	£7.99
_____ Red Earth and Pouring Rain		
_____ *Vikram Chandra*	17456 6	£7.99
_____ Pig Tales *Marie Darrieussecq*	19372 2	£6.99
_____ Hullabaloo in the Guava Orchard		
_____ *Kiran Desai*	19571 7	£6.99
_____ The Last King of Scotland *Giles Foden*	19564 4	£6.99
_____ Headlong *Michael Frayn*	20147 4	£6.99
_____ Lord of the Flies *William Golding*	19147 9	£6.99
_____ The Remains of the Day *Kazuo Ishiguro*	15491 3	£6.99
_____ The Unconsoled *Kazuo Ishiguro*	17754 9	£7.99
_____ The Poisonwood Bible *Barbara Kingsolver*	20175 X	£7.99
_____ Immortality *Milan Kundera*	14456 X	£7.99
_____ The Unbearable Lightness of Being		
_____ *Milan Kundera*	13539 0	£6.99
_____ The Buddha of Suburbia *Hanif Kureishi*	14274 5	£6.99
_____ Aunt Julia and the Scriptwriter		
_____ *Mario Vargas Llosa*	16777 2	£7.99
_____ Amongst Women *John McGahern*	16160 X	£6.99
_____ A Fine Balance *Rohinton Mistry*	17936 3	£7.99
_____ Birds of America *Lorrie Moore*	19727 2	£6.99
_____ Our Fathers *Andrew O'Hagan*	20106 7	£6.99
_____ The Bell Jar *Sylvia Plath*	08178 9	£6.99

**To order these titles phone Bookpost on 01624 836000
Or complete the order form below:**

I enclose a cheque for £ _____ made payable to Bookpost PLC
Please charge my: o Mastercard o Visa o Amex o Delta
o Switch Switch Issue No_____

Credit Card No _____ Expiry date _____

Name _____

Address _____

_____ Postcode _____

Signed _____ Date _____

Free postage and packing in the UK.
Overseas customers allow £1 per pbk/ £3 per hbk.
Send to: Bookpost PLC, PO Box 29, Douglas, Isle of Man, IM99 1BQ
fax: 01624 837033 email: bookshop@enterprise.net
http://www.bookpost.co.uk